THE CODEX OF TYLER GRAYSON

CREATURES AMONG US

BY
RICHARD GIBBARD

First published by Richard Gibbard in 2019

Printed in the United States of America
First Edition 2019

ISBN: 978-1-7339383-2-7 (E-Book)
ISBN: 978-1-7339383-0-3 (Hardcover)
ISBN: 978-1-7339383-1-0 (Paperback)

Special thanks to Beta Readers: Emilie Buck, DJ Fortner,
James Stevens, Josh Gardner, Gilda Gibbard, Diane
Hermanson & Jessica Young

Cover Illustration by Rebecacovers
www.fiverr.com/rebecacovers

Edited by Dustin Bilyk from The Author's Hand

www.authorshand.com

To my family and close friends, thank you for the constant encouragement to do more and be more, even when I didn't see it in me.

And a special loving thanks to my Mom and Dad who have been and continue to be my first and biggest supporters.

CHAPTER 0
THE FIRST SCRIBE
April 4th, 546 A.D.

"Don't let him escape!" the voice echoed out with an inhuman shriek, reverberating through the cavernous passageways.

Deep shadows crept in ominous shapes as a man poked his head around a corner for the briefest of moments. His eyes scanned the area as he wiped the sweat dripping from his sideburns connecting his brown hair to his bushy beard. Shaking his head, he looked through the darkness once more.

Had the fiends already reached his last obstacle? It was a question he could not answer as he squinted his eyes in the inky black, so with nothing more than a simple loincloth and a ragged pair of sandals, he dashed into the unknown. He had no protection, his sword still buried to the hilt in one of the abominations, lost forever, and stinging cuts and deep purple bruises littered his body, blood dripping from his knees and chest like water reaching the end of a trickling stream.

Come on, Clarius! You're almost there! Just a little more. The man spun his head around searching his surroundings, but something clutched in his trembling hands, cloaked by the small flap of his pale robe, was tempting him. Clarius ran his hands over its smooth surface as the small piece of fabric glided to the ground. Carefully searching for the opening, he gazed down at his prize.

In his hands he grasped a crimson, leather-bound book, the Codex, his treasure. Carefully opening the infernal manuscript, the pages glowed a fiery cobalt-blue.

"Incubus?" Clarius grinned, whispering to the book. "Hah! Is that what you call those infernal creatures?"

Jolting his head up, Clarius once again found himself squinting through the tunnel, its choking darkness yielding nothing to the eye.

"This way! This way! I see blue!" something screamed from the dark.

Caressing the Codex like a cherished pet, Clarius knew defeating the horde of demons barreling towards him was an impossible feat, even for the most skilled Magi. But as his raw, scraped fingertips ran across the book's leather binding, he could feel absolute power kissing his skin. The power surged through his hand, spreading through his entire body. It was electrifying! Empowering! Unyielding!

I can't. I'm as good as dead on my own. I've got to get out of here, now! But as he stared, mesmerized by the Codex, his thoughts started to wander. *Or . . . I could lay waste to any demon who dared chase me out of this hellhole . . .*

But why stop there? I could cleanse these accursed tunnels of those wretched demons! The might of Hades and all its demons wouldn't stand a chance against such strength.

I could bring the fight to them and watch their world crumble! Nostrils flared, eyes dilated, heart racing, the thought of ending the demon's terror and bringing victory for the Magi Order engulfed him. *I could even end the civil war. Without their demonic lap dogs, the Ebon Council wouldn't stand a chance.*

But before his feet could betray him a round stone struck his naked shoulder, clunked and then echoed across the rocky floor. Clutching the Codex, Clarius' muscles tensed, and his head spun around trying to locate his attacker. He smiled with relief as he spotted something familiar.

"I thought you said you weren't going to step foot down here?"

The tiny creature trembled in the darkness, trying to keep himself hidden.

"What are you doing here, Emmice?"

What at first appeared to be an unusually large rodent slowly crept into full view. His bushy squirrel tail flicked nervously as feline-like whiskers protruding from his snout scanned the area. His singular bulbous eye, which sat perfectly in the middle of his hairy face, squinted, unable to see clearly into the dark depths of Hell's Gate. Emicce looked into Clarius' eyes.

"Master, we must go now! You have the book."

Thrusting the book to the rodent's face, Clarius spoked with a harsh whisper, "Why? I can bring the fight to *them* now."

Emicce scurried down the wall of stone to Clarius and tugged at his master's tattered sandal straps, begging, "No, please, we must leave now, please!"

Clarius peered down at the Codex, then into his friend's quivering face, and his mind cleared. *I alone could change the very course of history, but is it worth the risk?* If he failed, if the demons took back the Codex, his whole journey would be for naught. Good, honest, caring people and creatures, like Emicce, ultimately would be the ones to pay the price for Clarius' arrogance. *Today's not the day.* Wrapping the Codex back into his robes, Clarius gave Emicce a smile and a quick nod of agreement.

"Okay, how do we get out of here?"

"We climb."

Clarius craned his neck towards the ceiling. A jagged wall, nearly thirty feet high, and as steep as a mountain cliff, separated them from freedom.

"Well done, friend," said Clarius.

"There! The Codex!" shrieked a terrible voice. A black silhouette could be seen behind them as flames rose from the depths of Hell. The fiery inferno cast a brilliant light, illuminating both their escape route and the onslaught of approaching demons.

With Emicce already climbing his way to the top, Clarius aimed the Codex towards the exit's ledge. With a colossal effort, he threw his prize into the air. The book spun like a discus, landing on the ground above. The stones trembled beneath him, so Clarius climbed. Cool air suddenly whipped down from above, the breeze a comfort as Clarius grabbed a protruding stone. But his enemies were close behind, cursing and screaming death threats in hissing voices. Clarius glanced back, horrified by the sea of demons hot on his heels.

Emicce leaped to the top, spinning on his hind legs. Grasping small stones scattered upon the ground, he launched them at the demons, and his aim was astounding as they bludgeoned his enemies, sending some plummeting to the rocky depths.

Clarius made it to the top and plucked the Codex from the ground, but Emicce grabbed his arm and frantically cried out, "This way! Hurry, Master!" Pulling himself to his feet, Clarius gazed down into the mouth of Hell's Gate, welcomed by a torrent of glowing demonic eyes fast approaching.

Again Emicce tugged desperately at Clarius' leg, begging, "Hurry, Master! We must run!" But he paid him no heed. Instead, Clarius raised a hand out towards the mass of demons, the Codex once again in hand, fueling him.

"Vastatio!" A gale force wind whipped wildly down into the tunnel, and the rocks protruding from the wall began to vibrate, snapping free like crumbling sandstone. The demons tumbled, crashing into one another before slamming to the ground below. Then, in another instant, their inhuman hisses were silenced with a monstrous thud.

Clarius stood in awe as an avalanche of stone and dust buried his demon pursuers alive, and all went silent. *Nothing could have lived through that*, he thought, but then the silence was followed by a deep rumbling as molten lava suddenly shot up from deep below. Clarius and Emicce dove aside, dodging the fiery clumps of stone and magma.

He stared at his palm then back down into the gaping chasm. The molten seas of Hades poured in and filled the crater with death, and in time it would solidify, protecting the human world from the foul demonic scourge, if only temporarily.

"Incredible . . ." Clarius said, turning to Emmice with an elated smile. "The Codex, its powers are just as the fables told." *Gods . . . To be on the receiving end of its power. Those poor Magi. Never again. Their greatest weapon against mankind is now our greatest weapon against them!*

Taking Clarius off guard, Emicce hung from his hand and pulled, begging, "Please, can we leave now? This place . . . more might come!"

I wouldn't be so sure, little one. With a satisfied smile, Clarius gave Emicce a reassuring nod. Holding the Codex protectively close to his chest, Clarius took his first step back onto earth.

Without warning, the Codex suddenly flashed with a powerful white light. Clarius and Emicce recoiled as the beams flickered in random intervals, but soon the flicker became a constant blinding brilliance. The winds swirled around them, kicking dust and debris into the air. Closing their eyes, they winced in pain as the radiant light forced its way through their eyelids and caused them to turn away and gasp, going on for what seemed like an eternity. But suddenly, and without any indication of letting up, the blinding light disappeared.

Slowly opening his eyes as they adjusted to regular light again, Clarius reached out for Emicce. "Are you . . . are you okay, my friend?"

Rubbing his eye, bloodshot and dry, Emicce crawled to Clarius. "Yes, I'm okay. What was that? A demon trick?"

The Codex still in hand, Clarius puckered his lips, heaved in a gust of breath, and blew the dust from the book's cover into the air. He caressed the surface, but the power, while still there, was dull and void of any blue light. Though confused, Clarius sighed in relief – the Codex was still in one piece. He opened the book gingerly, but the relieved smile on his face evaporated.

"Wait, where is it?" Clarius asked hysterically, his eyes shifting side to side.

Emicce tilted his head in confusion. "Right there in your hands, Master."

"No . . . I mean the writing, the text. Emicce, I – look!"

He revealed a blank page, then flipped to another, also blank. The next, empty. With each page he turned, the truth sank in. The Codex had wiped itself clean, not even a single drop of ink left on its pages.

Dejected, Clarius dropped to his knees, clutched the Codex to his chest and wept. All his pain, all his efforts, it was all for nothing. All he could feel now were his searing, bloodied gashes painting the earth beneath him red.

"Master, look," Emicce said pointing to the Codex.

Defeat still plastered across his dirt covered face, Clarius' eye flickered with hope. The Codex was glowing. A single glimmering page towards the front was brimming a rosy pink. Grabbing the book with shaking hands, Clarius opened it, but it was still empty. He stared as a faint word slowly appeared at the top. It read: *Ritserru*.

His eyes shifted to his little friend, Emicce. "It must know what creatures are nearby?"

"Ritserru? Me?" asked Emicce.

"Do you have a quill?"

"No, why?"

"This page is blank, but I can fill it in with your help."

"You think that'll help?"

Gently caressing the Codex, he could feel its yearning. *Yes, this is what it wants.*

"We just need to fill it again."

"I'll help, Master. But . . . there are so many blank pages!"

"Then we have our next task."

CHAPTER 1
THE TWENTY-FOURTH SCRIBE
September 6th, 2022 A.D.

Warm beams of light slipped through cheap plastic window curtains, giving the boxes and bags that littered the dusty bedroom dulled colors and shapes in the early morning. And just before the advancing sunlight could wake the dozing woman, the alarm clock buzzed loudly.

The jarring, high-pitched repetitive shriek made it impossible for even the heaviest sleeper to drift back into slumber, and with the clock reading 6:45, Charlotte Grayson reached over, stretched her arm to its limit, and turned off the irritating alarm.

Charlotte groaned before calling out to her son, "Tyler! It's time to get up, sweetie!"

Rolling onto her back, she looked up at the patches of water damage on the ceiling and sighed. Charlotte rubbed her coffee brown eyes and let out a yawn. Sunny Southern California may have wanted to start a new day, but Charlotte just wanted more sleep.

She was thirty-seven years old, now in the waning half of what she felt was a very forgettable age. She had thick and wavy auburn hair that felt as smooth as silk, even with bed head. Bouncing upright, Charlotte squinted her lightly freckled face trying to blot out the sun's rays. *Is it just me, or is the sun brighter in North Hills than it was in Reseda?* Trying to embrace the day, Charlotte took a deep breath before slowly letting it out. *Not the springy young girl ya use to be, huh?* Her gaze turned to her satchel, bringing a smile to Charlotte's face. *Though, I could probably still run circles around most of Tyler's classmates.*

Looking around the bland, ramshackle bedroom, Charlotte tapped her fingers against her thighs rhythmically in thought. *Not quite as open or colorful as the last place, but I'll make this work.* It wasn't the worst living situation she had ever been in, not in the slightest. But moving so many times for a financially "stable" job was starting to get old. How could someone make a house feel like home if you needed to pack up and move every other year? This wasn't what she pictured thirty-seven looking like.

Charlotte cracked her back as she turned to face her nightstand. Atop it was a miniature house she had painstakingly made out of a large cardboard box and a collection of decorations from several craft stores, though the finer points had been meticulously put together by its lone denizen.

"Good morning, Penelope," Charlotte said softly.

Emerging from the cutout door in the box came a small, plump fairy creature, known to the bearers of such knowledge as a Gadwen. She had fiery, rosy red cheeks that made it look like she was constantly blushing, but her round, full face gave her a comforting warmth. While her wrinkling and spotted skin showed her age, her innocent, almost childlike smile gave her a youthfulness that always seemed to spark smiles all around her.

She greeted Charlotte with a yawn. "Good morning, Charlotte! Sweet dreams I hope?"

"Not really. Just sleep, no dreams."

Penelope's warm smile faded into a frown. "Poor dear. This move is stressing you. What's a Scribe to do without her dreams?"

Charlotte shook her head before jiggling her ear as though trying to shake something free. "I don't think it's the stress. Probably just a Dreammite."

"Pesky little thieves! Restful night's sleep then?" Penelope asked.

"Mmm . . . yes," Charlotte said whilst yawning. "Best sleep I've had in months. Still kinda sleepy."

"Nothing a nice cup of tea can't help!"

"I could go for some." Charlotte's eyebrow raised with a knowing smirk on her face. "Would you like some too?"

Penelope played coy. "Oh . . . I *suppose* I could go for a drop." She pointed at the bathroom and winked.

"It's cherry flavored, isn't it?"

"It might be," Penelope said with a guilty smile. Charlotte pulled her bedsheets aside and hopped out of her cozy bed. As she made her way to the bathroom door, Penelope asked, "Do you remember everything on your agenda today?"

A short chuckle escaped Charlotte. "Oh, you already know the answer to that."

"I do say, child, you're perhaps the most forgetful human I've ever lived with," Penelope said rolling her eyes.

As the bathroom door swung open, both were greeted by a floating tea kettle with a small flame underneath it. The tiny embers danced in the door's wake

14

before returning to a calm. Charlotte grabbed the kettle by the rubber handle and waved her hand at the flame. *Extinguō.*

The flame flickered as though being blown by an invisible wind until it was put out. Grasping a cup and a figurine size cup from a nearby cardboard box, Charlotte poured the warm tea into her own cup and a small splash into the smaller cup, filling it to the brim.

Waving her hands over the nightstand, Charlotte mused to herself. *Flores.* The nightstand came to life as beautiful multi-colored flowers sprung seemingly from thin air. It gave the room much-needed warmth, and both of them smiled.

Penelope pulled out a chair from her home and sat amongst the flowers. "You do make the most beautiful magic I've ever seen." Taking her tiny cup, Penelope held it up. "Thank you, dear."

Charlotte held out her own teacup. "A toast to a productive day."

"Cheers to that." The two clinked cups and sipped at the warm black tea with a hint of cherry. Penelope glanced up from her cup as the steam playfully swirled and twisted at the surface. "Now as far as your day goes, of course you must drop Tyler off at school. You also have pens to pick up from Fosdur."

Charlotte snorted with disgust. "Foul creature."

Penelope shrugged her shoulders. "He may be a vile thing, but he does make exceptional writing utensils. As always, just bear with him."

"Easy for you to say. You're not the one he's undressing with his eyes," Charlotte said, looking over her glass as she sipped her tea.

Penelope shrugged again. "After that, you're meeting up with Marshall to investigate a lead he has on another creature for the Codex. By that time, Tyler will be out of school, but as you know, he'll probably—"

Charlotte scoffed with a not so subtle hint of disapproval. "Be with that succubus he calls a girlfriend, Nessa."

Penelope chuckled before saying, "Now, now, be nice. I'm sure she is a fine young lady. Mama Bear needs to let her cub grow up."

Too unsettled to finish, Charlotte put her cup down. "Something about the effect she has on him. I'm telling you . . . something's off about that girl."

"Well, you can look into that on another day because today's full. You also need to register your new residence with the Guild, pick up some imp-repelling garden ferns, grab dinner, and the most daunting of all . . . continue unpacking this dreadful mess."

Charlotte sighed as she scanned the room. Some boxes were stacked seven high in the corners. "Yeah, not looking forward to that . . . again."

"Might I suggest taking Charlie up on his offer? He can unpack while you and Tyler are out."

Charlotte answered firmly and with a stern look on her face. "Absolutely not."

"Do you have something against Charlie? I thought you—"

"No, I love Charlie. He's great," Charlotte groaned rubbing her head now, massaging a headache. "It's who he serves..."

"Oh...yes, I see."

Charlotte's face twisted into a conflicted grimace. "Yeah... can I get you another cup of tea?"

"Oh no, dear. This is quite enough for me. But you need to get ready," Penelope said tapping her fingernails against the cup as she sat back in her chair.

"Okay, I'll be out in a sec," Charlotte said walking to her bathroom. Penelope wasn't sure how Charlotte composed herself in such a short time, but she assumed magic was involved. No more than two minutes after entering, Charlotte emerged showered, blow dried, makeup applied, dressed for success and ready to take on a full day's worth of work. She turned to Penelope for her opinion. "Well... how do I look?"

"You look like a vision. Simply stunning."

Charlotte shook her head. "As always, you're too kind. Do you need me to pick up anything while I'm out?"

Penelope waved her off unable to think of anything. "Oh no, dear. I'm fine. I'm just going to do some housecleaning while you're gone."

"Cherries are on sale."

Penelope's face lit up as though she had just landed on a jackpot. "Oh, well then yes, please. I would like that very much."

Grabbing her large worn-in brown satchel, Charlotte turned to Penelope saying, "Then I'll see you tonight with a whole box full of cherries."

Penelope smiled, opened her mouth to say something, then snapped it shut before looking away. Charlotte came to a halt at the door.

"Is there something on your mind?"

"I did wonder on something . . . but no, it's probably nothing, dear."

"Let me have it, Penelope. Are my pants on backwards, because the magic isn't a perfected science and –"

"How is it that Marshall has a lead?" Penelope blurted out uncharacteristically. "Aren't you the one that feels the pull of the Codex?"

Charlotte smiled and suppressed a giggle. Her little Gadwen was always such a worry-wart. "Marshall has been at this a long time. I've learned to trust his nose more than the faint pull of the Codex. Plus, he has contacts overseas, and I've had to stay relatively incognito. Not to worry, Penelope."

But Penelope looked unsure. "Okay, as you say, dear. Have a lovely day."

CHAPTER 2
JUST ANOTHER DAY

Charlotte walked into the kitchen to find her son already hunched over a bowl of cereal. Walking past Tyler to the sink, she gently combed his messy auburn hair back and away from his face.

"Good morning, sweetheart."

Tyler styled his hair back over part of his face. "Good morning."

"Sleep well?"

"Piss poor," Tyler answered with his eyes fixed to his bowl. "Had another nightmare about Dad."

Charlotte pulled out a chair beside him and rubbed his shoulder. "I still get them too. You want to talk about it?"

"No," Tyler said glancing up at the mostly unpacked kitchen. It wasn't nearly as nice as their last kitchen. It felt small and displaced, and everything was discolored and outdated. *This would drive Dad nuts.* Tyler reminisced helping his father renovate their last home – the home they'd spent the last two years living in even after he was gone.

Stroking his hair away, Charlotte peered into his eyes. "If you ever want to talk, please come to me. I still think about my mother and how life would be different if she didn't pass when she did. I understand how you're feeling, especially at your age."

A boy my age? Unlikely . . . Tyler nodded, wanting to switch subjects before things got emotional. "Why'd we have to move?"

Charlotte sighed as she hung her head letting her hair cascade over top. "Tyler, we've been over this."

"Yeah yeah downsizing—"

"Yes, downsizing. I didn't make enough on my own to afford the other house," Charlotte interrupted.

"Then why do we have to keep moving every three to five years. Amanda's lived in the same home her whole life."

Charlotte understood her son's frustration. Uprooting so often wasn't fair to him. "Doesn't help that our old place was literally right down the street from Amanda, huh?"

"And the mall . . ."

She smiled at her son's teenage concerns. "And the mall. Listen, I know it's not much now, but we'll make this house feel like a home. And I promise, I'll do everything in my power to keep this one. Just gotta give me time. Okay?"

Reluctant at first, Tyler nodded and said, "Okay . . ."

Charlotte peered down at Tyler's torn jeans. She never understood the appeal of wearing partially destroyed clothing. But more importantly she spotted his large scabbed knee poking through the opening.

"Honey, when did this happen?"

"Fell during dance with Casey. But my alibi is basketball with Ballsy."

"Is that what we're telling people?" Charlotte chuckled. *Neosporin should owe me stock options with this kid.* "When's your next dance session? Maybe I can drive you two there."

20

"Next week, but I don't know. Casey and I are thinking about quitting."

"But I thought you loved dancing?"

"I do, and Casey really does, but I don't know. I'll talk with her more today."

Casey really does? I wonder why . . . Charlotte thought with a smile having seen the way Casey looked at her son. "Okay, well let me know." Secretly she hoped they would keep at it. If Amanda had been sectioned off to the "friend zone" then sweet and caring Casey would be great for her son. Anyone but Nessa.

"Best get going, Mom. I may have been late to first period a few times too many."

"A few times?" Charlotte stared at Tyler. "The semester just started. And I get you there ten minutes before the bell every day."

Tyler drew out a long, "Yeahhh . . ."

He gets that from me. Charlotte rolled her eyes and shook her head. "Grab your stuff and let's get in the car."

✹✹

Pulling up to the school drop-off, Tyler jumped out of the car. Charlotte leaned down to peer out the open door. "I love you, sweetheart."

Slightly embarrassed, Tyler waved back. "I love you too."

Closing the door, Tyler watched his mom pull away as Amanda waved to Charlotte passing by her.

"Sup," Amanda chimed as she pulled her long wavy inky black hair into a ponytail.

"Hey," Tyler said waiting for Amanda to reach him. Side by side, the two walked around to the front of the school. There was little less than ten minutes left before their first period. Usually, by now Amanda would strike up a conversation with Tyler. But today she was oddly quiet, anxiously fiddling and cleaning her glasses.

Unsure what had his talkative bestie so quiet, Tyler playfully socked Amanda's shoulder. "Yo, you okay there? You're rather—"

Amanda interrupted as though broken out of a trance. "I'm fine. I'm just nervous."

"Nervous? About what? It's week two! Nothing crazy's happening yet. No projects, tests—"

"Not schooling! My swim meet!" Amanda shot back with harshness in her voice.

Tyler held his hands up as though being held at gunpoint. "Oookay . . ."

Amanda bit her lower lip. "Sorry, you didn't deserve that. I'm just nervous. That's all. I'm alright."

"Hey," he said, getting Amanda's attention. "You'll do fine. You're a great swimmer."

She cracked a small smile. "The last time you saw me swim anything was back in fifth grade."

Wow . . . has it really been that long? "True, but you used to swim laps around me. With all that practice I'm sure you're that much better."

"Thanks, Ty," Amanda said cracking a smile.

"By the way, when're you gonna let me know where these meets are? I want to see you in action!" Tyler stared into her deep piercing brown eyes.

"I don't think you'd—"

22

Amanda was interrupted by Nessa coming up from behind Tyler, blindfolding him with her hands. "Good morning, baby."

Tyler's smile grew, and the familiar wave of adoration painted his face the moment she removed her hands. "Hey, Nessa."

Letting Tyler escape her grasp, he turned as Nessa wrapped her arms around his shoulders. Leaning in, she gave him a long passionate wet kiss. Long enough to get a supervisor's attention, but not long enough for him to break it up.

Nessa had smooth faultless tanned skin from head to toe. Her bouncy, shoulder-length bleach blonde hair only drew people into her sharp bronzed cheeks, her full pillowy pink lips, and her vibrant glacial blue eyes. The envy of many girls and the attention of most guys, Nessa was also gifted with a slender yet curvy hourglass figure.

Growing annoyed, Amanda inserted herself into the conversation with a falsely cheerful, "Heeey, Vanessa. Good morning to you too."

Nessa sneered as she looked Amanda up and down. "What is it, Morales? I can't be affectionate to my boyfriend?"

Amanda scoffed crossing her arms. "Ha! No, you can. Just try not to eat his face off next time. It's disgusting."

"Jealous?" Nessa winked as she gently stroked Tyler's chest with her velvety hands,

Ignoring the question to throw her own venom, Amanda answered, "How does it feel being made of 50% plastic and 50% spite?"

Nessa kept smiling and shook her head. "Mmm, very jealous." She ran her eyes over Amanda's body as though judging her figure.

Tyler groaned as he knew he couldn't do much to stop the impending verbal abuse the two girls would sling at each other. It wasn't the first, second or third time it had happened this school year. Luckily, the warning bell rang. *Saved by the bell.*

Nessa gave Tyler a quick peck on the lips. "See you at Nutrition." Turning to Amanda, Nessa gave another pitying scoff before making her way to the gym.

Amanda called out using her fake voice again. "Have a great day!"

"You too!" Nessa said with an equally fake voice, turning only for a moment to salute Amanda with a middle finger.

Although she had seen a lot worse than someone flipping her the bird, Amanda smirked at the gesture. "Wow, Tyler. You really picked a winner."

"Please, not today."

But Amanda wasn't finished. "I mean, she could probably be used as a decent flotation device in the case of an emergency. But please, please tell me you're into her for more than just those."

"There's more . . . can we please drop this?"

Amanda rolled her eyes before using them to burn a stare into Tyler's own eyes. "Fine, just saying you could do a lot better."

"Come on, let's get to class. I don't want to be late again."

CHAPTER 3
A HULDRA

It was another chilly late summer evening in Sweden. The lush greenery surrounding Stora Ålsjön Lake had yet to surrender to beautiful shades of red, yellow and orange. The sound of calm waves brushing against the lake's shoreline was only overpowered by the abundance of bird calls. The lake and its surroundings were secluded. Perfect for a teleportation Jump.

The subtle sounds of nature prancing through the trees and over the lake were interrupted by the sharp snapping sound of a tree branch before transforming into an ear-deafening thunderclap. Charlotte gathered herself as she stumbled forward onto the southern banks of the lake and scanned the area. *Okay, no one saw that . . . Phew! I'm in the clear.*

The crystal lake before her was like a postcard but better, with rich green leaves as far as the eye could see. The mossy, woodsy smell of the forest after a recent rain and the muddy musk of the shoreline mixed together in her nose. She let the pleasantly unappealing fragrance swirl in her head like a drag from a well-crafted cigar, then let it out. Charlotte was at peace, and she at once wished to stay there and take a small vacation away from all the stress and worry of home.

If only Tyler could see this . . .

But as she looked down at her satchel, she saw its contents started to glow blue. Opening her bag, she pulled out the source; the Codex. The book's massive size was light as a feather to its rightful Scribe.

Opening the Codex to the glowing page, Charlotte knew from the color that it was a completed page. She flopped past the section reading "Creatures to Regard" and landed on the page: 'Werewolf'. *He's here.* Charlotte kept still as she listened for the slightest noise. She heard a halting crunch approaching from behind.

"That was much closer than before, Marshall," Charlotte said turning to face a solitary tree.

Caught, Marshall stepped out from behind his cover.

Sporting a worn, gray trench coat and faded blue jeans, Marshall Dunn cracked open a water bottle and asked, "What gave me away?"

"The Codex of course." *His eyes . . . he's stressing again.* Marshall's sunny yellow eyes seemed dimmed or faded between his tired weathered eyelids. *Look at all the grey in his hair. He's aged ten years in a few months.* Although Marshall was well into his fifties, he never looked it as much as he did now.

"Welcome to Sweden, Char. Been here before?" Marshall asked throwing Charlotte the water bottle.

Charlotte wiped her mouth after downing the rest of the lemon-flavored water. "Nope. First time actually."

"First? Really? That's surprising." Marshall panned his hands over the lake. "Well take it in. Sweden is a beautiful

26

country. I lived here most my life. Nature, the food, the women."

"History, culture, and festivals . . ."

Marshall gave Charlotte a wink. "Priorities . . . I've got mine, you've got yours."

"Speaking of priorities, you said you had a lead on another creature," Charlotte asked, snapping the Codex shut.

"Oh, much better than a lead. I convinced her to do an interview," Marshall said pointing his thumb into the forest behind them.

Charlotte sparked up. "An interview? How did you get her to agree?"

"Oh, you know . . . I have my ways." Marshall grinned suggestively.

"Doesn't that ring on your finger mean anything to you?" Charlotte said not holding back her disappointment.

His upbeat mood soured immediately and he went silent. "Does yours?" Marshall asked pointing to the ring on her finger.

Charlotte rubbed the golden band. "Yes, yes it does. I loved the man I married, and I still do."

Marshall stared coldly at Charlotte. "And I love the woman I married. Both your husband and my wife knew exactly what they were getting into when they married us. Only, David paid the price."

Did he honestly just say that!? Charlotte turned away furious, and then snapped back around to glare at him with angry eyes. "I hope you and your children never have to experience what Tyler and I've gone through."

"I promise you they never will," he replied, tilting his head in a leading motion. "Come on, let's go. She's waiting for us."

The two walked alongside one another in silence as tiny ripples lapped up against the damp shoreline.

"Couple more days until the full moon. How is your family doing?" Charlotte asked.

"Just great."

She probed further. "Isn't it Maxine's first cycle?"

Marshall looked surprised that she remembered. "Yes, yes it is. Steph's gonna stay up with her—"

Charlotte interrupted. "Good mother."

"*Great* mother. The best . . . no offense of course."

"No, I agree from everything you've told me. Maybe I could learn a thing or two."

"Hey, 'nough of that, Char," Marshall said giving her a nudge. "Tyler turned out to be a fine young man."

"He did. Guess I got lucky. He's a saint compared to me at his age." *Of course, I was already scribing by then.*

Marshall grinned. "You know, it seems just yesterday Maxine was learning to walk."

"Time goes too fast," Charlotte replied. *And 'business' takes too much of it.*

"Can you believe Tyler and Thomas are both graduating this year?" Marshall said, shaking his head as he stared off into the distance. His eyes always seemed to be looking somewhere else these days. It worried her.

Charlotte groaned. "Don't remind me. I wish I could keep him young forever."

"You and me both," Marshall said. "But it's how it goes. While you're not lookin', they grow up. In the end, you can't protect them from the world forever. Lord knows I'd do anything to make life easier for them."

Charlotte peeked at her satchel with the Codex nestled securely inside. "I just hope someday this'll all be behind me. Behind *us*. I'd spend more time with him . . . and some grandchildren, hopefully."

Marshall pulled ahead into a clearing. "Well first things first, we have to finish that damn book."

Readying the Codex, Charlotte took out the pen she bought from Fosdur earlier that day. "Alright, where is she?"

Having crossed the tree line, above them Marshall and Charlotte heard branches bending under the stress of weight. Following soon after was a loud thud and twigs snapping under feet. The two turned sharply and were greeted by a slender young woman wearing a slightly tarnished, white knee-high sundress. Her tangled, uncombed chestnut hair ran midway down her back and its volume was only matched by the bushy chestnut tail creeping out from under her dress. She stared at the two taller humans, unsure of her decision to reveal herself. Her eyes examined the area for any more travelers.

The Huldra looked up to Marshall asking, "Just her, right, Mr. Dunn? No one else?"

With a smirk and a nod, Marshall introduced the two. "Charlotte this is Lynn, Lynn this is Charlotte. She's the Scribe I was telling you about."

Charlotte approached Lynn timidly and slowly. "Hello, Lynn, a pleasure to meet you. You're quite beautiful and much younger than I thought you'd be."

Lynn's face beamed and erupted into a wholesome chuckle. "I'm well over 400 years old, but thank you. Compliments never grow old."

With daylight slipping away there was little time for chit-chat. "If you wouldn't mind, I'd love to ask you a few questions," Charlotte asked.

Lynn nodded. "Please, ask away."

Charlotte snapped her fingers over the Codex. *Lux.* A small light surrounded the Codex, making it easier for Charlotte to write. Sitting down on a log, she started the interview. "Okay Lynn, tell me about Huldras as a whole." Lynn thought for a moment before answering:

"Most of my sisters populate Scandinavia. Though I will admit, when we're looking to explore, we'll usually hide our tails, don longer clothing, and leave our homes. But for the most part, we're forest creatures. We love the forest and all her children.

"I know it may sound a little vain, but we Huldras like to be seen as beautiful . . . then again, what gal doesn't, right? I also think I speak on behalf of Huldras when I say, if you are kind-hearted and treat nature with respect, there are few creatures more compassionate than Huldras. However . . . harm nature and you'll find out just how dangerous we can be.

"Huldras are similar in looks around Scandinavia with the exception of our tails. Swedish Huldras have fluffy, fox-like tails while Norwegian Huldras have thinner skin-covered tails with a tuft of fur at the tip like . . . well, like cows."

Lynn scratched her head trying to think of any other details. "Let me think, what else would you like to know?"

Charlotte put the end of her pen to her lips, thinking. "Are Huldra all female or are there males?"

"Only female as far as I know. But I have heard of a creature that others have referred to as our male counterparts. Hul-dre-kall? I think that's how you pronounce it. Supposed to be hideous. Might account for their supposed aggression," Lynn said fiddling with her messy locks.

I can feel it, almost there! "Anything else you can think of? It's almost finished."

"Hmm. Well, Huldras and human charcoal burners used to get along back in the day. We'd watch over their kilns while they slept. In return, they'd give us some of their rations."

While writing this down, Charlotte watched as the pink page turned baby blue. *That's it! One more entry in the bag. Wish they were all this easy.* Charlotte glanced up from the Codex saying, "That's everything I need! Thank you very much, Lynn."

"That's all?" It was then that Charlotte noticed Lynn was rubbing her head as though suffering from a migraine. Lynn whimpered, "I . . . I think . . . oh, something is *wrong*. Someone is—"

Before she could finish her sentence, a blue ball of plasmatic light came streaking across the dusky sky, flying past Charlotte before colliding with a tree. A loud snap echoed outwards as the collision sent shards of splintered bark everywhere.

"Magi! Run!" Charlotte exclaimed as another blue plasma ball just missed her head. Her loose hairs seared instantly in the ball's wake.

Lynn scurried across the leaf-littered forest floor with inhuman speed before disappearing into the thick overgrowth. As a barrage of blue lights streamed towards her and Marshall, Charlotte cast magic non-verbally. *Clipeum!* The hostile fire reflected off her glimmering shield in all directions. Tucking the Codex away into her satchel, the two took off into the dense forest as the leaves on the trees strobed flashes of blue and white while pops and snaps reverberated at almost deafening levels. Ducking behind two large trees, Charlotte and Marshall searched for a good breakaway.

Charlotte shouted to Marshall over the roaring spell bombardment, "How did they find us?"

Marshall shouted back as a spell zoomed passed his head, "Occucrypts? Tracker? You tell me!" Unholstering his sidearm, Marshall asked, "How're we gonna get out of this mess?"

With her adrenaline pumping, Charlotte only then realized the large bloody gash cutting through her hip. Only now did she feel the pain. *Gah! Must've got me back in the clearing*. The streaking burning sensation felt like someone had cut into her using a hot knife.

Charlotte winced as she held her hand over her wound and whispered. *Sana.* She watched as her skin sealed over her wound. *Still twinges a little . . . Strange.*

Bark covered the ground around them like shrapnel as a mighty spell smashed into Marshall's tree. He turned back to find Charlotte mending her wounds. "You hit?"

"I'm fine."

"You gotta get us out of here or we're toast!"

He's right. We have to Jump now! Charlotte thought as their assailants closed in on their position. Winding up for a Jump, Charlotte's heart sunk in her chest. She could feel the magic around her, but it was just out of reach, shimmering around her but impossible to hold onto. *I can't . . .* "I can't get us out . . . s-something's wrong!"

"What! What do you mean you can't get us out of here? There's too many of them, Char, and I think Kroll is with them!"

Charlotte shook her head. "I can't. Something's wrong, Marshall! I can hardly feel the magic around me."

"Well, any ideas?" Marshall shot back in frustration.

"We have to outrun them. When I feel a stronger pull of magic, then we'll Jump!" Charlotte said unable to offer anything better.

With their enemies now dangerously close, Marshall shouted over the howling screams of spells turning the surrounding forest into charred rubble, "Then we better get running!"

Taking a breath, Charlotte counted them off. "Okay, here we go. Three . . . Two . . . One . . . *Cadere!*"

The spell trembled outward from her location causing the ground beneath their unseen assassins to quake and tremble. Charlotte and Marshall took off into a sprint, for they knew her spell would only buy them a couple of seconds before a flurry of spells would bombard them as they darted through the dark and dense forest.

CHAPTER 4
MIDDAY

Tyler packed his Algebra textbook as he waited for the mosh pit of students crowding into the hallway to disperse. *Guess I'm not the only one who doesn't understand this crap.*

Already waiting for him at the door, Amanda asked, "How was class?"

"Math, my favorite," Tyler said sarcastically. "How about yours?"

"Fine, Mr. Haywood's pretty chill."

"Told ya."

Once the two were on the ground level, Tyler spotted Casey waiting at their regular spot. Casey was the youngest of Tyler's group of friends. At sixteen years old, she was always the one left behind once her friends graduated. Her middle-length, light brown hair bounced as she turned, and her honey brown eyes lit up upon seeing Tyler walking her way. She had full, round cheeks and a button nose giving her an adorable youthful grin.

Amanda nudged Tyler as she walked to the student store. "Be right there."

Tyler greeted Casey as he approached the table. "What's up, Case?"

"Heeey, not much, how about you?" Casey said as she scooted over to make room for Tyler even though there were plenty of seats around the table.

"Fine, teachers keep dog-piling the homework."

"Right? Tell me about it."

"Where's Ballsy and Zane?"

"Zane's coming. As for Ballsy, I don't know. Haven't seen him today."

"Or yesterday," Tyler said pulling out his phone. "Music?"

"Heck yea," Casey answered. Leaning against his shoulder, Casey pulled out her lunch while Tyler enjoyed his own bag of chips.

Amanda took a seat adjacent to Casey holding a tuna sandwich. "So what'd I miss?"

"Everything," Tyler answered.

"Damn it, again?" Amanda smiled as she took a bite. Tyler cringed. He didn't know how she managed to eat tuna every day. She'd been obsessed with it since they were barely out of their diapers.

"Know if Ballsy's here today?" Tyler asked.

Amanda shrugged. "Haven't seen him. He's been absent lately. What about Za—"

"Here," Zane whispered into Amanda's ear, causing her to jump.

Amanda gave Zane a death glare as he sat across from Tyler and Casey. "Seriously, dude? Every day!"

"You'd think you'd learn then," Zane said still laughing.

Zane stood just a smidge over six-feet tall with silky black hair he kept short and gelled back. He was rail-thin, lacking fat and muscle, but not gaunt or sickly.

"Mr. Chen, how ya doin' ya four-eyed freak?" Tyler joked.

Zane bowed his head. "Mr. Grayson ... I'm doing quite well, thank you. How're you doing ya soulless gingy bastard?"

"Mmm, quite well, quite well, thank you."

Amanda shook her head with a smile. "You two are dorks."

"What'll it be today, boy and girls?" Zane said pulling a deck of cards.

But before anyone could answer Nessa walked up and called out, "Hey, Ty-Ty."

"Isn't this a treat ..." muttered Zane, sliding his cards back into his pocket.

Casey immediately straightened up, creating space between herself and Tyler, her retreat unseen. Nessa was too busy locked in a stare down with Amanda the moment she started approaching.

"Hey, Nessa. How's it going?" asked Tyler.

"Much better now that I have you in my sight," she cooed, but still staring at Amanda.

"Wanna sit down?"

Breaking the stare off, Nessa smiled and took a seat next to Tyler. She turned to everyone purring, "How're we all doing?"

Zane shuffled uncomfortably. "Fine, you?"

"Okay, you?" Casey added but went unnoticed, sheepish and barely audible.

The atmosphere around the table turned cold. Amanda carried on eating her lunch not saying a word unless someone asked her something, and even then she answered curtly. Casey became rigid keeping her eyes to herself. Zane fooled around shuffling his deck, trying to feel out if anyone still wanted to play.

Zane offered the deck to Nessa. "Want in?"

Nessa smirked and shook her head. "I'm fine, thanks." Reaching over, Nessa caressed Tyler's hand getting his attention. He perked up at the touch and felt his heart hammer in his chest. "Hey, let's go for a walk."

Casey took a drawn-out, silent sigh of frustration as her eyes locked onto Nessa's hand holding Tyler's.

"Okay, sure," Tyler said before turning to his friends. "Catch you guys later?"

Amanda and Casey remained silent and just nodded while Zane answered, "For sure, man. See ya later."

"See ya in fifth, Ty," Casey murmured as Nessa pulled Tyler away.

Nessa immediately turned and leered at Casey much like a cat might look at a mouse before pouncing. And like a mouse, Casey shrunk as Nessa eyed at her, breaking eye contact before looking down at the floor.

Casey turned to Amanda once Nessa and Tyler were out of sight, both equally frustrated, but for different reasons. Amanda nodded. "Yeah, you and me both, Case."

✸✸

It was just past 3 PM when the school's dismissal bell rang and the halls filled with students eager to go home. Walking out of class, Tyler met up with Amanda before walking to her locker.

"Come on, worrying isn't going to help," Tyler said trying to calm Amanda's nerves.

Bending down to unlock her bottom locker, Amanda pulled out a couple books from her tidy space. "Yeah, yeah I know . . ."

"Win, lose or draw, you'll live."

Amanda nodded as she shut her locker and turned the knob. The two climbed down a flight of stairs to Tyler's locker and Amanda quickly changed the subject. "So what're your plans for today?"

Tyler was a little apprehensive to answer after this morning. "Nessa and I are gonna hang out. We're having dinner with Mom."

She suppressed a laugh. "Never mind, you're the one who needs all the luck today," Amanda said bumping Tyler's shoulder.

Tyler gave a half-hearted laugh, though he knew she was right. "Maybe they'll get along today?"

"Or they'll use the kitchen-wear as weaponry."

Tyler kept quiet.

Amanda stopped and grabbed Tyler's hand. "Hey . . . you know I'm only kidding, right?"

"I know, I'd just like it if you were a little nicer to her."

Amanda let go of his hand. "Nicer? *Me* be nicer? How about she tries it for a change?"

"She's actually a nice person if you'd just try to get to know her."

38

"I have! And she was a bitch to me. And poor Casey . . ."

"Casey?"

"Yeah! She's terrified of Nessa. And for good reason too. She keeps giving her death glares every time Casey pulls your attention away from her."

"Does she really?"

"Why would I lie? You know I just want to see you happy. We all do. And I can try to be nicer to her. But if she isn't gonna try too . . ."

"I'll talk to her, especially about Casey. That's not cool."

Amanda smiled, happy to have her friend back from Planet Nessa for a second. "Thank you. And maybe things'll change. Maybe she'll even become a part of the group?" Bringing him in for a hug, Amanda whispered with a light chuckle barely held back, "But if she tries to get between me and my bestie, I'll take her out." They both laughed. Tough words coming from someone who had never been in a fight her whole life.

Tyler peered into his locker asking, "So when do I get to see one of these swim meets?"

"It's not very exciting, you'd probably be bored," Amanda said trying to squash the topic.

"It's a race! How could it be boring? Even then, I'd like to be there for you."

Amanda backpedaled. "And the suits are ugly . . . and a little revealing."

Tyler gave a puzzled look as he glanced back at Amanda. "A one-piece swimsuit with a swim cap? "

Amanda rubbed her shoulder nervously. "Well—"

"As for revealing. Mmm, oh, I think you're right!" Tyler interrupted, flicking his finger against Amanda's thigh. "Seeing these babies would change my entire perception of you, harlot."

Amanda jumped, swatting Tyler over the head with her book as he ducked for cover. "You know I hate that!"

"Um . . . yeah? That's why I do it," Tyler said closing his locker. "But seriously, why can't I see you compete? It's almost like you don't want me there."

"No, I do. It'd be great to have someone else besides Mom and Dad cheering me on. It's just . . . complicated," Amanda answered.

Tyler stared blankly at her. "I think you're just being weird. But if you insist. Someday?"

Amanda nervously shrugged. "Someday . . . maybe."

Walking out to the pickup zone, Tyler waited with Amanda until her mom pulled up. First giving Tyler a hug, Amanda jumped into her mom's car. "Wish me luck?"

"Give 'em hell," Tyler said with a wink and a wave.

Tyler saw Mrs. Morales saying something to Amanda as she eyed him. Amanda moaned a drawn-out, "Mooooom . . ." before turning back to Tyler blushing. Watching them pull away, Tyler turned and made his way back to the front of the school where he saw Nessa waiting at the gate with her arms crossed and a displeased expression on her face.

That better not be directed at me. "What's that look for?"

"Is it *my* turn now?"

Seriously!? "Oh come—"

Nessa interrupted shouting, "Rolling your eyes at me now?"

"You're acting ridiculous," he replied, matching Nessa's volume.

"Oh! I'm acting ridiculous now?"

It was as though, very suddenly, Nessa's true nature had been unveiled. Tyler answered her with clarity, "Yeah, just a bit. You pick a fight with my mom every time we get together. My friends are terrified of you. Amanda, my best friend, can't even be in the same room with you. And now I can't say bye to her?" *Wait . . . why am I even with her?* "So yeah, I'd have to say this is a little—"

Seeing she had let things get out of control, Nessa flashed her baby blues. "Ty-Ty, stop. Look at my eyes."

Still steaming, Tyler peered into her eyes and immediately felt calm. His anger drifted away.

"I'm sorry, Ty-Ty. I didn't mean to make you mad," Nessa said with a pouty face.

"No, it's okay, I'm not mad. It's just—"

Nessa's phone buzzed grabbing her attention. "Hold that thought." Peeping up from her phone, Nessa smiled as though whatever she just read had made her year. "But you're right. It's not working."

"Wait, what?"

"We're over, deuces."

Before he could react, Nessa turned and walked away. Tyler just stared at her. *Wait . . . did she just break up with me?*

Slightly unnerving, Nessa turned around only to say, "Yep," before continuing her march to her car.

Yep? That was weird. Now without a ride, Tyler had an hour walk ahead of him. But as Nessa walked further away, Tyler started remembering how he felt before staring into Nessa's eyes. His anger returned to him. *I'd rather walk then be in a car with her anyway.* Tyler pulled out his phone and sent Amanda a text.

Amanda

> Well not sure if you've even left the school yet, but me and Nessa just broke up.

What??? Really? What happened in the last 2 minutes?!?!?

> It's really dumb

Ok... sorry? Congratulations?

> Lol yeah maybe both

Well don't worry buddy, it's that dumb bitch's loss anyway. There are other fish in the sea.

> Yeah, I guess. Sure I can't come by and cheer you on? Lol I'm free now

Maybe another day. I'll ttyl <3

Tyler heard someone yell out to him, "You're better off without her, brah!"

He turned to see Zane staring back from afar. "Think so?"

Zane squinted his eyes with an almost concerned look on his face. He smacked his lips answering, "You kidding? If she comes crawling back, run! Run as fast as you can!"

Tyler laughed. "We still on this weekend?"

"Heck yeah, man! Hopefully Ballsy isn't AFK still."

"Yeah. Let's see if Case wants in too," Tyler added.

"Case? She plays?"

"Yeah, played with her the other night. She's a pretty good marksmen."

Zane was surprised. "Huh, cool. We can make room in our squad."

"Okay cool, we'll talk more about it tomorrow. I've kinda got a long walk ahead of me," Tyler said as a tidal wave of anxiety crushed down upon him. His cheerful demeaner vanished.

"Uh, you okay? What's wrong?"

I suddenly feel awful. Like something bad's gonna happen. Something . . . ah, quit it man. Walk it off. I just gotta clear my mind. Tyler played it off. "Thought I forgot something. I'm good. See ya," he said before turning for home.

Zane grabbed his backpack and ran down the school steps to catch up with Tyler. But he stopped. Something told him to stay. To give his friend space and let Tyler be with his thoughts. Alone.

CHAPTER 5
PLAN GOES SOUTH

It was almost impossible to navigate through the dark Swedish forest without running into a tree or tripping over uneven ground. Even using magic to enhance vision proved nearly ineffective. The only smell Charlotte's nose could pick up was the aroma of dirt, moss, and dead leaves mixing with her sweat. She scrambled out of sight as she tried holding back her gasps for air. *Gotta keep quiet. I think we lost them.*

Listening, Charlotte could hear her relentless pursuers panting nearby. She glanced down at her watch in the dark. *It's past midnight and we've been running for hours. But look at them. They're just as winded . . . perfect.* Not only was Charlotte a much stronger magic wielder – even with her mysterious restrictions – but they didn't know where she was. This made Charlotte very dangerous, and they knew this.

"Everyone freeze!" one of the assassins hissed in an inhumanly deep voice bringing their hunt to an abrupt halt.

Marshall was right, it's that brainless psycho, Kroll. Ezekiel means business and he knew damn well where I was going to be. How?

Marshall pressed against her shoulder, trying to slow his breathing as they both scanned the area, unable to find anything in the choking darkness. They had to take a gamble if they wanted to go on the offensive.

Charlotte poked her head out from behind a tree, watching the blurry outlines of her attackers slowly creep forward. Then, as though igniting a lighter, she saw their eyes burn a bloody crimson red in the darkness. She quickly ducked back behind the tree before any could see her. From the far-off cries of owls to the echoing chirps of crickets, all manner of life was still. Only the sound of leaves blowing in the slightest wind kept the forest from being silent as the grave.

Charlotte swore under her breath. *Attack or wait them out? I have no idea how many we have, and though Kroll's a bumbling idiot, he packs a serious punch. Enough to kill Marshall . . .*

Taking one look back at Marshall, Charlotte listened to them spreading through the darkness, combing the area. They knew she was there.

Charlotte jumped out from behind her tree, and launched a spell before the nearest demon could react. *Somnum!* The demon collapsed to the ground, unconscious and possibly dead before his head even hit the dirt. She withdrew back behind her tree before another demon could spot her. The only thing the other demons could do was look at one another speechless and afraid. The line between hunter and hunted was gone.

"Where are you, bitch?" Kroll growled. "She's here! Find her!"

The tides had changed. Their attempt to intimidate her only showed their own intimidation. When another rushed to their fallen ally, Charlotte popped out again.

Parálisis! The demon froze like a plank. He could see Charlotte slipping back behind the tree but was powerless to move or speak.

Another demon called out to Charlotte, "You're outnumbered, girl! Give us the Codex, and we'll let you live!"

Silence.

Kroll shouted, this time closer, "You can't win!"

"You sure?" Charlotte whispered. All of them lunged forward and turned, ready to fire a spell, for each heard Charlotte as though she was whispering right behind them. The demons' eyes shifted back and forth as they panicked in silence.

Charlotte took her chance. She stroked the bark of the tree. "Lynn, forgive me. If I survive, I will return one day and plant ten trees in this one's place." Placing the flat of her palm against the tree, she whispered, "*Disseco!*" The tree snapped at its base, sending a ripple of sound through the forest.

The demons' ears perked and they all zeroed in on their position. But, unsure what trap she had placed, they slowly marched toward the tree, all ready to fire a life or death spell.

Charlotte gave the tree a light shove. *Dis!*

The severed tree thrust forward toward the demons like a speeding bullet. Only the demons spread far enough were able to dive out of the way while the unlucky were dragged along under the crushing weight of the wooden missile.

"Wow . . ." Marshall whispered before Charlotte grabbed his arm and dragged him to his feet.

They broke into a run as the few surviving demons scrambled to their feet. She fired raw magic at the nearest demon as she sprinted by him, and a flash of deep purple light lit the forest as her plasmatic ball hit its target. To their right, Marshall put a bullet in another, and the demon fell back groaning in anguish. The light and noise gave away their position, but they didn't have a choice now.

Something scurried past Charlotte towards her attackers. She could only make out what looked like a fox-like tail before it darted into the darkness, and then Charlotte heard Lynn pounce on a demon before dragging her helpless victim out of sight. *Whatever magic I have at my disposal, I doubt it'd be worse than whatever Lynn has in store.*

With a barrage of blue plasma illuminating the area around them, Charlotte ducked as one streaked towards her just missing her chest. Diving behind a downed and rotting tree, Charlotte thought to herself. *Six . . . six more and we're in the clear. Only problem is these six know exactly where we're hiding.*

The old, rotting tree shook violently as a volley of spells crashed against it. The pitch black forest strobed light with each spell, and even with only six left, popping out to fire her own spell was too risky, especially if Kroll was still among the living. Charlotte knew she had to make an escape. They wouldn't be able to find them if they could get enough separation.

Charlotte groaned in frustration. *I shouldn't even be in this situation! I've always Jumped in and out of danger before!*

"What's wrong? Out of gas?" Marshall whispered to her, ducking low as another spell flew overhead, reducing another tree in the distance to a fiery plasmatic smolder.

We might not make it out of this. If we're caught, trapped or even killed . . . the Codex will fall into his hands. That can't happen. I won't let it. She had to make sure the Codex was safe.

Charlotte knew it would be risky, but not doing anything would be risking everything. Placing a palm over the Codex, Charlotte closed her eyes. *Largior Tyler Grayson.* Instantly, the Codex disappeared into thin air. *Thank goodness that worked.*

A bolt of plasma smashed into their downed tree, sending a flurry of sharp wooden shrapnel in their direction. Marshall grabbed Charlotte and pulled her closer. "Char, we can't go on. You have to give them the book."

"What? Marshall, are you insane? You know what would happen!" Charlotte shouted pushing Marshall off her.

Frustrated, Marshall reached for her satchel and tried to dig for the book, but Charlotte pulled away. "There's a lot more of them then there is of us! I've only got two bullets left and your bloody magic isn't working at full capacity. What're you gonna do? Fight them all?"

Gritting her teeth, Charlotte snapped her fingers, trying to grasp another wisp of magic, but there was nothing. Without it, she couldn't hope to fight them even though she had already trimmed their numbers. *My connection feels even weaker without the Codex . . . I can't risk Marshall's life. And I have to come home to Tyler. He'll have no one.*

Marshall repeated himself, "Just give them the book!"

"How can you even suggest that!" *He knows what would happen if Ezekiel gets the Codex.* "I teleported it to Tyler with the last of my magic. I couldn't even if I wanted to!"

"Tyler? Why would you do that?" he said, growling in frustration.

"I had to, Marshall. I just hope he doesn't notice before I get back."

"Get back? Who's getting back? Now we have nothing to bargain with!" Marshall furiously beat his fist into the fallen tree. "Damnit, Char, why?"

Charlotte turned to Marshall giving him the best reassurance she could muster, "Hey, stop it! We're gonna make it!"

A large piece of the tree splintered off just to Marshall's right, nearly taking off his arm in the process. Running out of time and options, Charlotte planned aloud, "Okay, here's the plan. I'm going to try my best to find a last wisp of magic and create a blinding field with it. If they look at it or even face it with their eyes closed, it'll blind them long enough for us to make a final break. But it'll take everything I have, Marshall. I'm gonna need you to carry me out of here."

Marshall murmured coldly, "That might work."

"I can only hold it for maybe a minute, so you're gonna need to be quick, okay?" Charlotte said, winding up to cast the spell. Marshall muttered something under his breath and looked away, while Charlotte swirled her palm around and around as though winding up a lasso, "Three . . . Two . . . One—"

"I'm sorry."

The sheer force of the shot drove Charlotte to her knees as the Magnum bullet tore through her chest, and only after the shock had passed did Charlotte feel any pain. Her jaw clenched as short grunts of anguish escaped. She tasted blood as she tried to speak. Staring down at her white undershirt, she saw the exit wound penetrating the shirt as blood gushed out, staining her chest crimson. Her eyes bulged in pain as her vision blurred. Kneeling helplessly in the wet dirt, Charlotte wasn't sure what hurt more: the bullet wound or the heartbreaking truth. She had been shot in the back.

"Marshall, please tell Tyler –"

He let fly another gunshot, this one fatal as Charlotte fell to the cold ground, motionless. Her eyes were open, but the flickering light there had blown out like a birthday candle. Gun loose in his hand, Marshall stared down at his friend's lifeless body as the smoke trailed from the barrel.

"It's done!" Marshall called out, dropping the gun before running his hand through his hair.

The cautious steps of each demon quickened as they raced to Marshall's side. The infernal humanoids ranged in size, each sporting long charcoal black horns jutting out from their foreheads. They had blood red skin from head to spaded tail which made hiding their demonic identity all but impossible.

"Is this the best Ezekiel has to offer?" Marshall shouted, glaring hateful daggers into Kroll's chest as he lumbered forward in his wide gait with a terrible grin on his face.

"The Codex?" Kroll asked, paying no attention to Marshall's insult.

Marshall knelt over, picked up his gun and slid it back into its holster. He paced in frustration. "She teleported it to her son."

"Well then what're we waiting for? Let's nab it!" another demon laughed with wicked glee.

50

"This'll be like shooting fish in a barrel," cackled another.

"Hey!" Marshall roared furiously. All of them but Kroll jumped back in surprise. He pointed to them one by one saying, "Take the book. But don't harm the boy."

The choir bellowed in mischievous laughter. "Why do you care?" Kroll barked, taking a step forward. He towered over Marshall by at least two feet, but the Werewolf refused to be intimidated.

Marshall only repeated himself. "Don't. Harm. The boy."

"Oh, we'll leave the boy . . ." Kroll said with a throaty chuckle as he and the other demons merged back into the shadows. "So long as he doesn't resist. Now do something with the body, or I'm taking her filthy human head back to Lord Ezekiel as a trophy, mutt." And with that they were gone, leaving Marshall alone with Charlotte's lifeless body.

No, not alone. Lynn was there watching, he could smell her.

She'd seen everything.

CHAPTER 6
HOME INVASION

The walk home should have only taken an hour or less, but with no reason to rush home, Tyler took his time wandering through the valley. This did his anxiety wonders. Not completely relieved, but much better. With dusk now turning day into night, Tyler strolled into the front yard, fumbled with the keys to the front door and walked up the old brick stoop. Closing and locking the door behind him, he was unaware he had been followed the entire way home.

Almost tripping over a pile of unpacked boxes, Tyler caught himself on the last step of the stairs. *Really, Mom? Don't have to be a klutz to trip over this mess.*

He picked himself up and marched into the kitchen. *Let's take a quick break,* Tyler thought as he flopped his backpack onto the discolored counter. Turning on the TV for background noise, Tyler sat for a moment. *Anything I can do to stall writing that paper?* He turned to see the empty pots and pans atop the stove.

That'll do. Tyler texted his mom, "Don't pick anything up, I'm making dinner." He knew she would appreciate the gesture and he could relax a little before tackling tonight's homework or neglecting it altogether. His mom always loved it when she came home and he had dinner ready. His father had a passion for cooking and Tyler loved learning from him, perfecting family recipes and even improving on a few after his passing. He wished he was here to try some of his new concoctions.

He peered into the freezer and refrigerator. *Minus the capers, I've got everything for Dad's chicken piccata. I know this one like the back of my hand.* He could hear his father's voice at the back of his mind, "Make this for a special girl and her heart will flutter." Tyler laughed. *Definitely not the intention tonight. But Mom always loved that dish.* He wondered whether it was the recipe his dad had used all those years ago that had captured his mother's heart.

It was an elegant delicious Italian dish that filled the senses and the stomach. *After everything she's been going through, she deserves a meal like this and more.* Filling a pot with water, Tyler slid his backpack across the counter to make a clean prep area. But as he did, he caught a glimpse of something in his backpack. *Huh? What the heck is this?* It was an old leather-bound book. *And it's glowing blue?* Turning off the water before the pot overflowed, he grabbed his backpack and pulled out the Codex.

Tyler stared at it for a moment, baffled how it found its way into his backpack. He picked it up, and found its leather cover was soft to the touch and worn. It was very old. *Huh? It's so big, but it's super lightweight . . . weird.*

Opening to the first page, Tyler read: 'Property of CG.'

It's Mom's penmanship . . . 'CG' . . . Charlotte Grayson. Sheepishly, Tyler opened the book to the glowing page. He looked down at the parchment. "Succubus," he read aloud the word scorched into the top of the page. *Huh? Succubus is burned in. But the rest is written in pen . . . or maybe quill.*

The doorbell startled Tyler as its melody rang throughout the house. He paused, for the first time in his life considering it was a door better left closed, but then the doorbell rang again, so Tyler slipped the mysterious book back into his backpack and walked to the entrance.

Opening the door, Tyler was greeted by Nessa looking up at him with pouty eyes. "Hey, Ty-Ty."

"What do you want, Nessa?" Tyler said not in the mood for any more drama.

"Tyler, I know you're mad. I messed up bad. I'm sorry."

Tyler stared at her blankly. "So you pull that stunt earlier, say you're sorry and everything is supposed to be okay?"

Nessa drew back, her eyes welling with tears. "Please, Tyler. Can we just talk."

"I'm not stopping you, what do you wanna say?"

Nessa scratched her head. "Mind if I come inside? It's a long drive to your home from school."

No it's not. It's twenty minutes max. Tyler had half a mind to tell her off, but there was something about Nessa standing there that made him want to hear her out. Opening the door wider, he let her inside, and as he did he could feel his head growing cloudy. For a moment he couldn't stop looking at her, how beautiful she was. And a fleeting thought told him he'd been a fool to ever let her walk away. "Y – you want some water?"

"Yes please," Nessa said walking into the house.

"So what is it?" Tyler asked, walking to the kitchen and grabbing her a glass from the cabinet.

Turning back to Nessa, he saw she was looking around the room. "You guys have a nice little place here."

The house is an unpacked mess . . . hardly 'nice'. Maybe she's just trying to make small talk before she apologizes. But as she kept snooping around, Tyler got an odd feeling that she was searching for something. Moving to the counter, Tyler slid his backpack toward him, immediately drawing her attention. *This is starting to get really weird.*

Nessa smiled as she walked to the counter. "So how about that water?"

Tyler slung his backpack over his shoulder and handed Nessa a glass of water. Her eyes remained fixated on the ordinary backpack.

"I thought you were thirsty?" Tyler said watching Nessa put the glass on the counter without even a sip.

"Oh yeah," Nessa said as though waking from a trance. She gave him a half smile before downing the entire glass.

Tyler just wanted this bizarrely developing conversation over. "You had something to say?"

"Yeah I did—hey can I dig through your backpack for some paper? I've got a big essay to write tonight."

"Here you go, keep it," Tyler said handing Nessa a spiral notepad sitting on the counter.

Nessa took the pad with a hint of frustration steaming from her careful smile and chuckled. Nessa added, "Okay, how about a pen?"

Tyler pointed to a cup stuffed full of pens by the fridge. "No pen, no problem." Nessa stood there silently thinking out her next move. "How about a big leathery book? Need one of those too?" Tyler asked.

She looked him dead in the eye, but showed no hint of recognition. *She's good.* "What? What do you mean?"

"This book," Tyler said opening his backpack enough to flash the glowing book.

"Oh, you found it!" Nessa cried out, unable to pry her eyes from the tome. "I was looking all over for that! Thank you!"

"This is yours?"

Closing the gap between the two, Nessa reached for the Codex. "Yes, it's mine."

Tyler pulled the backpack away from her. "You're lying."

Nessa's eyes met Tyler's with her hand still reaching out for the Codex. "Tyler, let me see the book."

"Okay, what's going on, Nessa?" Tyler asked as he stepped back to create space between them. "The second you stepped inside you started snooping around. What's so important about it?"

Nessa only repeated herself with a more demanding tone. "Let me see the book."

Tyler closed the zipper and flung it over his shoulder. "No, get out of—"

As he spoke, Nessa closed her eyes and took a deep breath to compose herself. But when she opened her eyes again, her pupils had turned to slits. Tyler took another step back.

Nessa asked one more time, her voice now deeper and carrying a lisp from her forked tongue and keen fangs, "Let's try this again, Ty-Ty. Give me the Codex!" A pair of large void black bat wings fanned out from behind her, and patches of torn membrane littered the damaged pair of

56

wings, immediately turning her stunning beauty into something out of a horror movie.

Tyler stared, unable to comprehend what was happening. He felt his knees go weak, but he managed to take another step back. "W – what the hell . . ."

"Basically." With her eyes glowing a fiery red, her flowery pink lips turned chalkboard black, and she let out a hiss as her skin changed to a blush red. "Give me the Codex *now* and I won't hurt you . . . badly."

"Nessa . . . just hold on a sec—"

"NOW!" Nessa roared, lunging forward at Tyler with her sharp black nails outstretched like talons.

Ducking out of the way at the last second, Tyler jumped left just as Nessa whipped herself around. Dragging behind, her long, spaded tail sliced through his forearm, drawing a thin line of blood. The hairs on the back of his neck stood on end as she hissed peering at him with a demonic grin. She crouched down to lunge, but both were caught completely off-guard when one of the blunt and heavy wooden kitchen cabinets unhooked itself from the wall and fell forward.

Nessa didn't even have time to wince before the cabinet crashed down onto her head. Between her face getting sucker punched by the cabinet and banging the back of her head against the counter, she was knocked out cold. Maybe worse.

Tyler tried to form words as he stood silently over her unconscious body. Every time he opened his mouth, his words were stolen, leaving his mouth ajar. *What just happened?* Opening his backpack, Tyler took out the still glowing book, the source of his current misery, and opened it to the blue glowing page.

"Succubus..." *The book, did it sense her?* He wondered staring down at Nessa and then back at the book.

Two more pages started to glow blue. Tyler panicked as he flipped to the nearest page: *Gadwen.* This page was full of information; even the margins brimmed with his mother's writing. Tyler opened to the second glowing page: *Brownie.* Like the Gadwen, this page was also filled with information but there was much less.

Tyler jumped when he heard something bumping into glasses and other dishes in the remaining cabinets. It sounded like a mouse but bigger, and he recoiled when something thunked against the cabinet door. *Something's struggling to get out.* Another attempt and the creature managed to swing the door open.

Seeing Tyler standing there mostly unharmed, Penelope sighed in relief. "Oh, thank goodness you're okay." She peered down at the Succubus. "It's going to be impossible living with your mother now."

"W – what are you?" Tyler asked gazing at the tiny creature. *This can't be real.*

"My name is Penelope and I'm a Gadwen."

Tyler's eyes widened. "Gadwen! You're in the book!"

"Yes, of course. That's the Codex of Creatures. Every mythical creature has its own page," Penelope said pointing at the book.

"This isn't normal," Tyler said leaning himself against the kitchen counter.

Penelope's ears perked up. A low-pitched rumble came from a stopped truck just outside. "I'll tell you everything later, sweetie. We need to get you out of here. It's not safe. You invited a demon into your house, and the power of the Oath has been temporarily broken."

"What Oath?" Tyler was startled when he heard something moving behind the downed cabinet. He stared down at the Codex then back to Penelope. "Let me guess . . . a Brownie?"

Penelope nodded and called out, "Charlie, the coast is clear."

Popping out from behind the cabinet, Charlie examined the Succubus and giggled. "I'd say I hit my mark, huh?"

Charlie was no more than two feet tall with a plump physique. While his arms and legs looked almost too small for the rest of his body, his nose was large and freckled. Much like his species' name implied, Charlie was covered in miniature brown clothing from head to toe.

Penelope hopped down from the cabinet. "Yes yes, good work. But we have to get Tyler out of here before—" A loud crashing noise came from the front. The door cracked down its center as something tried forcing its way through the deadbolt. Penelope reached for Tyler's hand. "They're here! Hurry, we have to hide!"

But before they could leave the destroyed kitchen, the front door flung open, smashed into the wall and left a small crater in the drywall. Stepping through the cracked door frame, three demonic creatures peered at Tyler with their burning crimson, slitted eyes. Their noses flattened like a snake's, and large, curved horns protruded from their foreheads, each white at the base but discoloring into a smoky black towards the ends.

Another page started to glow and Tyler quickly glanced down at the Codex. *Incubus.* Shifting his focus back to the intruders, he watched as the one at the front pointed to the Codex with his blackened, razor-sharp forefinger.

"Tyler Grayson! Give us the Codex and we will leave peacefully!" the Incubus shouted with a deep booming voice.

Feeling his heart beating faster, Penelope squeezed his hand. "Don't listen to them, sweetie! Demons cannot be trusted!"

The Incubus reared his yellowing jagged teeth at Penelope. The flames in his eyes raged like a firestorm as his narrow slit grew even smaller. "Unless you wish to be fed to the hellhounds, not another word, *Gadwen.*" His eyes shifted back to Tyler. "Give me the Codex *now* or suffer death."

Pulling out the Codex, Tyler looked down at the old book. *What's so important about this thing?* Penelope pulled Tyler back by his collar, her tiny wings beating faster and faster. "Don't give it to them!"

Tired of waiting, the Incubi growled as they crouched down ready to pounce on Tyler. But before they could, Charlie ran in front of Tyler and lunged at the lead demon, dwarfed by his size. "Back! Back, you beasts!" he cried as he swung a sharp kitchen knife at the fiends.

The creature drove them back a step, but with one mighty swipe, Charlie was flung through the air before smashing into the wall. A weak groan escaped the Brownie as he struggled to pick himself off the floor.

The leader grinned and moved forward to attack. But two steps in, he dropped to his knees and began to desperately gasp for air. He clenched around his neck as though trying to strip invisible hands choking him. The other demons stared at one another, unsure and panicked as they watched their leader suffocating, and that's when an older man with a slight limp walked into the room, The expressions on all three demons turned from panic to unbridled terror.

The man stood an inch or two shorter than Tyler with short sandy white hair and a well-trimmed beard. He had a moderately healthy physique, though an old man gut had grown in over the years. Wearing a grey overcoat with matching slacks, he was a well-dressed man if not a little out of touch with the style of the day.

The man glanced down at the demon. "You hurt my friend," he said pointing at Charlie with his eyes. "So how about this? When you can tell me to stop, I'll let go."

"St . . . ah . . . awp!" the demon gasped, struggling at his windpipe.

Unsatisfied, the old man extended his hand and crushed it into a fist. All anyone could hear was a distinct bone-crushing noise, and the demon's eyes rolled back as he fell to the floor, dead.

"Ezekiel will hear of your actions!" the other two demons hissed at the man.

Raising an eyebrow, the old man smirked. "Oh, will he? And who's gonna tell him?"

With the snap of his fingers, the two demons burst into flames. Even though they were creatures of the underworld, there was no fire in hell as searing and all-consuming as these, as their tortured, agonizing screams reverberated through the home and sent shivers down Tyler's back.

His heart pounding in his chest, Tyler wondered if he and the tiny fairy grasping his hand were next. The old man stared at Tyler for a moment, taking him in, before walking to Charlie's aid. "You alright there, Charlie?" he said, pulling the Brownie to his feet.

"I'll be fine, thank you," Charlie said, a giant red bruise forming on top his bald head.

"Get him some water," the old man said to Tyler in a demanding manner.

After everything he just witnessed, Tyler didn't hesitate and quickly stepped into the kitchen, up and over Nessa, and grabbed a glass of water. He gave it to Charlie and backed away, still watching the man closely.

"What? Quit staring! I ain't gonna hurt you," the old man said aggressively. Turning to Penelope, the man nodded. "Penelope."

"Jon . . ." Penelope greeted the man half-heartedly.

"I save both your hides and that's the 'hello' I get?" Jon chuckled as he limped to the front door checking for more intruders.

"I don't like you," Penelope said, crossing her arms across her tiny chest.

Jon nodded, unfazed. "Well, not the first time you've said that."

"Excuse me," Tyler said, inserting himself into the conversation. "Thank you for saving us, but . . . who are you?"

"I'm your grandfather," Jon said staring the young man square in the eyes.

Tyler was taken aback. "Grandfather? My mom said both of my grandfathers were dead."

"Not surprising."

"Why?"

Jon pointed to Penelope. "Well like your little friend there, your mother didn't like me very much."

"Wait, why—"

Jon interrupted. "Save it. We can talk later. Right now we need to get you and that cursed book back to my place."

Tyler stepped back. "Woah, thanks for saving me, Gramps. But I'm not going anywhere. My mom's gonna be home any—"

"Damn it, boy, just listen! Don't make this harder for me than it already is," Jon said with a painful look on his face.

"I'm staying right here," Tyler said, taking another step backward.

"Just like your mother . . ." Waving his hand over Tyler's eyes, Jon grabbed him as his body fell limp. Jon's spell had slipped Tyler into a deep sleep.

Penelope shrieked, "Tyler! Really, Jon?"

Jon snarled with contempt. "You coming too or am I leaving you?"

She glared at Jon as she held out her hand. Forming a link, Jon held Tyler upright in one arm while holding Penelope's hand with the other. Charlie wrapped his arms around Jon's left leg, and with a loud thunderclap the four of them Jumped to safety, leaving behind the remains of three demons, and what had been Tyler's life, forever.

CHAPTER 7
A PLACE TO HIDE

The roaring boom of thunder rippled through the sleepy lane, and the four landed gracefully on the front porch of Jon's property. With Tyler still slumped against him, Jon waved his hand over the locked door and it opened to his will. Penelope was nauseous and weak in the knees after Jumping. Helping her onto a comfortable cushion, Charlie rushed into the kitchen and got her a cup of water.

"Put him there so we can keep an eye on him," Penelope said pointing to a nearby couch.

Jon dragged Tyler into a bedroom instead. "No, he needs a bed and a place to hide. He'll soon be—" He was interrupted by another crackling wave of thunder – another Jump. "It's him . . ." Jon said as he rolled Tyler into bed and locked the door behind him.

A calm knock came from the front door, each thud drowning out all other sounds in the house. Everyone was still. Everyone was quiet. Even Jon had an uncertain look on his face. As Jon made his way to the door, Charlie held Penelope's hand while positioning himself slightly in front of her.

Opening the door, the three were greeted by a pair of red glowing eyes stepping through the shadows into the dim light of the porch, extinguishing into a steel blue color once they caught the light. The man strutted with each step, dressed in a fine black business suit, matching pants, and a ruby red tie. His skin was a lighter shade of crimson, and his short hair was a natural bleached white despite appearing to be in his thirties. But his most notable feature was a large, pale scar that ran just under his chin up through his ear, severing flesh from his right ear lobe.

He rested his arm up against the door frame and peered inside. "Jon," he said as his eyes met Jon's.

"Ezekiel . . ." Jon replied unenthusiastically with an unamused scowl on his face.

"Now now, old friend. Have I caught you at a bad time?"

"Who else do you want to take from me?" Jon said coldly staring at him despite knowing firsthand what Ezekiel was willing and capable of doing.

Ezekiel played coy as Penelope shifted uncomfortably. "Who else? Why . . . I don't know what you mean."

Jon marched forward with his finger pointed at Ezekiel, forcing the man to step back into a proper posture. "Is that right! Then why the hell is my daughter dead?"

Penelope cried in disbelief. "What? Charlotte's . . . no!"

Ezekiel smirked as tears broke the rims of Penelope's eyes. He turned back to Jon and gave him a smug smile. "Oh, *that*. Nothing personal, old friend. But as you know, she was the Scribe and, well, I need the Codex."

The creature's grin sickened Jon. It took everything in his being to stop him from screaming. "You've ruined everything and everyone I've ever loved."

"Come now, Jon … Ruined everything? No. You … *you* ruined your own life. Not me."

Jon stared blankly at Ezekiel and then looked away. "What do you want? Why the hell are you here? To gloat?"

"Jon, do you play me a fool?" Ezekiel laughed, taking immense joy in the conversation. "What have I always wanted? The Codex, Jon. Hand it over."

"Sorry to disappoint you, but it's not here. Now get off my property!"

"Of course it is, Jon." Ezekiel smiled as he licked his lips and scanned the room.

"My daughter hated me," Jon reminded him while blocking the doorway with his body. "What makes you think she'd teleport it to me?"

"She gave it to her son. Your grandson."

Jon kept silent. "Tyler? We've never even met. Why would he be here?"

Ezekiel's face turned dreadfully serious. "Because a certain Succubus told me she saw you take Tyler and those two with you."

That caught Jon off-guard. "This is none of my business . . . now leave!" he demanded, trying to close the door, but Ezekiel wouldn't be dissuaded.

"She also found the Incubi I sent to follow her … dead. How did they die, Jon?"

"Are you accusing me?" Jon said, feigning outrage.

"Innocent until proven guilty," Ezekiel said with an amused chuckle. "But with that said, Tyler has the book and you brought Tyler here. May I speak with the boy?"

"Out of the question. You have a knack for killing my family."

66

The fiend's expression turned sinister. "Then we're at an impasse, old friend."

Jon pointed out into the horizon. "No, we're not. I teleported that cursed bundle of paper and ink as far away from here as possible. Now go find it like a good boy."

"Oh really? Where?" Ezekiel scoffed.

"Back to Sweden."

"Sweden, you say . . . Here's the problem, Jon. How do I know you're not lying to me again?"

"Have I not proven myself to you after everything I have done?" Jon said coldly.

Ezekiel answered with a demented smile, "That was long ago . . . prove it."

Jon just stared at him, insulted but indifferent about his reputation with Ezekiel. "If the Codex is here, can't you sense it?"

"Jon we have an Oath. I'm a man of my word, and I'm magically bound to that Oath. I can only do that here if you give me permission."

Jon stepped aside. "Not a foot inside . . ."

Ezekiel bowed. "Very well. Thank you for obliging."

Thrusting his hand out with his palm extended, Ezekiel closed his eyes and felt for magic. He smiled as he sensed the magic flowing from Jon and even faintly in the other three. But that was all. He had felt the radiant power pouring from the Codex before, but it was nowhere to be found in this home.

Ezekiel's eyes welled with anger. "How?"

Jon leaned in forcefully. "It's not here!"

"Where!" Ezekiel roared as he turned sharply to the two smaller creatures. "Tell me what you know, or I'll—"

"You'll do nothing. As a part of your Oath," Jon reminded him.

"Yes, of course," Ezekiel said composing himself. "Where in Sweden?"

With the power now in his hands, Jon shrugged. "Haven't the foggiest. It's a big country. I suggest you start looking."

Ezekiel's smirk turned bitter. "I will." Marching off the porch, Ezekiel turned and snapped, "You have quite a lovely home, old friend. But please do remember, I am only bound to my Oath when you're standing in your cage. And if you're lying to me . . ."

"Trust me, I'm well aware."

A familiar boom of thunder echoed behind him as Ezekiel disappeared into a flash of dark red light. Once he closed the door, Jon was bombarded by Penelope. "Tyler has the Codex! How did you—?"

Jon interrupted and pointed to Charlie. "You've spent too much time with my daughter, Gadwen. Brownies can hide objects, even magical objects. Even from someone with as much command over magic as Ezekiel. Well done, lad." Charlie looked up at Jon and gave him a firm salute.

"And what happens when his search comes up empty?" Penelope asked as Jon peered in on his sleeping grandson.

"Tyler and the Codex will be long gone. Safe and away from here."

Even Charlie was amazed by the bold statement. "Umm . . . how you gonna manage that, Master?"

Jon shifted with unease. "I'm still working on that. But he's safe in these walls. In the meantime, you two look after him. Knocking him out and then forcing him into a Jump may have taken a little more out of him than I anticipated."

"Yes, of course, Master."

Jon turned to Penelope. "You are free to stay or leave if you wish."

"Leave?" Penelope scoffed. "With my poor Charlotte g – gone . . . well, I'm not leaving Tyler's side! It's the least I can do for a dear friend."

"Very well," Jon said opening the door for her. "If either of you needs anything, I'll be upstairs figuring this mess out."

He closed the door and left Charlie and Penelope alone, staring down at Tyler's limp body. Penelope wiped away a tear and slumped her head before looking over at Charlie, who was fighting his own battle with his emotions. "She was supposed to bring me cherries. She didn't even like them, knew most of them would go bad before I could finish half. But she always brought me cherries, Charlie."

Charlie patted her gently on the back and stuffed a pillow under Tyler's head. "How on earth are we going to tell him she's gone?"

CHAPTER 8
AWAKENING

Tyler woke in an unfamiliar room. The small crackling flames from the room's fireplace provided heat and lighting, giving the room a mysterious, warm glow. Groggy, he slowly sat up with stiffness in his back. *My back . . . need to stretch. Feels like I've been sleeping for days.* Cracking his back, Tyler pushed the warm white bed sheets aside and turned.

"Evening!" Charlie said with a cheerful grin.

Tyler flinched in surprise. *Wait . . . It's the Brownie! Charlie, was it?*

Penelope popped up from a chair, waking from her own slumber. "Oh, thank goodness. You've been out for quite some time, dear."

"This is real? I . . . I have to be dreaming, right?" Tyler asked.

Jumping onto his bed, Penelope floated to Tyler's side and patted his hand. "Unfortunately not, sweetie. But you're safe now."

This isn't normal . . . Wait! That means . . . Tyler stretched out for his backpack and grabbed the Codex. "This thing . . . this book. It's what those things are after?"

"Yes, dear. Those things were Incubi. Well, and one was a Succubus."

70

Tyler sat back as he remembered Nessa's demonic transformation. "I was dating a Succubus?"

Penelope gently rubbed Tyler's hand trying to comfort him. "If it makes you feel any better, I've heard men complain that they've *married* a Succubus."

This made Tyler chuckle. "That's just . . . never mind. Mom's never gonna let me forget this one."

Penelope peered over to Charlie before returning to Tyler. "Sweetie, there's something—"

"Wait! The book has her initials." He opened to the front cover and pointed. "See right here. Why does my mom have this thing?" *Does she even know demons want it so much?*

"Your mother was a Codex Scribe, Tyler. Her job was to travel all over the world and fill in the empty pages."

"My mom?" Tyler snickered.

"Yes, dear. She was quite the talented Scribe . . . and Magi to boot."

"Magi?" Tyler said with a tilt of the head.

Penelope cautiously tried not to overwhelm him. "Yes, people or beings that can use magic."

The room grew quiet. Tyler just sat there staring at the Gadwen as though waiting for her to finish her joke.

When she just stood there unsure what else to say, Tyler broke the silence. "You're . . . Are you serious? Magic?"

"Is magic really out of the realm of things considering what you've seen?" Penelope asked.

"Yeah, I suppose you're right."

Charlie held out a glass. "Here. Drink this."

"Ummm . . . what's that?"

The glass glistened with a purple liquid. "It'll help. Between Jumping and Master putting you under, I'm surprised you weren't out cold for a whole week."

Tyler cringed as he took a gulp of the strange concoction. "Where's my mom?" He turned to Penelope. "You told her where we are, right?"

Penelope shrunk. "Tyler. I don't know how—"

"Penelope . . . stop." Charlie interrupted.

"He needs to know, Charlie," Penelope said in a voice harsher than she intended.

Can I get an answer! They're starting to freak me out! Tyler cut in, impatient. "Know? Need to know what? Where is my mom, Penelope?"

Charlie answered again, "It's not our place to say."

Penelope gave the Brownie a stern look. "Then who, Charlie?"

"I will," said Jon as he walked soberly into the bedroom, steeling himself for the news he was about to deliver.

"Where's my mom?" Tyler asked nearly toppling over as he stumbled towards Jon.

Jon cleared his voice as he peered over at the two tiny creatures staring back at him with uncertainty. "Tyler. I've never been good at this . . ."

Tyler shook his head. "No . . ." He could feel a sick wrenching feeling deep in his gut.

"Tyler . . . I," Jon groaned as he took a deep breath. He looked his grandson in the eyes and saw fear and anxiety staring back. "I don't know the details, but Charlotte, your mother, was betrayed by a friend, twice. First by giving away her position. And then he . . ."

Everything in Tyler's body told him to get out of there. His legs were shaking. "I've got to get home. This is all some sort of twisted nightmare."

"You can't, child," said Penelope, rushing to his side and grabbing his arm. "They will be waiting for you."

"I don't care!" he shouted, shrugging the Gadwen away. "I've got to get home. I have to!"

"Tyler," said Jon, shaking his head, still in disbelief himself. "Tyler, she's gone."

"Liar!" Tyler's voice cracked, and his knees finally gave way. He crumbled to the floor, trembling.

Jon ignored the insult and reached for the frightened boy. "Tyler . . ."

"No! Don't touch me!" Tyler said slapping his grandfather's hand away as tears welled in his eyes.

Jon's short fuse ran out, his emotions all out of whack. He lunged forward, grabbed Tyler violently by the shoulders and shook him. "Wake up! Do you think this is something I want to do? Do you think this gives me pleasure to tell my grandson that his mother is dead?"

Charlie and Penelope raced to Jon pulling at his arms trying to tear him away from Tyler. "Stop it, Jon!" Penelope shouted.

Unaffected by their efforts, Jon leered into Tyler's frightened eyes and repeated, "Do you think I want to tell my grandson that his mother isn't coming home? Do you?" Jon let go of Tyler and gave him a slight shove. Unnerved, Tyler sat cautiously watching the old man pace angrily. Jon threw himself into a chair and hung his head in defeat, covering his eyes as he let out an unrestrained weep of agony. "A parent should never have to bury their child . . . and I can't even do that."

"You couldn't find her?" Charlie asked as he comforted Penelope.

He shook his head. "They took her body, Charlie. Found only blood . . . just my baby's . . ." Jon choked.

Tyler couldn't believe this was really happening. *This is all just a twisted dream. This can't be real! Demons? Magic? My mom's . . . This is just a nightmare! I have to wake up! Wake up! WAKE UP!* Tyler looked up as his tears broke the brim of his eyes. He first saw Penelope and Charlie huddled together, and, nightmare or not, Tyler's heart retched to see the heartbroken Gadwen sobbing uncontrollably into her hands. Charlie stroke her forehead while handing her a handkerchief.

He straightened, wiped away the wetness on his cheek with the back of his hand and approached Jon. "How did it happen?" Tyler said through clenched teeth.

Jon remained still as though not hearing the question. In reality, he wasn't composed enough to answer. He kept replaying his daughter's final words, spoken to him through a familial mind-link she created seconds from death. It was the only reason Jon knew any of this was taking place. *'Marshall, please tell Tyler . . .'* Then a loud bang snapped their connection.

Charlie cleared his voice and answered for Jon, "Her Adjutor betrayed her. Coward shot her in the back."

A fire at the back of Tyler's mind raged unfamiliar. *Is this what it feels like to want to kill someone?* "Adjutor?"

"A Scribe's assistant. Your mother only had one, a Werewolf by the name of Marshall."

74

Marshall? Never heard her mention a Marshall ever. "What's his last name?" Tyler asked, clenching his fists. He wanted to hurt someone, smash something, make someone pay.

Charlie shook his head. "We don't know. Your mom never talked much about him."

"I know what you're thinking, Tyler, but you have to let it go," Jon said, lifting his head. He could see the anger growing in his grandson's eyes, and while the feeling was unfamiliar to Tyler, Jon saw himself in the boy and needed to crush it before he got himself killed.

Tyler stood to tower over Jon, gazing down at his grandfather with piercing angry eyes. "You want me to let it go? A man . . . no! A *friend* of hers murdered her in cold blood! And you want me to let it go?"

Standing to meet Tyler's fiery gaze with his own, Jon said with the utmost seriousness in his voice, "Yes. That's what I want you to do."

Tyler scoffed. "First my father, now my . . ." *Wait!* That's when it struck him. Tyler turned to Penelope. "My father, how did he really die?"

"Tyler . . ." she said, looking away.

"Penelope! Did demons have anything to do with my father's death?"

"He . . ." she said before turning to Jon as though looking for approval.

Tyler grew weak in the knees as he reached for a chair. "Oh my God . . ." *My mind is playing tricks on me. You can't believe any of this!*

Jon knelt in front of Tyler. "Your mother did a great job covering her relations from her enemies. But they ultimately found out she was married. On that night when your father was working late, they sent Fire Sprites into the building."

Tyler dropped his head, breaking his stare. He felt so tired, so overwhelmed and so angry. He just wanted everyone to go away, for all of this to go away. "Why didn't my mom just give them the damn book so they would leave us alone?"

"That's no ordinary book," Jon said pointing to the tome on Tyler's bed. "That's the Codex of Creatures."

Tyler stared blankly at his grandfather. "Who cares what book it is? She . . . she put all of us at risk!"

"It's not that simple, boy. That book has been in your lineage for over a millennium."

"Why the hell should it matter? What's so special about it?"

"Your ancestor, Clarius Melis snuck into Hell itself to retrieve this book. When complete, whoever wields it becomes imbued with its powers."

"Powers? Like superhuman strength or something?"

"Yes, but strength is just one of the many things this book offers. Its wielder would become a one man army."

Reaching out and grabbing the Codex, Tyler flipped through its pages. The unfamiliar burning rage surfaced. It was as though merely touching the book invited the foreign emotion to make a home within Tyler. He listened deeply as a noise pierced his ears. It sounded like a kettle overboiling mixed with a torturous shriek of someone down a long hallway. Then silence.

Tyler peered up. *No one else heard that?* "When complete? But there are empty pages everywhere."

"It was erased long ago. Ever since then Codex Scribes, like your mother, have been filling in the blank pages."

Tyler closed the Codex. "So . . . demons want this book." *Marshall works for the demons then. Marshall . . .* Even thinking his name sent hateful spikes down his spine.

"Yes, but only because their master seeks the Codex. Ezekiel."

"Ezekiel?" Tyler asked. *Marshall works for Ezekiel.*

"Yes. He's over seven-hundred years old and with your grandmother and mother gone, the strongest Magi there is."

"Stronger than you?"

Jon seemed reluctant to admit someone was better than him. "Yes . . . stronger than me."

Tyler placed the Codex on a table and instantly felt a wave of relief, though the rage still steamed dormant below the surface. "But why? What did Mom have to gain? What does Ezekiel have to gain besides power?"

"Both sides are fighting for the same end goal. To complete the Codex. But for different outcomes. With the Codex complete, the Scribe could seal the link between our world and the underworld forever, binding the seal to the Codex. This would mean that all demons on our plane would be sent back from which they came, never to return. Earth would be purged of demonic influence forever."

"But if Ezekiel gets his hands on a completed Codex?" Tyler asked.

"Then he could forever open the link between both worlds. Demons would pour out of the underworld, raising havoc and ruin throughout the globe. And the only force they would answer to or serve would be their master, Ezekiel. His magic would be unrivaled in strength. On a whim, he could obliterate millions without breaking a sweat. Uprising humans, mutinous demons, it would not matter. The era of demons, and the reign of Ezekiel would last until the end of earth."

Okay . . . so them getting it's pretty bad. "Wait. Why not hide the Codex somewhere? A place no one can find it? Then none of them could –" Jon gave him a telling stare. "It calls to them, doesn't it?" *Of course, it does.*

"If left alone, yes. A distant relative of yours found out the hard way. Besides, though the link is far weaker than it used to be, Ezekiel is powerful enough to still periodically bring a demon into our world. Playing keep-away will not solve the problem."

Tyler sat there silent for a moment before asking, "So with my mother . . . gone, who's gonna keep it away from Ezekiel? Who's gonna finish it?"

Jon was unsure how to answer. "It falls to her Adjutor, an appointed family member, or her next in line. Her Adjutor has aligned with the enemy, so he's out. She never appointed a family member. So technically, the duty falls to you."

Tyler sat there with a knot in his throat. His palms and forehead starting to sweat. "Me? It's my job now?" He stared down at the Codex timidly. *I . . . I can't do this. I'm not even eighteen yet!* But then his expression changed. *But it's a weapon. It could help me find Marshall. Find him, and . . ."*

Jon scoffed in a less than reassuring tone. "Yeah, and you wouldn't last a day out there with Ezekiel's demons looking for you."

His grandfather's bluntness reeled Tyler back to reality. "Thanks, Gramps."

Jon got up and stepped into Tyler's comfort zone. "What? You want me to tell you that you can do it? That it was your destiny? It's the job you were born to do? Tell me, if you couldn't handle one Succubus on your own, how are you going to fight off Ezekiel's forces? How about finding and documenting dangerous creatures? Taking on scribing? You'd be in over your head, boy."

"Then you do it!" Tyler responded coldly as he shoved the Codex at his grandfather. "If you're so strong, then be a man, take the book, and kill the son of a bitch responsible for murdering my mom!"

Jon stared deep into Tyler's eyes as the room grew uncomfortably quiet. He knew this wasn't Tyler, not completely. He grabbed the Codex and lobbed it onto the opposite bed, never breaking eye contact.

"Wanna try that again?"

"I'm . . . I didn't . . ."

"That book has brought me nothing but suffering. I don't want to see it, let alone possess it," Jon said scowling at Tyler. "Besides, I'm an old man now. Scribing is a younger man's job."

"Then what? Wait here until they come knocking?"

"He and his minions can't touch us here. He's bound by his own magical Oath he gave me. You're safe here."

Tyler stared at his grandfather with a curious yet disturbed look plastered across his face. *Gave him? How did Gramps get him to do that?* "Okay, so we're safe here. But I can't stay here forever. I'll have to leave eventually."

Jon sat in his chair. "Yes. Eventually. But for now, you need to stay with me until I figure out how to hide you or parley with Ezekiel to leave you alone."

"Would he do that?"

Jon appeared uncomfortably uncertain. "I don't know. But if you no longer possess the Codex, then he gains nothing by hunting you."

"Who's brave enough to take this thing from us?" Tyler asked leering at the Codex.

Jon reached out and took the Codex. "I don't know. Someone trustworthy. The Magi Guild might help me find a suitable Scribe to take over on your behalf. For now, leave this all to me. For now, sleep."

With that, Jon made his way to the door. "Gramps." Jon turned. "The Codex . . . it's never left my family's line?"

"Correct."

"It's sad . . . I'll be the one who lets it leave."

Jon shook his head. "Know what's sadder? A young man dying for the sake of a family tradition he didn't even know existed."

Tyler nodded and watched Jon leave with the Codex in hand. *Okay, it's over . . . but it doesn't feel over.* Crawling into bed, Tyler stared at the ceiling. Charlie and Penelope caught each other's peripherals while staring motionless at Tyler.

Penelope broke the still as she crawled up onto Tyler's bed asking, "Are you okay, sweetie?"

Tyler said nothing and just nodded his head. *This . . . this just can't be real.*

Charlie rubbed his arm awkwardly. "You can talk to us, Tyler. We're both here for you."

Tyler kept his focus on the ceiling not wanting to acknowledge the two creatures. "Thank you . . . but I'm still not convinced this is real. It's all in my head, or I'm having some kind of mental breakdown. I could snap out of it at any moment now. I just have to wait." *Magic isn't real. None of this is.*

Penelope reached out and patted Tyler's hand, concerned more than ever. "I really wish this was all a nightmare, but it's not, dear."

Rolling over, Tyler stared at the tiny fairy fluttering above him, and blinked to see if she would disappear. But her rosy, wet face still stared into his, her concern and love for him evident. "If it's not a nightmare, will you be here when I find out?"

"I'm not going anywhere. Better dreams, sweetie," Penelope said woefully.

CHAPTER 9
REALITY

Tossing and turning in his bed, Tyler gritted his teeth as a nervous sweat formed on his squinting forehead. Trembling, incoherent pleas escaped his locked jaw as he jolted his head from one side to the other. Jolting upright, he couldn't remember anything about his nightmare. Nothing, except how it ended. All he could hear in the choking darkness was his mother's terrified scream before a loud gunshot brought her to her knees and then to the wet, cold ground. Even now he could've sworn he still heard the echoing bang as he felt his back drenched in a cold sweat.

With his vision still blurry and his heart in his throat, Tyler collected himself. *It's all just a . . .* Looking around he could see nothing had changed. He was vaguely able to see the outlines of the room with the fire now only small embers. In the darkness of the room his mouth hung open for a moment before tears ran down his face and his stifled whimpers broke the silence. A sickening, almost vomit-inducing churning in his gut overwhelmed him as the truth sunk in. Tyler heard a tiny thud hit the floor followed by a petite creature jumping up onto his bed.

"It's okay, sweetie. I'm here, I'm here," Penelope said rubbing his arm.

82

"She's really gone, isn't she?" Tyler's words choked out of his mouth.

Tears welling in her eyes. "I'm afraid so. She was a wonderful, wonderful woman."

"It's too soon. I'm not ready," Tyler said coughing from his hysteria.

Penelope helped wipe away his tears. "No one is ever ready to say goodbye to the ones they love, let alone someone as special as your mother."

Tyler tried to compose himself. "The last thing I said to her was that I loved her." His composure slowly crumbled. "But I rushed it . . . embarrassed others would see me."

Penelope reached out and grabbed his hand firmly. "She knew how much you loved her. You were her world."

"But it's not enough." Tyler buried his face into his arm as he took a woeful gasp. "If I'd known that it was the last time I'd ever see her, I would've told her how much she meant to me. Sorry for all the times I was a pain in the ass. How much I love her. And now I can't! I miss her. I miss her so much."

With Tyler's wails no longer held back, Penelope wrapped an arm around him while gently brushing his hair with her tiny hands. "Me too, Tyler. Me too."

"What's his name?" Tyler asked with grief still in his eyes.

Penelope looked puzzled. "Who are you talking about?"

"The man who killed her. What was his name again?" Tyler asked, his nostrils flaring and his body trembling now in anger rather than sadness. Anger was easier.

"I don't want you going after him," Penelope said.

Tyler murmured angrily, "He betrayed her. He has to pay for what he's done—"

Penelope grabbed Tyler by his hair and pulled his face upwards. Eye to eye, she pointed a stern finger at him, "Don't you talk like that in front of me ever again! You're a good boy, Tyler. You're not a murderer. He'll pay for what he's done in one way or another, but that is not for you to decide."

"How do you know what I am? We've only just met!"

"Child, I have known you all your life. Every birthday, every new home, every bump and bruise. I know exactly the young man you are."

Tyler sniffled, still shaking in his rage. "I can't let it go, Penelope. I just can't. She was such a good person! She didn't deserve to die, and her killer is still out there. Breathing, laughing, probably in a warm bed. *Marshall* doesn't deserve mercy!"

"No one deserves death, Tyler. Not even the worst of the worst," she said, grabbing his palm firmly with both of her hands. "You have to let go of this anger. Your mother wouldn't want to see you like this."

"I can't! I can't stop feeling this! Even if I had the choice."

"There is always a choice, sweetie. And you've done so well so far."

"This is like nothing before."

Penelope loosened her grip. "No. This is harder, and you're not alone in any of this. I feel angry, too. Charlotte was like a daughter to me. Even I want to see Marshall face justice, but—"

"Then let me—" Tyler interrupted before Penelope cut him off.

"But! When and how is not up to me . . . or you."

"Then what? It's not fair! I don't know what to do or what to feel," Tyler said breaking down as he stared into Penelope's eyes and saw her fear.

Penelope brushed his cheek. "I don't know either, dear. All I know is that I'll always be here for you. But you must promise me! Tell me that when everything is said and done, you won't go looking for Marshall. Knowing your mom, she'd want the same. She'd want you to forgive and live a happy life. So promise us both."

Tyler couldn't bring himself to speak. He gasped for air. "I – I can't . . ."

"Sweetie, close your eyes and just breathe . . . Just breathe," Penelope said as she stroked his hair. After several minutes, Tyler calmed down. "Now open your eyes and promise me." Tyler shook his head. "I'm sorry, but I can't . . . but I'll promise to try." *Probably get myself killed if I tried hunting him down anyway.*

Penelope leaned in and kissed his cheek. "Then that'll do for now."

"How long did you know my mother?" Tyler asked moving over and inviting Penelope to sit with him.

Penelope smiled as she dug deep into her thoughts. "I remember your mother coming home only days old. I had been living with your grandmother since I was a young Gadwen."

"How was she? Growing up?"

A laugh escaping her. "Troublesome, cunning, a smart mouth, generous, kind, and always with a smile on her face. Much like you."

"Apple didn't fall far from the tree?" Tyler asked wiping his eyes.

She shook while grinning. "No. Not very far at all. I've had the privilege of watching you both grow up . . . you more from the shadows. I've never met kinder gentler souls than you and your mother. Your father was a rather good man too, considering everything. All the risks. The complications. But your father never second-guessed his feelings about your mother."

"I miss him too." Tyler peered to his backpack, only then remembering Jon had the Codex. "All this, all for a book." Penelope agreed with her silence. "Hey, Penelope. Can I ask you something?"

"Anything, sweetie. Ask away."

Tyler peered over to find Charlie was still fast asleep. "My mom said Gramps was dead, and you don't like him. Besides his winning personality, what's the problem?"

Penelope also checked to make sure Charlie was asleep before speaking any ill towards his master. "Jon . . . has done a lot of good in his life. But he's also done a lot of bad things too. I don't think it's my place –"

"Bad things?" Tyler asked trying to dig more information out of her. *What? Did he kill someone?*

She shook her head and just repeated herself. "Bad things. But you're his flesh and blood. You're his only family. He'll do right by you. You need to trust him. Jon will figure this out."

86

Tyler sighed as the clock flashed 3:48 AM. "Will you still be here tomorrow? I don't want—"

"Why does everyone think I'm going to leave?" Penelope interrupted. "If Charlotte was the closest thing I had to a daughter, well, you're the closest thing I have to a grandson. I'm not going anywhere, Tyler. However long I have in my golden years, I'll be right here."

"Thank you, Penelope."

Penelope leaned in and kissed Tyler's forehead. "Best get some more sleep. If you need me, I'll be right over there."

"Penelope . . ." Tyler said as Penelope turned to climb down.

"Yes?"

"I don't want to wake up alone again. Can you sleep the rest of the night here?" Tyler asked as he slid over to make room.

Penelope laid down beside Tyler and pulled the warm covers over herself. "I'll be right here if you need anything."

✸✸

He woke the next morning and the realization hit him like a brick to the face. Life was never going to be the same. The only real family he had left was gone. No warning, no body to grieve over, just gone.

Wiping his eyes, Tyler tried to think of anything else to make the pain go away. But instead, Tyler's mind turned to the memories he'd shared with his mother. Each memory played through his head crystal clear. Big or small, weeks ago or years ago, Tyler relived a lifetime.

How did she do it? Balance such a dangerous job, commit to a marriage and raise a son all at the age of twenty? Twenty rang in his head for a moment. *I'm almost twenty. There's no way I could do that.*

Penelope rolled over upon hearing Tyler. He could see the genuine pain and concern in her eyes as she stared up at him. Pain for the loss of her dearest and oldest friend. Pain for the son she reluctantly left behind.

Penelope reached out and stroked Tyler's face. "I know, dear. Me too."

Tyler tried to keep his composure. "She deserved so much more. She deserved to pass old and happy. Not in the dirt . . . Not alone and sc—" Tyler gasped for air. He couldn't bear to think of it.

Penelope shook her head and said, "Your mother was one of the bravest people I've ever known. She may have felt many things in the end, but fear was not one of them." Tyler nodded but said nothing. "What do you say we hold a ceremony today in memory of her?"

"How? We're not supposed to leave the property. Where can we hold it?"

Interrupting Tyler and Penelope's conversation, Charlie walked to his bedside and said, "I know just the place."

✲✲

The sun marched closer to high noon. Using Jon's backyard, Tyler, Penelope, and Charlie set up Charlotte's private ceremony against the property's back wall. While the front of the house blended in with the neighborhood, the back was

88

vastly different. The spacious two-acre parcel was covered with lush grass with the exception of a well-maintained dirt track bordering the edges of the property. Towering green ferns budded up against the yard's sturdy cement brick wall. Pruned and grown by Jon, this natural wall was artistic and kept neighbors from seeing into his property. Towards the back of the lot stood two small three-tier cherub water fountains surrounded by red and yellow rose bushes, and centered between them was the mural of a dark-haired woman smiling.

Charlie stood at the foot of the fountain garden with a floral bouquet of Whengid's Glory in hand. He peered at the mural and held the wreath as though showing the woman his flower arrangement. Placing the self-rooting bell-shaped wildflowers between the fountains, Charlie soberly returned to Tyler and Penelope's side. "Will this do?"

Tyler nodded. "They're beautiful. She'd like this."

"They were your grandmother's favorite. A lovely perennial, very invasive though."

"Are you sure Gramps will be okay with us planting them?" Tyler asked.

"I keep these grounds. I'll take care of it."

That's okay then. Don't want to get on Gramp's nerves. Tyler stared at the mural. He could see his mother's resemblance. "So that's my grandmother?"

Penelope smiled. "Miel. Wonderful woman." Her sentiments were echoed by Charlie.

"Was she the Scribe before Mom? Or was it Gramps?" Tyler asked.

"She was the Scribe and an amazing Magi," Penelope said.

Charlie snickered, "An understatement! On top of her other achievements, your grandmother fought Ezekiel in what many consider to be the greatest magical duel of the modern era."

"Really? My grandmother?" Tyler asked staring proudly at the mural of a woman he had never known. *Wish I'd gotten to meet her.* "I guess this is the perfect place for Mom's ceremony."

Penelope held Tyler's hand and looked back at the house. "Is Jon joining us?"

"No . . ." answered Charlie.

Tyler shifted his eyes to Charlie, incensed. "No? This is for his daughter!"

"I think that's exactly why he won't be joining us, sir. It's best we let him grieve in his own way."

"I'd be here if I was him," Tyler snapped.

Charlie was quick to defend his master. "Well, you are you and Jon is Jon. Don't go changing yourself for anyone. Nor should you expect it either."

Tyler said nothing but nodded. *Fair enough.*

"Shall we begin?" Penelope said, and Tyler nodded. She stepped forward and looked down at the wreath as though talking with Charlotte. "Charlotte. You were a fantastic friend, a loving wife, and an amazing mother. I have your son with me, and I'll watch over him, I promise. You did . . . such a good job with the little time you had." Tears welled in Penelope's eyes, and Charlie quickly pulled at Tyler's leg in a plea to give her the space she needed. "It's not fair that you're gone. But I just wanted to make sure you know that I always have, and always will be, so very proud of you, dear. I love you."

Penelope walked back and took Tyler's hand from Charlie. Both wiped the tears from their eyes as Charlie stepped forth. "Hey, Lottie. I never thought ... well, I honestly hoped I'd already be gone before this day came. You were always my favorite Locke. Don't tell your father though," he said, forcing a grin as he looked over his shoulder. "I'm sorry parts of your life weren't as they should have been. But what you did have, you had in spades. I've never met anyone like you. I guess you were just that special. Which makes me special, because I got to witness a beautiful life. Miss you lots, Lottie."

Stepping back, Charlie turned to Tyler, bowing as he gave him the floor. Tyler took a deep breath. Kneeling before the flowers, Tyler could feel his heart in his throat, and the words came out without thinking about them. "Hi, Mom. Things have gotten pretty crazy in the last twenty-four hours. I just wish you were here so I could tell you ... how much you mean to me. I'm sorry. I'm so sorry for all those times I caused you trouble. You were an amazing mother and I hope you knew that. I couldn't have asked for better. I love you. I wish I had told you that more. I just wanted to tell you that and ... I miss you, Mom." Tyler broke out into tears. Hunched over, his body gasped for air between trembling sobs. Now at his side, Charlie and Penelope comforted him, all sharing the pain together.

Charlie helped Tyler to his feet. "Let's go inside. I'll make some comfort food while Penelope and I tell you about your mother's adventures."

Penelope shot Charlie a death glare. "Charlie! Not now, he's—"

Tyler interrupted. "No. I'd really like that right now, actually."

"Really?" Penelope asked.

"Yes. I want to hear about the adventures she had—but only the good ones for now."

Charlie smiled. "Well, where do we begin?"

CHAPTER 10
LEGACY

Everyone was sound asleep after a long and emotional day. Everyone except for Tyler. It was lights out at ten, and Tyler knew that was his chance. He waited and listened for his fellow roommates to fall asleep. *I can't tell if Gramps is asleep. For tiny creatures, these two snore a lot.* Tyler laid silently as he watched the clock. At 10:30 PM, he made his move.

Thirty minutes is long enough. He's asleep, Tyler thought as he slowly slipped out of bed. Creeping his way out the bedroom, he closed the door behind him before searching the dimly lit house for the library.

It was a modestly sized room with bookshelves running the length and height of the walls. A large wall-sized window looked out into the backyard. There was a single large table which ran the length of the library, and trinkets and miniature statues decorated the bookcases, mostly unnoticed by Tyler who was trying to adjust to the darkness.

Anchoring a hand to the table, Tyler shifted his eyes back and forth. *Okay . . . where is it?* A moment later, Tyler watched as the room tented a tranquil blue. Seeing the glowing source, he reached out and pulled the Codex from its shelf. Peering back to make sure he closed the door behind him, he took a seat and opened the Codex.

Let's see, let's see . . . okay. Brownie. Yes, I know Charlie's here. With this acknowledgment, the page lost its blue shine. *Alright. Let's see, one more. My guess is . . . yes, Gadwen. I know this too.* Just like before, the page's glow faded. *Hmm, no other creatures around, huh? Oh well, not what I was looking for anyway.*

Kicking his legs out, Tyler skimmed through the Codex, and he immediately noticed two trends with the book. First, the creatures were separated into three sections; creatures to behold, regard, and fear. *Okay, hmm. So wondrous harmless creatures at the front. Civil and moderately dangerous creatures in the middle. And nightmarish dangerous creatures in the back.* Tyler also noticed under each creature entry was a signature. *I think these are Scribe signatures. My ancestors.* Flipping through the pages, Tyler searched for his mother's name. *Ruth . . . Ruth . . . Mallidy . . . Ruth . . . Eric . . . Ru—Christ! Ruth cornered the market on fluffy creatures.* Skipping a healthy portion, Tyler continued his search until finally. *CHARLOTTE! Here she is! One of Mom's entries. Let's see . . . Huldra.*

Teetering his chair back and forth, Tyler read his mother's entry, unaware just how recent it had been. *Scandinavia! I wish I was there, traveling.* He had always dreamed of traveling the world himself. Tyler closed his eyes and smiled as he pictured his mother's journey in his head. Hiking, exploring, discovering different cultures.

What else? Tyler asked himself as he turned the pages looking for more of Charlotte's entries. Tyler found her next creature. *Piptipine. Found mostly in central America. A small raccoon-like creature with poisonous quill-like fur. Bites and stings can cause various skin issues such as psoriasis.* Tyler read on until the distinct sound of someone clearing their throat ejected him from the pages. Nearly toppling backward, Tyler saw Jon standing in the doorway peering in at him.

"I thought I made it clear? Lights out at ten," said Jon.

"No lights," Tyler answered with a smirk.

Jon stared at him, unamused. "Why? What does reading any of that do for you?"

"I don't know, It just helps. I can picture her traveling. Smiling. Being happy. Exactly how I want to remember her."

Jon shook his head. "That book was a burden upon your mother. Just like all other Scribes. She had to leave her husband and son daily, knowing she risked her life every time."

Tyler glanced down at the Codex then back to Jon. "I know my mom. She was a happy person. Burden or not, part of her would've loved this."

"Think what you want. She wanted to be with her family."

"How do you know? When was the last time you two even spoke to one another?"

Jon's posture stiffened, his demeanor grew cold. The question clearly cut deep. "August 13th, 2000. She was fifteen."

"You . . . remember the date?"

"One of the worst days of my life." Jon winced as though shaking the memory from his head. "Hard to forget those kinds of days."

An uncomfortable silence enveloped the room. Neither of them said anything for a while.

"Can I ask you a question?" Tyler finally asked. Jon hesitated, then pulled out a chair and sat down. "All these signatures . . . They're all my relatives. Right?"

"Yes," Jon answered curtly.

"Any famous?"

Jon chuckled. "In the regular world? No. In the magical world? Plenty."

"Like who?"

"Hmm . . . well, most known was Mallidy. Great scholar and Magi. Her twelve published works are the benchmark of magical literature. Lived to be 391 years old."

"391! That's insane! How?"

"Magic. No one understood magic better than Mallidy."

Goosebumps ran down Tyler's arms. "Who else?"

"Eric the Undying. Hulking man. Legend says he carried two swords, each weighing over a hundred pounds. He was a monster hunter."

"Monster hunter?"

"Eric only sought the world's most dangerous creatures for his entries. He knew eventually every creature needed to be documented. Sparing future Scribes the danger, he would take on the horrors of the world. To this day, he is the only Magi known to have fought and killed a Scrimjaw."

"I'm guessing Scrimjaws are bad news?" Tyler asked.

"Your worst nightmare doesn't hold a damp matchstick."

Jon continued naming more Magis and their accomplishments much to Tyler's fascination.

"You know so much! Did you learn this all from your parents or a secret school?"

Jon scoffed in revulsion. "I was four when my parents left me for dead. My magic . . . frightened them." Tyler recoiled trying to figure out some sort of apology, but Jon steamrolled on, saying, "I learned everything as a refugee. I was housed at the Magi Guild's headquarters. Of course, nowadays the Guild is nothing more than a poorly run booster club."

Tyler could tell the conversation was going to run sore if he let Jon reminisce further. "Can I ask you for your honest opinion?"

"Shoot."

"With training do you think I'd make a good Magi . . . a good Scribe?"

Jon looked mortified. "You don't know what you're asking about. You have a life. Don't flirt with that idea."

Tyler closed the Codex. "That didn't answer my question."

Jon froze. He wanted to lie, but Tyler asked for his honest opinion. "You have the pedigree. You'd need the best master you could get to steel you for the harsh world out there. But, yes, perhaps you would be a good Magi . . . and Scribe."

That was all Tyler needed to hear. He pulled the Codex to his chest. "Charlie said you trained Grandma and my mother. Would you train me?"

Jon stood from his chair. "No."

"Then I'm going off into the world unarmed," Tyler said sternly.

Pulling the chair aside, he leaned over and yelled, "Don't be a fool, boy! You wouldn't last. Ezekiel would hunt you down and you'd be dead before the weekend!"

Tyler tucked the Codex under his armpit. "Then train me."

"You want me to train you to be a Magi?"

"Yes."

"I don't train a bastardized version of Magi. You would need to become proficient not only with magic but the sword as well, and I don't believe you're capable," Jon said hoping this may deter him.

"You don't know what I'm capable of," Tyler said, slamming the Codex down on the table. "Teach me both."

Jon groaned in frustration as he stumbled towards him. "What the hell changed in twenty-four hours?"

"I know too much." His answer halted Jon's advance. "Between you, Charlie, and Penelope, I've learned so much about my family. I can't go back to regular life knowing what I know. If this is what my family has done for generations, then I don't want it to end with me."

Jon latched onto Tyler's shoulder with his gnarled fingers. "You don't understand the gravity of what you're asking, boy."

"If I were brought up in the magical world, we wouldn't be asking who the next Scribe would be, would we?"

Jon said nothing.

"I've always wanted to travel and explore the world."

"It's not all fun and games."

Does he honestly think I don't know that by now? "I know . . . Mom would still be here."

98

"You really want this? To throw away a safe and long life ahead of you?" Jon asked, placing his forehead in his palm.

Tyler corrected him. "I want to step into the next chapter of my life doing something that matters. My family's legacy . . . *Mom's* legacy."

Jon said nothing. *Maybe not now, but there's more than legacy on his mind.*

"Please, just give me a shot."

"A shot?" This caught Jon's ears. "Give you a shot?"

"That's all I'm asking of you."

Jon thought for a moment before answering. "Fine. I'll give you a taste tomorrow. If you aren't up to snuff, you must promise to give up Scribing."

"And if I am?" Tyler asked.

Jon smirked. "Then I'll take you under my wing."

Tyler stuck his hand out in confidence. "Deal."

Taking his grandson's hand, Jon motioned for Tyler to forfeit the Codex. "We start at six in the morning. Now. Bed!"

Tyler marched back to his room without another word, leaving Jon with his thoughts. Jon turned to a picture of Miel hanging from the wall and sighed. "He gets his tenacity from Charlotte, who got it from you. Either that or he's a fool."

CHAPTER 11
BETRAYER'S REWARD
Washington DC

Marshall walked down the cold sterile hallway towards the only elevator in the building. Stepping aboard, he pressed the button for the 13th floor, watching as the elevator doors slowly closed. Resting up against the back wall, Marshall battled with an image stuck in his head. It was the same haunting image he'd seen since he pulled the trigger. Charlotte. Facedown. Dead.

As the indicator above sped towards the 13th floor, Marshall's heart rate quickened. He was angry and upset. Angry at himself. Upset knowing there was no way to change what he had done. *Just remember why you did this,* Marshall told himself, trying to overcome the guilt consuming his heart and mind.

When the elevator opened, Marshall was met by a familiar face. *Ezekiel's standards must be low if they let these monsters into the building.*

With a faint smile upon his face, a man greeted Marshall. "So good to see you, my old friend." The gaunt pale-skinned man held out his hand as though welcoming Marshall to the other side.

100

Passing the man with a nod, Marshall only murmured, "Romen."

"My my, not in the mood for small chat? Since when did Ezekiel invite dogs to sit at his table?" Romen said flashing his inhuman, long and jagged teeth.

Marshall stopped and turned, staring the frail-looking beast in his yellowing eyes. "Funny, I was wondering when vampires were allowed . . . well, anywhere."

Romen's smile vanished as his yellow nails inched out into claws. "You dare—"

"Oh, I'm sorry. I forgot. You Vampires don't like that name. Strigoi, right?" Romen hissed. "Just run along, Romen. I have no business here with you. Not today at least," Marshall said shooing the fiend off.

Roman smiled and bowed with fake sincerity. "Good night, Mr. Dunn. Say hi to the bitch and kids."

Gripping the door handle, Marshall stepped into Ezekiel's office. Seeing Marshall enter, Ezekiel wrapped up a phone call while motioning for Marshall to take a seat. The room gazed out into the bustling city below, a cover for Ezekiel's more secretive operations. It was painted in cyan blue with dark wood floors and decorative molding. Marshall's eyes caught two potted plants off to each side of Ezekiel's desk. *Fake, like everything else about this charade.*

"Apologies for the wait, Marshall. Welcome back," Ezekiel said, beckoning him forward.

"Vampires? And I thought you couldn't sink lower." Marshall answered ignoring his greeting.

Ezekiel chuckled. "We created the S&W Pact for a reason, old dog. I suggest you get with the program and start playing nice. Now . . . how was your trip?"

Marshall couldn't hold back the disgust on his face. "I've had better. Sweden will never be the same, thank you."

Ezekiel opened his desk and pulled out a celebratory bottle of bourbon. "Oh, come now. Wipe that look off your face. You have secured a better future for your family."

"Have I?"

Ezekiel poured himself a glass. "Oaths are not made to be broken. I'm a man of my word. Your son and daughters will have bright futures."

Marshall stared blankly at Ezekiel. "And what about Tyler. No father. No mother. What about his future?"

"Victim of circumstance."

Marshall let out a throaty canine growl. "She didn't need to die! Your 'men' botched up the whole mission! If you would have—"

"Would have what, Marshall?" Ezekiel asserted. "Let her go? Try again another day? Give her another chance to hand it over?"

"Yes . . ."

"No. I've been chasing Scribes for centuries now. I gave you clear orders. The Codex in hand or Charlotte Grayson dead. And you delivered."

The two sat silently for a moment as Ezekiel enjoyed his drink. "Where's my son?"

"Safe, I assure you. And you'll be happy to know his memory has already been modified to never remember his . . . *stay* with us."

"His kidnapping, you bastard."

"His stay. And I'm sure you'll be elated to hear that he is already fast asleep in his own bed." Ezekiel took another satisfied sip of his drink.

"And what of me? What am I to do now?"

Ezekiel leaned back in his chair. "Tyler Grayson now has the Codex, despite what his grandfather says."

"I won't kill a boy, demon!"

Ezekiel laughed at Marshall's outburst. "Oh, you are feisty! But I don't need you to handle him."

"Leave him alone! He's not a Magi. He's not even a Scribe," Marshall barked, failing to keep the desperation out of his voice.

Ezekiel seemed entertained by Marshall's growing concern. "Why do you care? You haven't even met the boy."

"He's . . . her son. Just leave him alone."

Ezekiel reached into his desk and pulled out a file handing it to Marshall. "Never mind her son. You asked what's next. Here it is."

"What are these?" Marshall asked.

"My word," Ezekiel said.

Opening the file, Marshall read the document to himself. It was his newly secured federal position. His new work location, schedule, and even his new six-figure salary.

Marshall almost couldn't believe what he was reading. "H–how?"

Ezekiel chuckled swirling his bourbon. "I own this country. And when I have the Codex in hand, you can expect a raise."

Money for college. A better house. Not living off of coupons. And weekends off. I . . . I can see Steph. The kids. Marshall collected himself as he tucked his files into his coat. "When do I start?"

"I'm sure you are aware the Magi Guild will be hunting you for some time."

"Ha! The Guild . . ." Marshall scoffed.

"Don't be so cocky. Just keep low and be ready for my call. For now, I want you to report to your new position Monday. Until then, go be with your family."

Marshall rose from his seat. "Just like that?"

Ezekiel smiled before tipping back the last half-ounce of bourbon. "Just like that."

CHAPTER 12
ONE SHOT

6 AM felt like it came minutes after Tyler snuck back into bed. Jon gripped Tyler's shoulder and gave him a silent but firm shake. When their eyes met, Jon motioned for Tyler to follow him. Crawling softly out of bed, Tyler gently closed the door behind him, leaving Charlie and Penelope sound asleep.

Tyler walked into the kitchen to find Jon making some sort of concoction. The room was small with outdated fading wooden furniture, appliances, and yellow wallpaper. *Everything's so old. Looks like a picture from the 1950s. The room even has an old people smell.* Jon poured the brown-colored drink into two large glasses then turned to Tyler.

"Here. It's breakfast."

The drink had a thick creamy texture reminding Tyler of a chocolate malt, but after a quick sniff test he soon found this was far from a chocolaty treat.

"What is it?"

"Breakfast. Now drink," Jon said already halfway done with his drink.

Putting the drink to his nose and giving a sniff, Tyler jerked his head back in repulsion. Whatever it was, it smelled past its prime. *Probably testing my willpower. Ugh . . . this is gonna suck.* Throwing the drink back, Tyler downed it as fast as he could. The lukewarm beverage coated his throat as he swallowed it in several large gulps. He flinched a little from the overbearingly unpleasant taste. *Oh . . . it's got a spoiled milk aftertaste.*

"That's a good way to upchuck. How's your stomach?" Jon asked collecting Tyler's glass.

"That's nasty." Tyler pardoned himself as he burped.

Seeing he was going to keep his breakfast down, Jon turned and washed the glasses. "Yeah, not my favorite either, but you can't duplicate the results with any other substance. Helps keeps your mind sharp and ready to learn. Also enhances muscle memory and growth. Your body will react to each day of training as though it were ten days. Get a year's training done in little over a month. Now, let's see what you're made of."

Following Jon out to the backyard, Tyler tried his best to ignore the nasty taste still swirling in his mouth. Jon handed him a wooden practice staff with one hand and took one for himself. "Before we start, I must ask the basics. What do you want from me, Tyler?"

"For you to teach me how to protect myself and become a powerful Magi."

"Powerful? Good. Now, why?"

Tyler paused for a moment, shaking away the thoughts of Marshall, his mother's killer, from his mind. He bit his tongue. "As I said last night . . . it's my family's legacy. I'm next in line."

Jon looked at him, unbelieving, for a moment, then pressed on. "I want more than just a call to duty from you. Why else?"

"I need to keep the Codex away from Ezekiel."

106

"Why?"

"Why else? Because it's what he wants, and he's the reason my mother is dead," Tyler blurted out. "Because with it he'll open a demon floodgate. Because if he gets it, he'll probably kill people like you, me, and anyone else who stands against him."

"Good . . . so you know the stakes. Almost."

"Almost?"

"There is one more power the Codex wields. One over the creatures themselves."

Tyler didn't like the sound of this. "Over them? What is it?"

"The one who possesses the Codex holds immense power over mythical creatures. If a creature's page is filled in, the possessor of the Codex can bend that creature's will as they see fit."

"You mean creatures like Penelope? Like Charlie? Their pages are filled in. If Ezekiel gets his hands on the Codex—"

"He could effortlessly make them do his bidding. Yes. As could you."

Tyler stepped back. "Me?"

Jon nodded. "The possessor. Currently, that is you."

"But . . . I-I'd never—"

"Good, let's hope you never have to test your resolve. But now, do you fully understand the stakes?"

"Crystal clear . . . let's start?" Tyler asked.

Jon smiled. "I have one last question. And it's important. How will you achieve all this?"

"By . . . listening to whatever you say?" Tyler answered cautiously.

"Very good, smart like his mother. Now," Jon said, and moved into a squatting position before placing his staff on both knees, the stick perfectly balanced. Pointing to the ground, Jon ordered. "Do as I do for five minutes."

"Five Minutes? Come on, Gramps. That's ridiculous."

Jon had already closed his eyes to meditate. "Do you give up?"

"No," Tyler said while getting into position.

"Then do as I say and don't ask questions."

At first, Tyler struggled to get low enough to keep the staff on his knees. *Okay, Tyler. You can do this. It's just like 9th Grade P.E. only worse.* "Like this?" Tyler asked balancing the staff against his knees.

Jon opened an eye to check Tyler. "Good. Now, close your eyes and listen to what I say." Tyler closed his eyes and took a long deep breath. "Don't speak. Only listen. By now you're probably starting to feel the fatigue of your muscles straining. I want you to focus on that feeling, then against what logic has taught you. I want you to convince your mind that the feeling isn't there."

"What?" Tyler broke the silence, and before he could receive any more direction he was on his behind, legs shaking from barely a minute in the squatting position.

"Up!" Jon's voice harshened and Tyler snapped back up to his feet. "What did I say?"

Tyler sighed. "Don't speak."

"Then shut up and do as I say," Jon snapped. "Again!"

Tyler bent his shaking legs and tried to relax into position. He laid the staff on his legs, and this time he listened, forcing feeling into his legs. *Oh boy. Haven't felt this kinda burn in a while.* He could feel his shaking muscles

108

straining again, ready to give out. *Okay, I feel it. But it doesn't exist, Tyler. You're not getting tired.*

"Very good," Jon said in a low voice. "Feel the tension pass."

Alright, Tyler. Just listen to Gramps. I gotta be halfway done . . . maybe. He lost track of the seconds in his head, keeping his eyes shut as his legs shook. *I'm shaking but I don't feel a thing. This is easy.* Then the burn grew more intense. *I feel fine. Wait . . . I feel . . .* A tingling sensation enveloped his legs, then like dandelion seeds in the wind it dissipated, and Tyler felt the burn fade away. He stood perfectly still and comfortable. *I'm . . . I'm doing it! Have I always been able to do this?*

Jon glanced over to find Tyler completely at ease. "Very good, now I want you to block out all sounds. If you have to indulge in a sense, let it be smell."

Tyler kept his eyes closed as he breathed in the sweet aroma of flowers wisping through the slightest of winds. *Hmm, orange blossoms.* As he breathed deeper, the traffic far off in the distance, the city wildlife, and any other man-made noise in the area simply disappeared. He felt at peace. He was in touch with his body like never before.

"Alright very good. You may get up now," Jon said, grabbing his staff.

Opening his eyes, Tyler rose to his feet and held his staff loosely in his hands. "How? How did I do that?"

Jon motioned for Tyler to follow. "It's in your blood, boy. Your mind is a very powerful tool and weapon. From now on, whenever I give you a task, I want you to think about how you can make it a mental workout. Even if I tell you to lift a pile of bricks. Understood?"

Now standing close to Miel and Charlotte's flower garden, Tyler nodded. "You got it."

"That was well done by the way. Your mother did a full thirty minutes on her first day too. She'd be proud her son kept up with her pace."

Tyler looked confused. "Thirty minutes? You said five . . ." Tyler checked his watch. The clock read several minutes past 6:30. *I was doing that for thirty minutes?*

Jon stretched his back out against his staff resting on his shoulders. "I needed to break through to you first. If five minutes was 'ridiculous', what would thirty be?"

Makes sense. Tyler nodded silently.

"Go put your watch on a table. I don't want to be responsible for breaking it."

Tyler did as asked. "Break it? How?"

"Get into a ready stance," Jon said as he held his staff at the ready.

"What? We're going to fight or something?"

Jon grinned at the naive young man's question. "No, I'm going to fight you, and you're going to try to block my assault. Now if you are feeling gutsy, you can try to counter. But I can assure you . . . I'll make you pay for it. Now, staff up."

Tyler raised his staff. *Okay, this shouldn't be too difficult. He's an old man and I've got pretty good hand-eye coordination. Just block his swings.*

Taken by surprise, Tyler found himself backpedaling as a flurry of swings came from his elderly grandfather. Although he blocked the first set of strikes, the next swing crushed down on Tyler's hand, forcing him to drop his staff, fall to one knee and clench his hand in pain. But Jon wasn't done as he shoved the end of his staff into Tyler's chest, sending him falling back onto his butt gasping for air. He stared up with fury at his grandfather pacing around him.

Jon kicked Tyler's staff to him. "Never, under any circumstances, do you drop your weapon. If disarmed, fall back to a secondary defensive position or magic. But never willfully throw down your weapon!"

Tyler picked up his staff as he peered down at his reddened fingernails. "Willfully? You crushed my fingers!"

"By the end of the day, I'll have done a lot worse to you," Jon beamed.

Tyler broke ready position, frustrated. "How is this a test? How is this a fair chance?"

Jon broke stance as well. "Did you like having your fingers smashed, boy?"

"Yeah, loved it! Please, do it again!" Tyler snapped back.

"I'll beat the sarcasm and piss right out of you," Jon said restraining his frustrations with a well-disguised smile.

"Of course I didn't like it!"

Jon placed his hand on Tyler's shoulder and pulled him in closer before whispering, "Exactly. So if you become my student and I teach you how to hold a weapon so you're not killed on your first day outside, you're gonna listen real nice and close now, aren't you?" Tyler's frustration fell from his face, and he nodded. "Oh, and by the way. You asked for a shot. Not a fair one. Life isn't fair. None of this is fair! You either figure it out or take your lumps. Got it?"

Tyler nodded. *Oh, Christ . . . he's gonna beat the crap out of me.*

Stepping back several steps, the two raised their staffs once again before Jon charged in with another whirlwind of strikes. Seeing an opportunity, Tyler stepped forward and swung. Jon promptly batted Tyler's staff away before striking him across the lower rib cage with a loud thud. Tyler fell to the floor with the wind knocked out of him, again.

"I told you that was going to be a bad idea," Jon mocked as he paced around Tyler, who was on his hands and knees sucking air.

Catching his wind, Tyler grabbed his staff. "Why not teach me how to do this first so I can save a few broken ribs!"

"I can teach you how to be unblockable. I can also teach you how to be impenetrable. But I only have right now, when you're weak, to teach you just how much you don't want to get hit. I've found it helps keep students focused."

"Rather you teach me first," Tyler said rubbing his bruised ribs.

"I have my ways of teaching. Someday, God willing, if you have students of your own, you can teach them your way. Now . . . staff up. Unless you give up."

Tyler didn't say a word. Grasping his staff, he brought it up into a ready position. As Jon charged towards him, Tyler understood now. *The test is to endure. I can't beat him. I can quit, but I can't do that and become a Scribe.*

Jon had brought his lesson back into meditation under the midday shade of a tree nearby, and Tyler silently rejoiced no longer being a human punching bag. With his grandfather already in meditation, Tyler sat facing his mother and grandmother's flower garden. *I hope this jackass treated you two better than me.* Tyler noticed that the

Whengid's Glory was rooted in the earth and had already grown an inch or two taller. *How is it growing so quickly?*

Closing his eyes and remembering his grandfather's words, Tyler focused on the pain radiating all over his body. *Okay, just got to pinpoint the pain. Of course, it'd be a whole lot easier if my entire body wasn't pulsing.* It took him a while to convince his mind to ignore the pain. But, like before, Tyler felt the soreness in his muscles, the throbbing of his bruises, and even the stinging of his wounds seemingly fade away. He knew he had just gone through the wringer, but he couldn't feel it anymore.

"How's the pain level?" Jon asked, now standing over him.

Tyler kept his eyes closed as he breathed in the fresh air. "What pain?"

Jon growled, "Boy, don't get smart with me."

Tyler opened his eyes, frustrated to be pulled from his meditative state. "What? I did exactly as you said. I made it a mental exercise and the pain went away."

"You . . . disciplined your mind to ignore the pain?" Jon said, his own frustration wavering.

"Yeah? I used my mind. Just like you said to do, right?" Tyler asked, confused by the question.

Jon raised his eyebrows and gave a satisfied nod. "I've never met a first-day student who went through the thrashing you endured without quitting. Nor control their mind enough to ignore the pain. Not even your mother. Not completely anyway."

"Impressed then?" Tyler asked giving a cocky grin.

"Slightly," he murmured with an emotionless stare.

Extending his arm out, Jon waved it over Tyler and whispered something under his breath. Although Tyler had managed to push the pain aside for a moment, he watched in stunned silence as his bruised and beat body healed itself right before his eyes. In seconds, his body was unmarked, fresh as it was when he first woke up this morning. *Amazing!* Tyler peeked down at his hand to find his purple nails were flesh colored and healed.

"How did you do that?" Tyler asked eagerly.

"Tyler, what languages do you know?"

Tyler was taken back by the question. "Languages? Umm, I know English and a little Spanish. But that's it, why?"

"Have you ever heard of the 'dead language'?"

Tyler thought for a moment before asking, "Latin?"

"Yes. The base of many modern-day languages. But more importantly, it's the language of magic."

"Language of magic, how so?"

Jon pointed to a yellow rose in the garden. "If you extended your hand over this rose and told it to turn red in Latin, it would."

"That's insane. So to use magic, I just have to say whatever I want, but in Latin?"

Jon shook his head before it stalled and morphed into a nod. "Well, more or less. It also depends on your connection to the magic around you. It's in the air we breathe, the water we drink, even in you and me. If you can feel the connection and harness it, then you're almost there."

Almost there? Tyler was seating more on his knees than sitting crossed leg. "What's the rest?"

Jon motioned for Tyler to rise. "Your skill and conviction. Compare it to this. You can have all the

114

conviction in the world, but if you don't know how to hold a sword, you won't accomplish much. Likewise, you could be a master swordsman, but if you have no conviction, you might as well lay down your sword and not fight. It's when you have both conviction and the skills to handle yourself and your weapon that you become an unstoppable force. Same goes for magic."

"Okay then, what's next?" Tyler asked, rejuvenated.

Jon took a deep breath, as if resigning himself to a fate he never wanted. "We must get you an Ancori."

Tyler froze. "I need one? As in, I'm gonna be a Magi?"

Jon turned and asked, "Unless you no longer wish to—"

"No no, I want to. I want this An . . . well whatever you called it."

"Ancori. Then follow me. Lucky for you, I've found plenty during my journeys."

CHAPTER 13
THE MANIFESTATION STONE

Tyler sat patiently in the library waiting for Jon to return. *Huh, this room looks even bigger in daylight.* His eyes shifted back and forth as he scanned the bookshelf for titles he may recognize. *Medieval Magics, C.H.I.P: Through History, An Art Most Dark, Famous Magi . . . oh, one by Mallidy: The Complete Guide of Potioncraft.* The idea of reading an ancient ancestor's work intrigued Tyler, but before he could leave his seat, Jon walked through the library door carrying a small rusted lockbox. *Is everything in this house old?*

Pulling out a seat for himself, Jon worked the lock and key. "Are you ready?"

"What? Is something gonna jump out at me?"

Jon glared at Tyler with a scowl expression. "Ancori are stones. Gemstones. Here, take a look." Opening the box, Tyler was captivated by the shimmering jewels in Jon's collection. "Go ahead, touch them," Jon said as he laid the five gems on the table.

"They're beautiful. But why do I need one?"

Jon fiddled with a rough uncut Garnet between his thumb and fingers. "The real question is, why wouldn't you want one? Ancori are magic-infused gemstones. In fact, most

116

of the world's gems hold magic in them, to varying degrees of course."

"So there's magic in them?"

"Correct, but it's what you can do with their magic that makes them special. One perk is casting nonverbal spells through your thoughts."

Tyler's mouth hung agape. "You mean I'll just have to think of a spell, and it'll work? I can think of several uses for that."

"There's more. Regardless of stone, their magic will amplify your magical proficiency. More so, each gemstone favors certain magic. Spells your Ancori favors will improve even further."

"Wait, I understood amplifying my magic. But what do you mean by favoring spells?

Jon tapped the red stone with his forefinger. "Take Garnet for example. It would naturally empower your magic, but if you were casting defensive spells or protections, it would produce even stronger effects."

"That's awesome! So I just pick one?"

Jon shook his head and handed Tyler a turquoise-colored stone. "Viable pairings will give off energies. If you feel them, then it's a viable Ancori."

"I feel something when I hold this one. Feels kinda like a buzzing feeling," Tyler said rolling the stone in hand.

"That's energy, and that buzzing means you and Amazonite are a match. Should you choose it, of course."

Tyler said nothing but smiled as he admired the tiny precious stone.

"Did you ever want to be in the medical field?" Jon asked.

Tyler nodded. "Yeah, a doctor . . . how did you know?"

Jon pointed to the Amazonite. "Amazonite has been known to gravitate towards people with healing hands."

Huh, it's kinda like that metaphysical stuff Amanda's into. Wish I paid more attention now. "Okay, what're the others?" Tyler asked as he gave Jon the Amazonite.

One by one, Jon handed each gemstone to Tyler and named them. "Garnet . . . Malachite . . . Tiger's Eye . . . and Onyx."

"I see," Tyler said, rubbing his temples. Something was pressing at the back of his mind like a vice, and he began to lose focus. Each time a new gemstone touched his palm, the throbbing grew worse. "I – I don't want any of these," he muttered, taking in deep breaths. He rose to his feet and stepped away toward a bookshelf at the back of the room. Suddenly, a calming sensation rolled over him like a tide. *Good . . . stepping away from them helps. But, wait?* He suddenly knew something he shouldn't have known.

"What is it, Tyler? You reacted well with the Amazonite, even a permanent match perhaps. Come here, sit down," said Jon, motioning to the chair.

"You're not showing me everything."

"Excuse me?"

"When I touch the Amazonite, I felt its power. I don't feel it in any of the others. But I can clearly feel a second source of energy similar to the Amazonite . . . perhaps stronger."

"And it's not any of these other stones?"

"No, those ones hurt to touch. But there's a sixth stone, isn't there?"

Jon remained still glancing down at his box then back to Tyler. "There is a sixth stone."

"Can I see it?" Tyler asked, shaking away the cobwebs. Now more than ever, he could feel its presence, almost as though it was shouting to him.

"Choose from these five."

"Why don't you want me to see the other stone? If its calling to me so strongly, shouldn't that mean it's a really good match?"

Jon was taken aback. "It's calling to you? What does it say?"

"Well it's a stone, so no words. But it feels like its crying out to me."

"I . . ." Jon was unsure what to make of this. "You can feel it, but if I don't like what I see, it's off the table."

Tyler watched as Jon tapped on a hidden compartment in the box, releasing a single dull gemstone. It was much smaller than the rest, but as though reacting to Tyler's presence, the stone's dullness vanished into a shimmering brilliant color.

"What is it?"

"It's you're birthstone . . . Citrine." Jon pulled the small gemstone from the box and hovered it over Tyler's hands. "You ready?"

My birthstone? Why wouldn't he lead with this? Tyler nodded eagerly. When the gemstone left Jon's hands and fell into Tyler's the energy was electrifying. Its radiance turned the orange-brown stone to an almost yellow color before returning to normal. Suddenly, the energy pulsing through Tyler almost caused him to drop it onto the table. His arms shook. Jon peered at Tyler's gleeful face as he held the stone, the loose hairs on Tyler's head rising as though teeming with static.

Tyler glanced up at Jon. "I think we have a winner."

"So it would seem." Jon stared down at the gemstone inspecting its glow. It looked bright, vibrant, and full of life. Nothing about it reminded him about the way he acquired the stone so long ago. Maybe in Tyler's hand it would serve him well.

"Okay then, now what?" Tyler asked, innocent to the process.

"Palm out." Tyler hesitantly raised out his right palm while Jon placed the Citrine stone in the middle of his grandson's hand.

"Tyler Grayson, I will be taking you on as my Magi apprentice. Do you accept?"

"I do."

Placing his own hand over Tyler's, Jon shook his hand causing sparks to fly. There was an initial jolt of pain for a second, but it faded away into a slowly dissipating tingle. As soon as Jon let go of his hand, Tyler looked down at his new Citrine Ancori socketed into his palm. *Wow, weird . . . but not the least bit uncomfortable. It's almost like it's always been there.*

Tyler peered up to find Jon holding up his right hand, a dazzling white pearl was visible to Tyler now that he had his own Ancori.

"This is your official welcome to training camp, boy. May God have mercy on your soul."

Tyler stood from his seat proudly beholding his Ancori as it beamed majestically in place. "When do I get to use magic?"

CHAPTER 14
MEETING THE ADJUTORS

"Master, dinner is ready," Charlie said opening the door as the clock struck six in the evening.

Jon gave Charlie a nod before turning to Tyler. "That'll do for today. Time for supper."

"Will I get to learn any Latin tomorr—?" Tyler asked.

"Don't concern yourself with the pace or the daily lectures. That's my job."

"Alright. But should I practice or make flashcards or something for afterward?" Tyler asked still testing how much he could push his grandfather's patience.

Jon just put his arm around Tyler. "No. When it's time to train, you train. When it's time to rest, you rest. You're eager, but you need to unwind when you can. Trust me, if you're going to take up scribing, you'll rarely get uninterrupted rest. Take it now."

"Alright, alright," Tyler said wiping the sweat from his brow.

"Just a heads up. I'm not sure how picky an eater you are, but never insult or lessen the good deeds of a Brownie," Jon warned as they neared the back door. "A Brownie never forgets."

Tyler assured Jon, "I don't care what he puts on my plate, I'll happily eat it." *It has to be better than Gramp's sour milkshake . . . right?*

"That-a-boy. Now, go take a quick shower then meet us in the kitchen for supper."

After taking a nice refreshing cold shower to rinse off the dirt and grime of a hard day's work, Tyler walked into the kitchen. Jon, Penelope, and Charlie sat around the kitchen table enjoying their supper. Tyler walked to the empty seat and sat.

Charlie immediately pushed a bowl of soup in front of him. "I hope you like Brown Windsor Soup."

"It looks incredible," Tyler said peering down at possibly the most appetizing bowl of soup he had ever seen.

Charlie waved his hand as though inviting Tyler to eat his masterpiece. "Looks are one thing, tastes are another. Please, eat."

The brown seasoned soup had chunks of stewed beef and slow-cooked tender mutton. Giving the soup color, chopped pieces of carrot, onion, and parsnip gave the soup a hearty full appearance. The steam danced and whirled whimsically upwards into Tyler's nose. *Oh, it smells so good!* Taking a spoonful, Tyler savored every carefully crafted flavor.

"This is amazing," Tyler said with a low trembling moan of approval.

"Thank you, sir. Glad to hear it. Cooking is my passion."

Tyler perked up. "It was my dad's too."

"Soup's good, Charlie. As always," Jon said already halfway done with his supper.

Penelope happily ate her supper having complemented Charlie several times before Tyler and Jon arrived. Charlie puffed out his chest proudly knowing everyone enjoyed his soup. He went to grab his spoon, but then the doorbell rang.

Without missing a beat, Charlie got up saying, "I think I'll break out my family's recipe for Beef Wellington for tomorrow night's supper."

Tyler turned to Jon as he watched Charlie head for the door. "Wait, is Charlie going to answer the door?"

"He's just checking for me. Probably some salesmen or someone wanting to know if I've heard the good news," Jon said finishing his bite.

Charlie returned and motioned to Jon. "Master, the Adjutors have arrived."

Jon glared at the clock before throwing his napkin onto the table. "I guess the Guild is as bad with telling time as they are with a checkbook. I clearly said to come by at 8 PM, it's—"

Adjutors? "Should I com—" Tyler asked already pushing his chair out.

"No, you eat! I'll take care of this." Jon said, guiding Tyler back into his seat.

Pulling his chair back in, Tyler watched as Charlie ladled another scoop of soup into his bowl. "Thank you, Charlie. But I'm not that big of an eater."

"Nonsense! You're a growing young man and a trainee to boot. I know how to feed a Magi. Now sit and eat," Charlie said adding another scoop.

Tyler glanced over at Penelope as she smiled back enjoying her own miniature bowl of soup. *Well, it was mighty delicious. I could probably put down another bowl.*

After his third helping, Tyler waved his hand over his bowl. "Thank you, Charlie. Really, it's fantastic, but I am so full."

Charlie smiled as he placed the pot of soup back on the table. "Mark my words, by the end of training I'll be making another whole pot just for you."

Walking back into the kitchen, Jon pointed to Tyler. "Good, you're finished. Follow me."

"Thank you again for dinner, Charlie."

Charlie waved him off as he turned to Penelope. "He sure does say 'thank you' a lot."

Penelope proudly reminded him. "Well, he is his mother's son."

Taking Tyler into the basement, Jon stopped just outside the door. "Okay, let me make something clear. These are applicants. If you want one to be your Adjutor, great. But if none of them feel right, then we can send them all packing. The Guild will send us another group tomorrow. Do you understand?"

"I gotcha," Tyler answered. *Still not sure I even want an Adjutor . . .*

"It's ultimately your decision," he said before adding, "and you damn well better take my input into consideration."

Tyler wasn't sure he wanted his grandfather's input, but he shrugged and motioned toward the area where the potential Adjutors were waiting. "Alright, let's see them."

124

Opening the door, Jon brought Tyler into the well-lit room. One wall was filled with weights, pads, and other gym equipment Jon had collected over the years. The other was one continuous full-size mirror. Standing at attention, the four possible Adjutors stood in a line facing Jon and Tyler. They were all wearing face-covering brown robes with an odd-looking symbol over the chest. All of them, both male and female, wore the same robe. All of them except one.

"Excuse me, but where are your robes?" Jon asked noticing the night-blue tank top and faded black straight jeans.

A woman in her mid-twenties replied, "In my bag where they belong."

"Name," Jon asked bluntly.

"Erika."

"Full name?"

"Erika Demopoulos, and you?"

Jon turned to Tyler and pulled him in closer. "Not her." Tyler gave him a nod before Jon turned back to Erika and the group of would-be-Adjutors. "Not wearing the traditional Adjutor robes . . . care to explain?"

"You want us to scrimmage, don't you?" Erika answered, sizing up her fellow Adjutors.

"And you feel this will make the difference?" Jon asked.

Erika grinned. "No, I've had over two millennia of combat training. I just like looking good when I steamroll someone."

"Shame you won't get to show us," Jon said pointing to the door. "Get out!"

"Sorry, old fella. But he's the boss, not you," Erika said, unintimidated.

Jon said nothing, but his blood was boiling.

Erika turned to Tyler. "How about it? Care to see what I can do for you? Or should I leave because I like to wear clothes from this century?"

Tyler could feel the room's eyes on him. *Is this really a fight over clothes? I don't feel insulted. I just want the best ... who cares?* "I'll see what you can do. But if I end up picking you, would you wear the superhero cape?"

"If I have to," Erika said chuckling as Jon scolded Tyler.

Doing his best to ignore Erika, Jon pointed to the first in line. "Name please, sir."

"Nicoli Agnes, Satyr." The smaller yet well-built man unveiled his hood. The only evidence of his Satyr nature was the two horns curling out from his forehead around his ears. His goat-like lower body was covered by his robes, but from his reading Tyler knew he had hooves somewhere down there. His curious side wanted to see.

The tall but slender man standing next to Nicoli stepped forward. "Patrick Jones, Elf." Tyler stared at Patrick. *Elf? He seems normal to me ... oh, his ears.*

Standing beside Patrick was a seemingly ordinary woman. "Athena Elias, Harpy." Unlike Patrick, Tyler couldn't make out a single distinguishing harpy feature. Her large brown hawk-like back wings and her talon legs were covered by her robes.

Tyler turned to Erika. Her earthy brown hair ran midway down her back and complimented her chestnut eyes. She had a sharp jaw that rounded out at her chin and

126

small facial dimples when she smiled. Erika also had a smooth Mediterranean nose hinting to her Greek heritage.

Erika followed her fellow Adjutor's lead. "Erika Demopoulos, Siren."

"Okay, let's take a quick look over your Guild scores," Jon said rifling through their files. Not wanting to read Erika's files, he saved them for last. Nicoli was fine but excelled in nothing. Patrick was wise but rigid. Athena was inexperienced but charismatic. Then there was Erika. Jon stumbled through each page seeking out her flaws. But with each page turned, his eyes grew wider in disbelief.

Erika grinned as Jon turned to her with his hardened face. "How're my numbers?"

"You know the Guild will disband you for falsifying scores," Jon replied, shooting her a frightful look.

Erika's face grew cold and leering. "That's quite an insulting accusation. Give them a call, old man. They'll back up my numbers."

"You scored a 122 on Athletic Prowess, a 115 on Creature Knowledge, a 127 on Problem Solving, a 133 on Archery . . . and a 155 on Swordsmanship!?"

"What's it out of?" Tyler asked peering down at Erika's notes.

"155.3," Jon said curtly.

"Wow, almost perfect? Impressive!" Tyler said turning to Erika.

"There's three more pages, and not one score below 97," she said.

Jon argued, "I'm a 126 Swordsmanship. The Guild scored you higher than me?"

"I've got years of practice on you, old man." Erika shrugged.

Patrick scoffed. "Her files are old. She hasn't been to the Guild in decades."

Erika kept her calm demeanor. "Care to find out if my skills have doled?"

Jon withdrew to his desk. Frustrated Erika was still even in consideration, he turned to Tyler. "It's your interview, judge them however you want."

The four stared at Tyler waiting for him to conduct his meeting. Clearing his voice, Tyler thought for a moment before asking, "Okay, fight or flight?"

Nicoli flashed his double-sided war ax. "We fight, we do not run."

Patrick agreed holding up his broadsword. "It's the conviction of one's blade, not the number of blades."

Athena laughed. "Numbers don't hurt your odds. I say wait for the right opportunity, then fight or run."

Erika pointed at Athena. "She's the closest. The answer is . . . it depends. If it's an unintelligent beast, fight, flight, or outsmart it. If you can speak to it, you can always try to outsmart it."

"Always?" Nicoli asked, shaking his head with a smirk on his face.

Staring him down, Erika repeated herself. "Always. Right, old man?"

Jon kept quiet in his seat not saying a word. Shifting his eyes over to Tyler, he gave him a stern nod.

"You need an Adjutor who uses their head to assess the situation," Erika said, then turned to Nicoli, "Not one that runs into battle like an idiot."

128

Nicoli gripped his ax tighter, waiting for Tyler to let him show off his combat skills so he could take Erika down a peg.

Tyler quickly thought another question off the top of his head. "Okay, favorite movie?"

While most appeared confused by the unrelated question, Erika answered, "*The Shawshank Redemption*, or maybe *Edward Scissorhands*."

With the others unable to name a movie, since their lives were dedicated to training and service, Tyler moved on. *Okay, no moviegoers, huh? How about books?* "Okay, who's your favorite author?"

The others sighed in frustration unable to give Tyler an answer while Erika rattled off, "Truman Capote."

Reading *In Cold Blood* this year in American Literature, Tyler nodded. Although Tyler was having fun with the interview, he knew he needed to keep the questions more relevant if he wanted everyone to answer him. But with every question, Erika always had the best answer no matter how many answered before or after her. At least in Tyler's eyes.

After several minutes, Tyler asked, "Okay, one more question, then I want to see you all in action. If I tell you to take the Codex and run, leaving me behind, what do you do?"

Patrick quickly answered, "I would never leave you behind. It is my duty to protect you. If need be, I'd stay behind, and you would leave me."

Everyone nodded and agreed. Everyone, except for Erika.

Jon noticed this immediately. "You're bound by your Oath to protect the Scribe. Did you not hear Patrick's answer? Or do you have another?"

Erika panned to Jon then back to Tyler. "Okay, kiddo. So, they're right. By Oath, I couldn't do what you asked. But if we are going to work as a team, it's more important that I trust you. So my answer is, if I can trust that you have a plan, then I'd do as you asked."

The only person in the room satisfied with this answer was Tyler. Everyone else saw this as willfully breaking a part of the Adjutor's Oath.

Nicoli stepped forward with his ax in hand. "Come now, throw her out. She is not fit to be an Adjutor!"

"Throw her out yourself," Tyler said with a smirk. "Let's see what you're all made of."

The moment had come. It was time to spar. The four stepped back away from one another as they drew their weapons. Erika pulled out her off-white cyan Greek Machaira; a curving blade with an inner wrist guard.

When the Adjutors were ready, Tyler counted them down. "Okay then, 3 . . . 2 . . . 1 . . . go!"

The other three Adjutors immediately turned on Erika. Tyler sighed to himself. *They turned it into a three vs. one. This is bullsh – oh!?* As quick as the fight began, it was over. With her blade at Nicoli's throat, her foot pressing down on Patrick's head, and Athena reeling on the floor from a well-positioned punch to the sternum, Erika held them in position waiting for Tyler to call the match.

Amazing! All Tyler could mutter was, "Wow . . ."

"Want to see a rematch?" Erika asked pushing Nicoli away, stepping off Patrick, and pulling Athena to her feet.

130

"No need."

Jon scrambled from his chair calling out, "Tyler! A word!" Taking him aside, Jon leered into his eyes. "I'm telling you, she's trouble. Don't pick her."

"Why not? Because she's rough around the edges?"

Jon pulled Tyler in closer by the collar. "Adjutors are disciplined and follow an Oath. From what she's shown me so far, she follows no one's rules but her own."

"She has clear combat skill when outnumbered, she has great scores, and she seems pretty relatable," Tyler argued confidently in his judgment.

Jon growled, "Tyler, just stop for a moment and think with your head! The bigger one! Don't make the same mistake as –!"

Tyler cut him off before he could finish that thought. "Who said I wasn't thinking with my head?" Tyler said with a chuckle.

"Boy!"

"I am thinking this one through, and my gut says she's a home run. Trust me. She came from the Guild. You said it yourself. They're a reliable source, right?"

"I trust no one, and neither should you, but it's your call. For your sake, I hope you're right." Jon loosened his grip.

Returning to the group, Jon pulled Nicoli, Patrick, and Athena aside, "Come, follow me."

While the other two went silently, Nicoli turned one last time to Tyler. "Watch your back, kid."

With the others out of the room, Erika took a playful shot at Tyler's shoulder. "If I'm right about what you're doing, then you're making a good decision."

"I think so too. We're a team now. I've got your back, and I trust that you have mine. But . . ."

"But?"

Tyler pointed to Erika's belongings. "But, you're gonna need to wear the superhero cape."

Erika gave a heavy sigh. "Aw, really? Do I have to?" She waited for Tyler to tell her otherwise, but then realized he wasn't going to back down from this stance. "Fine, as you wish, boss." Tyler chuckled after Erika finished draping the robes over herself. "What?"

"You're right . . . those things aren't from this century."

"See? They're hideous! Can I *please* ditch this thing?" Erika almost begged.

"Okay . . . around me, you don't have to wear them. But if Gramps is around, you have to wear them. Deal?" Tyler said extending his hand.

Erika reached out, hesitantly taking his hand. "I guess I could do that if it'll keep the old man off my case."

CHAPTER 15
CATCHING UP

Charlie and Penelope had just finished moving their belongings into another room when the clock struck 10 PM. Giving the new Scribe and Adjutor their own living quarters, the two walked out as Jon stood in the doorway.

Seeing Tyler and Erika already on their respective beds, Jon checked his watch before glaring at Tyler. "Lights out." With the snap of his fingers, the room was plunged into darkness followed by the sound of Jon closing the door behind him.

No library trips tonight. Both listened in silence as Jon made his way up the stairs to his own room. The second they heard a muffled door shut, Erika's side of the room lit up. *Christ, that's bright!* Soon Tyler could hear music coming from the earphones in Erika's MP3 player. Not giving it much thought, Erika started humming along to the song.

I guess she's got no intention of turning in this early. Guess I'll check my . . . Tyler froze as he pulled aside his bedsheets. *Crap! I haven't checked my phone in days.* Tyler scurried to his backpack and grabbed his phone. *Ah! It's dead!* Tyler caught Erika's attention.

"Got a phone charger?"

"Knock yourself out," she said pointing to her wall charger.

Tyler plugged in his phone and waited for it to reach 10% before taking it back to his bed. *Fourteen unread messages?! Crap! I hope none of my friends went to my place looking for me. Let's see. First message . . . Amanda.*

Amanda

Hey, sick or something? *Wed 10:21 AM*

You must be resting =/
Hope you feel better soon, text me
when you get this *Wed 3:12 PM*

Good night <3 *Wed 9:04 PM*

Are you okay, I'm starting
to get worried *3:19 PM*

Please text me *8:22 PM*

Hey I'm so sorry, Amanda
A lot has happened the last
couple days, hard to explain

DUDE! You scared the crap out of me!
I was starting to freak myself out ='(
I'm glad to hear you're ok
Tell me about it tomorrow?

I'm not going to school tomorrow
either, meet up this weekend?

134

??? okay sounds good
Mall?

                              Sounds good, good night!

Good night! Jerk! <3

Ballsy, Zane

Ballsy:
Yo Tyler, out two days?
you okay? *4:11 PM*

Zane:
Like you're one to talk
Out for three days this week

He's fine, I feel ya, bra
breakups suck *4:11 PM*

Ballsy:
Is that it? Better not be
or I'll have to slap some
sense into you
You're better off without her *4:12 PM*

Zane:
She hasn't been to class either
Must be taking it hard too
But Ballsy's right *4:12 PM*

Ballsy:
There are pleeeenty of girls
who'll be all over you Ty
You one fine ass white boy *4:22 PM*

Zane:
^ Lol should I give you
two some privacy =P

You need time?
We can reschedule Gamefest
Right Ballsy? *4:24 PM*

Ballsy:
I think he could use Gamefest
But if you want we
can hold off *4:25 PM*

Hey guys, long story, I'm fine though
Yeah, let's raincheck Gamefest
And no, it's not about Nessa
I'm better off, she's a little she-devil
Ttyl, night

Ballsy:
Adda-boy!
Night, Man

Zane:
Savage! \m/

Casey

Hiya! Missing a lot right now
Don't worry, I've been taking
136

good notes
Hope all is well! ^_^ *3:12 PM*

Hey, Zane just told me
about Nessa, what a bitch!
I'm sorry, Ty :/ *3:26 PM*

> Hey Case! Thanks =)
> Hope all's well too

> Haha, yeah I'm totally ok
> But thanks for asking!

OK, I'm here if you
ever want to talk :)

> Thanks, Case!
> Good Night!

Night!! ^_^

Tyler plugged his phone back in before turning to find Erika still in her own world listening to music.

"Erika . . . Erika!" Tyler whispered. *She can't hear me.*

After a few more attempts, Tyler grabbed one of his pillows and tossed it at Erika, landing right on her face.

Erika brushed the pillow aside as she pulled out her earpiece. "Hey!"

"Shhh!"

"What?!"

"What're you listening to?" Tyler asked trying to break the ice. *Probably should've aimed lower, she looks pissed.*

137

"Currently ELO . . ." Erika answered.

"I thought I recognized the song! You like classic rock?"

"Yep . . . you?" Erika said as she powered down her MP3.

"Yeah, one of the few genres my mom and I agreed on," Tyler said before asking, "What other kinds of music do you like?"

"I love music."

Tyler sensed Erika's lack of enthusiasm. "Oh yeah, being two thousand years old, right?" She just nodded which prompted Tyler to ask, "Yeah okay, so how old are you actually? You can't be more than twenty-five, right?"

Erika sat up in her bed and said, "Okay, sorry if I come off as a bitch here, but having time to lose myself in my music is . . . well, it's important to me."

"Oh, sorry I—"

"It's fine. How would you know anyway?" There was a still before Erika answered, "2125, I think, give or take a few years or decades. I've lost track."

It took Tyler a moment to realize she was answering his question. "Wait. You're serious? You mean to tell me you're that old?"

"I'm that young, thank you."

"Sorry. But I mean. How? You look . . . well, amazing for 2125 years old—young," Tyler backpedaled.

"Is my age really the most mind-blowing thing you've encountered in the past week?" said Erika with a furrowed brow.

"Ha, fair point. So, being a Siren . . . What, do Sirens live for ten-thousand years or something?"

138

"We're immortal, we never die natural deaths."

"That's crazy! So you can never die?" Tyler asked with fascination in his eyes.

Erika shook her head. "We can't die natural deaths. But we can still die from unnatural causes or—yes, we can still die."

"Never getting old . . . That sounds amazing."

Erika shot back saying, "Isn't all it's cracked up to be. Gets boring at times . . . and lonely," she said with a hint of sorrow in her voice.

"Lonely? Seriously? If *you* couldn't find someone in two-thousand years, I'm screwed."

Statuesque, Erika redirected the question, "You seem like an above average guy. No luck?"

"Ha! Above average, huh?" Tyler said chuckling at her bluntness.

"You're seventeen, aren't you?" Erika asked waiting for Tyler's nod. "Yeah, not really into jailbait. So, no luck then I take it?"

Tyler answered as he teetered back and forth. "Well, yeah I've had girlfriends before. The last one was a Succubus though."

Erika peered at Tyler with judgmental eyes. "Oh, well, that's a thing. To each their own I guess."

"I didn't know she was a Succubus! She tried killing me last time I saw her," Tyler said defending himself.

"Well, it could be worse, right?"

"Umm, how?" Tyler asked tilting his head.

Erika shrugged. "I don't know, you weren't supposed to ask me how."

"So seriously? No one, in two thousand years? I don't believe it," Tyler said shifting the focus back to Erika.

"Believe it," Erika said, though her smile faded.

The room went silent. *Ugh . . . batting a thousand tonight, Grayson.* Tyler changed topics asking, "So besides living forever, anything else I should know about Sirens?"

"We're amazing singers," Erika answered bringing a smile back to her face.

"Really? No wonder music's a big thing for you," Tyler said perking with interest. Erika reached for her earpiece when Tyler asked, "Mind showing me?"

"Never paid attention in history class? A Siren's voice will lure men to her," Erika said laughing at his naivety.

"Oh, come on, I thought that was just mythology. Your voice can't be that powerful. No offense."

"Let's make it interesting. If I can get you to walk over to my bed with only my voice, you buy me dinner." Erika grinned as she dropped her MP3 onto her bed.

"Sure, and if I can resist, what do I win?" Tyler asked.

Erika hummed as she warmed up her voice. "Ha, whatever you want, kiddo. Literally, whatever the heck you want."

When Erika was ready, Tyler sat upright and listened as Erika quietly sang a beautiful song. *Huh, feels like it belongs to a song from the 1920s.* But as each lyric left Erika's mouth and entered his ears, it was like the song was born anew. More colorful. Warmer. No longer outdated or hokey sounding. It was just beautiful. So beautiful in fact that when Erika stopped, bringing Tyler back to reality, he found himself mere inches away from her face.

Umm s-she's awfully close. Tyler grinned nervously before looking around. *Wait! I'm . . . I'm on her bed!?* Tyler peered back at Erika as she smiled victoriously. "How did—"

Giving herself some breathing room, Erika gently pushed Tyler away. "I love seafood and Chinese. *Authentic* Chinese." Tyler just nodded knowing he somehow lost the bet. "Now, back to bed," Erika said pointing to his side of the room.

"How are you not singing for a living?" Tyler asked still unsure how he ended up on Erika's bed without noticing.

Erika scoffed and rolled her eyes. "Are you kidding? I'd be mobbed at my own concerts. I sing by myself."

"That's sad."

"What? Singing alone?"

"Well that too, but your voice. It's . . . special. Sad the world will never get to hear your gift."

"Huh, guess so. Is what it is, though. But . . . thanks." Erika glanced down at her phone and saw the time. "Well, we should be off to bed. The old man wants to start when?"

"6 AM sharp."

Erika shivered in revulsion at the thought of waking at such an ungodly hour. "Old people I swear."

CHAPTER 16
A LITTLE HELP

The next morning started with another day of Magi training. As the sun arched past noon, Tyler found himself once again face down with the wind knocked out of him. He slowly picked himself up giving Jon an irritated grimace. *Fourth time today, Gramps!*

Jon patted Tyler on the back and helped him to his feet. "You're getting better. You aren't leaving yourself open as much now."

"Thanks, Gramps. It means so much to hear that from you right now," Tyler said still gasping for air.

Jon smirked as he straightened Tyler's hunched over posture. "Smartass. Ready?"

"Please, can I take five?" Tyler asked.

"You know the rules then."

Tyler dropped to his hands and knees before getting into a pushup position. *Fifty pushups . . . five minutes. Let's go.* Meanwhile, Jon turned to find Erika leaning against her planted practice weapon as she flipped through songs.

"Bored?" Jon asked coldly. Erika bobbed her head from side to side still unaware of Jon's death glare. "Excuse me . . . Erika!"

Haha, she still doesn't hear him. He's turning red! Tyler grabbed his weapon and tapped Erika's shoes, getting her attention, then tilted his head in a gesturing motion towards Jon.

"Oh! Are you finished borderline abusing your grandson?" Erika asked before Jon could get in a single scolding word.

Tyler couldn't help but chuckle even though it hurt to laugh. "Nope, the pain train's still rollin' through town."

"Care to join practice?" Jon asked crossing his arms.

Erika put her MP3 player away. "Oh? Is that what we're calling this? Okay, want me to take a turn at beating him or do you want me to actually help train him?"

"Go for it," Jon scoffed.

"Up," Erika said giving Tyler a hand.

"Please, I just need five," Tyler grunted. *I feel even more torn up than yesterday.*

"Kiddo, just get up," Erika said in an almost sweet reassuring tone. Taking his hand, Erika pulled Tyler up to his feet and handed him his practice weapon. "Okay, let's say I'm winding up to swing at you and I'm this close. What do you do?"

"Step back . . . and block?"

"So you actually want me to wind up and take a swing at you?" Erika asked with a furrowed brow.

"No, no I'd rather you not."

"My thoughts exactly. I mean you could fall back into a defensive position. But wouldn't it be infinitely better if you could take away my momentum and be positioned to land your own blow?"

"Yes, how?" Tyler asked all too eagerly.

143

"In slow motion, please. Pretend you are going to wind up and swing down at me." Tyler took up his staff and did as she asked. Erika took an aggressive step forward as he neared the end of his windup, their eyes now locked mere inches from one another. "Now, how's that angle you're gonna need to take?"

"It'd be very difficult," Tyler answered seeing her point.

"Best of all, I have complete control. You can't do much in your current position. But for me, I could stab you in the . . . well take your pick where. I could punch you, kick you, knee you."

"Okay, so if I can close the gap, go for it? But if I can't, it's okay to fall back into a defensive position?" Tyler asked dropping his stance.

"Yes, exactly! Just remember, if someone's bold enough to wind up for a swing, they're pretty much telegraphing what they're doing." Erika turned to Jon. "Hey look, old man. One minute in and he's already learned something from me."

Jon rolled his eyes. "Low bearing fruit. You mustn't be well-versed in the Old Disciplines."

"The Five Disciplines. You're applying Mera-su, improving pain threshold and avoidance. But very outdated by Kena-su," Erika answered affirming her knowledge.

"Very good, I'm surprised you actually know of them. But Kena-su is only effective if you can keep up the pace. I'm training him to be a thirty-minute soldier, not a three," Jon said having heard this argument before.

"You plan on training him, right? I'll have his back, so between the two of us, he'll be ready and protected," Erika said pointing to Tyler.

"Ask any of the previous Scribes if training and an Adjutor was enough." For the first time, Erika didn't have a comeback. "You may be his Adjutor, but I am his Master. He will follow my teachings."

"Fair enough," Erika said, yielding the argument out of respect.

"Crap! No . . ." Tyler cried holding his right hand.

"What's wrong?" Erika asked.

Tyler held out his hand. "My Ancori chipped. I . . . I didn't even—"

"Oh, little lamb." Erika chuckled.

"What?"

"That's normal," answered Jon as he took the broken fragment. "Your raw Ancori is being cut. Once your training is complete, it will take on a new shape."

"What shape?"

"That depends solely on you."

"What's your shape?" Tyler asked taking a breath of relief

Jon held up his palm to reveal a perfect circle. "The Sphere. It stands for one's endurance. Now. If you'd like to continue our training . . . staff up."

Erika withdrew to the side letting Tyler square off with Jon once again. But as Jon stared down his tired grandson, he didn't call for the ready. Maybe he was pushing Tyler a little too hard. He stared into Tyler's eyes, and for a moment, he saw his daughter's eyes staring back and he quickly turned away. He was training Tyler just as hard as Charlotte. Training him not to be acceptable, but exceptional.

Charlotte was exceptional, Jon thought. *And yet Charlotte's . . . gone. Tyler has to be stronger, faster and smarter. He can't end up . . .* Jon turned back and peered into Tyler's confused eyes. *For you two, I'll pour everything I have left into him.*

Jon lowered his weapon and pointed to the patio. "Water break. Ten minutes, then I want you both back here—without electronics."

Slugging down some water, Tyler turned to Erika still listening to her MP3. "Thank you."

"You're welcome?"

"Hey. Just curious, you know there are a lot of better ways to listen to music now, right? I mean, MP3s are kinda ancient," Tyler said as he filled his cup.

Erika answered as she lovingly patted her MP3 player, "I've had this thing for so long though. It was my first music player . . . it's special. And besides, if it isn't broke, don't fix it."

"Oh my, I just realized something," Tyler said laughing.

"What?" Erika asked pausing the song.

Tyler replied sarcastically, "I just realized . . . that was such an old person thing to say!"

"Ha haaa, very funny," Erika said half amused and irked.

Tyler lifted his cup when a text message came through.

146

Amanda

Heeey, change of plans
I'm gonna be out of town this
weekend mind if we hang tonight?

> Hey! Um sure, shouldn't be a
> problem, 10:30 okay for you?

10:30? Why so late?
The mall will be closed

> I really can't get out earlier
> I'll explain more when I see you
> Meet you outside the North End

Ok fine, nothing like a little
curfew law breaking

> My thoughts exactly
> Okay, g2g
> See you tonight.

"Erika? You think there's any way Gramps would let me meet up with a friend after training?"

"Oh yeah, totally. I don't see him forbidding it at all," Erika answered sarcastically.

Tyler watched as Jon stepped inside the house for a moment. "Seriously though. Just meet up and come back. No back alleys or shady places. It'd be fine, right?"

"Oh, completely fine. I mean, what, there's only a demonic army hunting you."

"Point taken," Tyler said with a sigh.

"So we're going out tonight, then?" Erika asked stretching side to side.

"But you just said—"

"You only asked how the old man would feel. I'm down for a little adventure," Erika interrupted as she picked up both of their practice weapons.

"Oh um, you want to come too?" Tyler asked taking his practice weapon.

"Wherever you go, I go . . . kind of my job now." This was met with a silent nod before Erika asked, "So, who are we meeting up with anyway?"

"Amanda, a friend of mine since forever," Tyler said as he prepared himself for another round with his grandfather.

"Oh, a girlfriend, huh?"

"No. I mean she is nice and all, but no, just friends," Tyler said quickly to clarify.

Erika smiled smugly. "Mhhm, sure. And how're you gonna explain me being there too?"

"I'm gonna tell her everything. So, I'll just introduce you as my Adj—"

Erika interrupted Tyler, "Are you crazy, kid? This isn't exactly common stuff in the

non-magical world."

Tyler cut in between breaths. "Yeah, I know. I was kinda in that world up until a few days ago. But Amanda will believe me."

"Or think you've gone insane," Erika said jabbing at the naïve Magi trainee.

"It'll be fine, trust me."

148

CHAPTER 17
PAST CURFEW

Jon walked into Tyler and Erika's room at ten o'clock for lights out, as had become custom. But to his surprise, both were sound asleep in their respective beds. *Perhaps the rigorous day's training wore them out?* Jon thought to himself. Waving his hand over the light switch to disable it, he gently closed the door before climbing the stairway to his bedroom.

The sound of Jon's lock clicking into position was barely audible. But as though on cue, Tyler threw his sheets aside and climbed out of bed already dressed and ready to leave.

"You ready?" Tyler whispered to Erika as she climbed out of bed dressed.

"Yep, let's hit it," Erika replied as she slung the strap of her pink purse around her shoulder and ruffled her hair out.

"I honestly didn't take you for the kind of girl who likes pink . . . well, anything," Tyler chuckled as he pointed at the purse.

"I'm not," Erika said reaching into the purse pulling out a small dagger. "And if we run into any trouble–" the dagger extended into a large rapier "–trouble won't expect wittle pink purse girl to run them through."

"Got one in there for me?" Tyler whispered as Erika's weapon shrunk back to normal.

"If need be. Now let's move – the last bus for an hour leaves in five minutes."

The two hardly made a sound as they snuck from their bedroom into the living room and out the front door. Tyler carefully locked only the bottom lock. Now outside, Tyler put the spare key he grabbed from the living room table into his pocket. Tyler and Erika tiptoed through the front yard and out the front gate.

"It squeaks . . . close it slowly," Erika whispered cautiously.

"I've done this before. Don't worry . . . there, we're in the clear."

The two stepped lightly until Jon's house was out of sight before breaking out into a full-blown sprint for the bus stop.

Tyler waved at the bus driver as they watched the last bus pull into the station well ahead of them. *Come on! Look this way! Look this way!* The driver glanced up after closing the door behind several passengers just in time to see Tyler and Erika running down the sidewalk.

"Thanks for waiting," Tyler said, gasping as the two boarded the bus.

The driver seemed amused. "Hey, fastest I've seen two kids run for anything in a long time. Take a seat."

The two took a seat behind the bus driver. Erika reached into her purse and pulled out a bottle of water.

"Lucky he waited," she said, taking a couple sips before offering it to Tyler.

"Yeah would've blown the whole night," Tyler said taking a gulp of water. "Thanks."

Tyler peered out his window to find someone running up the sidewalk just as the bus pulled away. *Shoot, that sucks. Maybe the driver will pull over if I tell him . . . wait.* Tyler squinted as he peered out into the darkness at the figure. *Something about him feels off. I can't put my finger on it. Hmm . . . I'll just keep my mouth shut.*

Once the man was out of sight, Tyler turned his attention to the people around them. *Everyone seems pretty normal.* But then he crossed eyes with a man sitting several seats back. The man's emotionless glare was fixed solely on Tyler. He could feel his heartbeat racing as he turned away but kept the man in his peripherals.

"Erika . . . Erika . . . four o'clock," Tyler whispered trying not to move his lips.

"One sec," Erika said as she calmly turned and found the man still looking their way. Seeing Erika glance his way, the man winked at her and puckered his lips. Erika returned a disgusted grin. "Just a creep, relax. I'd imagine most demons looking for you would be closer to your Gramp's place."

The bus pulled up to the Northridge Mall stop several minutes later. Tyler and Erika briskly made their way to the North End. The two were hardly alone as mall-goers crowded the parking lot near the restaurants. Passing the movie theatre, the two walked down the dimly lit cobblestone path as the sports bar erupted with cheer. *There she is!* Tyler recognized Amanda sitting on a bench up ahead.

Erika nudged Tyler. "Oh, looks like you've got some explaining to do. The girlfriend looks a little put off."

Tyler shot Erika a look before calling out. "Hey! What's up?"

"Hey! I've missed you," Amanda said wrapping her arms around him.

"Missed ya too."

"I see you've brought a girl with you," Amanda said before turning to Erika. "Hi, girl."

"Sorry, Amanda this is Erika. Erika this is Amanda."

"Oh, I like her, she's sassy," Erika said smiling as she shook Amanda's hand.

"Thanks." Amanda gave Erika a wincing smile before turning to Tyler. "So, is Erika the reason you've dropped off the face of the Earth?"

"No, well, not really. It's a long story. Let's all go somewhere quieter. It's a lot to take in."

After walking and talking for the better part of an hour, Tyler reached into his backpack and pulled out the Codex. "So, now I'm in charge of filling in the Codex."

Amanda said nothing as she gave a cautious nod.

"So yeah . . . that's about it. Please say something."

"Tyler, are you doing okay?" Amanda asked as she nervously scratched her head.

"Told ya she'd think you went nuts," Erika jabbed Tyler.

"I'm telling you the truth!" Tyler said holding the Codex. "Look, I'll show you! Here is the . . ." All three peered down at the Codex as a page near the middle glowed a baby blue.

"Okay, cool trick, Ty," Amanda said anxiously.

Checking around him. *I don't see anything. Where is it?* Tyler rifled through the Codex towards the glowing page. "I'm not doing it, the Codex knows there's a creature nearby."

"Okay, I believe you! Now put the book away." Amanda adjusted her glasses as she strained to see movement in the dark.

Tyler shrugged off Amanda's comment. "No wait, I'm almost . . . see look! 'Merfolk'. There's a . . . Mermaid or Merman nearby? Huh? Out here? But there's no water." Just then another page started to glow closer to the back of the Codex. This page was pink.

"Pink, what does pink mean?" Erika asked.

"Blues are creatures with information filled in, pinks are new pages . . . new creatures!" Tyler explained as he raced towards the pink page.

Amanda could feel the hairs on the back of her neck standing on end. *This isn't funny!* she thought. Her heartbeat raced as the terrifying feeling of someone or something watching them sent a shiver down her spine.

Amanda tried closing the Codex. "Okay, enough! Let's get out of . . ." Amanda suddenly screamed when she turned to find someone standing behind Tyler and Erika.

Tyler jumped away from the figure as Erika reached into her purse for her dagger. But then they realized it was just a young boy no older than ten. More kids hid barely out of sight while this brave one approached the three young adults.

"Sorry, I didn't mean to scare you. Can we get a ride to the movie theatre?" the boy giggled.

"It's okay," Tyler said breathing a sigh of relief. He pointed towards the theatre. "The theatre's right over there, kid."

"Please, sir! We just need a ride to the movies. Please!"

"Look, it's right there," Tyler said turning and pointing at the movie theatre just down the pathway.

But as Tyler turned his back on the innocent looking kid, its eyes turned a soulless black. With Tyler's back turned, the creature raised its arm, ready to strike, as unnaturally long and jagged fingernails snapped out like a switchblade.

"Tyler!" Amanda screamed as she pulled him towards her. Tyler could feel and hear the creature's claws *swoosh* just by his shoulder.

Erika drew out her dagger into a rapier just as a second fiendish child charged towards them. Tyler and Amanda repositioned themselves as the initial creature circled its prey, crouched over like a tiger about to pounce. The creature's smile grew unnervingly wide as it imitated childish laughter with a sinister distortion.

"Erika! Sword!" Tyler shouted keeping his distance from the slowly advancing creature.

Erika pushed off one of the swarming monsters to throw her purse, but as it flew, another black-eyed creature darted between the two and nabbed it out if the sky. It hissed at Erika before hurling the purse into the empty parking lot.

Crap! Think, Tyler, think! The black-eyed child lunged itself at Tyler and Amanda without warning, and he pulled Amanda toward him just in time. *That was a close shave.* But

154

the creature was already crawling towards them as another crept up their side.

"Erika, a hand please!" Tyler shouted only then realizing she was dealing with no less than five of her own.

"I'm a little busy right now!" Erika yelled as she clipped one across the chest.

Tyler felt Amanda's hand trembling in his own. *I brought her into this.* Tyler stared down the fiend as it licked its lips ready to end their young lives. *It's now or never!*

Tyler raised his hand, closed his eyes and shouted, "*Dis!*"

An invisible force flung the creature back with such power it pinballed off one store's outer wall. The devilish creature fell to the floor and struggled weakly to its feet.

It–it worked . . . Tyler smiled, examining his hands as though discovering them for the first time. *I did it! I used magic!*

He glanced back at the remaining creature. Its soulless eyes quivered as it backed away slowly. *Ha! Fat chance, pal!* Tyler's Ancori glowed as he waved his hand as though clearing a table. "*Dis!*"

The creature was instantly picked off its feet and flung through the air. It shrieked terribly as it slammed into two of the other creatures busy dueling with Erika. Tyler was not only capable of using magic, but he was strong with the only Latin word he knew. Unprepared for this, the creatures gathered, took one last menacing glare at Tyler and fled off into the night.

"What the heck was that?" Amanda asked in a demanding tone as she picked her glasses off the floor.

"I don't know. Did you see their eyes?"

"Not those things!" Amanda shouted. "You! How did you . . . you tossed those things around like toys, Tyler. Without even touching them!"

"You know magic?" Erika asked as she jogged back with her purse in hand.

"Wait, so everything before? It's all true? Everything?" Amanda added.

We need to move. They could be getting back up for all we know. Tyler started walking towards a more populated spot near the theatre and asked them to follow. "Yes, everything is true, Amanda. Now let's get outta here."

Erika insisted as they walked closer to the theatre, "How did you do that? The old man hasn't even taught you magic yet."

"I looked it up on my phone earlier today. Now let's move!"

Hidden away in a small cove a few feet from heavy foot traffic, Erika stood guard as Tyler pulled the Codex out.

"Damn, it's gone," Tyler said. The glowing pink page had disappeared.

"What were those things?" Amanda asked.

"I don't know. But they had to be the pink page, right?"

"Your guess is as good as ours," Erika said.

Huh? Really wish I knew. I'm gonna need to fill them all in eventually. Tyler turned to the still beaming baby blue page. *Merfolk?* Tyler scratched his head. "A Merfolk is still close."

Erika extended her palm over the Codex asking, "How close?"

156

The page radiated a brilliant, almost blazing, blue. Any brighter and it would have startled the mall goers around them.

"I'd say pretty damn close." Erika's eyes met Tyler's as the Codex returned to a normal glow.

"Yeah, but it'd be hard to miss a guy or girl with fins! Hmm . . . let me read."

Erika eyes shifted to Amanda. "Unless she has legs."

"Wait, he said you're a Siren? Maybe it's confusing Merfolk for Siren?" Amanda asked, backing away.

"I don't think the Codex makes mistakes," Erika said, zeroing her stare on Amanda.

Amanda just stared at Erika wide-eyed and shook her head in quick jolts.

"Hey, kiddo . . . In all the years you've known Amanda, has she always been a great swimmer?"

"Yeah, how did you know?" Tyler froze. He peeked up from the Codex and saw the concerned look on Amanda's face. "No way! Really?" Tyler gasped. "Amanda? Are you a Mermaid?"

Amanda could only smile nervously. "Maybe a little."

Tyler fell back against the wall rubbing his brow.

"Having one of those 'my life's a lie' moments?" Erika asked, smiling over at him.

"Yeah, it's been happening a lot this week," Tyler said with an unsure chuckle. He turned back to Amanda. "All this time? How did I miss it? Legs! You've got legs!"

"Not exactly something I'm allowed to share with the world. You're my best friend! If I could've told anyone, you would've been the first person to know."

Yeah . . . that makes sense. Things could get dangerous for her if people found out. Tyler attempted to connect the dots. "But you've got legs. Mermaids have fish fins, don't they?"

"We can change back and forth between fins and feet, carefully."

"And all those competitions, I couldn't come because—"

"It's not a regular competition. Most of the girls don't want outsiders knowing their 'secret' identity," Amanda interrupted.

The Codex's illumination faded.

"Can I see your fins?" Tyler asked not thinking too much into it.

"No!" Amanda blushed.

"Why not?"

"I don't want you to see me like that," Amanda said. She was composed but growing more anxious by the moment.

"Oh, come on, like that's going to change how I—"

"I. Said. No. Drop it!" Amanda glared at him.

"Kid, you better leave it be," Erika inserted.

Tyler didn't understand what was so wrong, but he conceded. "Okay, sorry. Was just curious. It's not every day you find out something like this."

Amanda's face was on fire. Her eyes held back a slowly gathering ridge of tears. It felt like the world around her was getting bigger and she was the embarrassing center of attention. "I'm sure you can read all about everything in that stupid book," she said.

"Amanda . . ."

158

"It's getting late, we should call it a night, yeah?" Amanda said shrugging.

"Yeah, probably not safe out here," Tyler said, embarrassed now. "We'll walk you to your car."

"Thanks."

The entire walk to Amanda's car was silent. Mercifully, Amanda got one of the first parking spots entering the lot. She opened her car door and hopped in without a word. Backing out from her spot, Amanda rolled down her window. "Text ya later?"

"Please."

"Okay. Night."

"Night."

Once Amanda pulled away, Tyler turned to Erika. "We should go. Bus leaves soon."

Erika reached over and zipped Tyler's backpack closed. "Well, that was a good outing."

"Yeah, the best," Tyler scoffed.

"Hey, one good thing came out of this. Not only did you use magic, but you used it well. And without proper training!"

"I did do that, huh?"

"Sword skills may take a little getting used to, but I'm sure you're a natural with magic." Pulling out her MP3 from her purse, Erika offered Tyler an earpiece. "Music?"

"Sure," Tyler said as they started their trek home.

CHAPTER 18
CAUGHT

The pair walked down the sidewalk as they skirted into the wee hours of the morning. It was a relatively quiet drive and walk home as they both enjoyed Erika's playlist. But Tyler's mind was somewhere else, something Erika noticed as they neared home.

"Seen that look on a lot of men before. What's on your mind?" Erika asked seeing an unsure look in Tyler's eyes.

"Nothing."

"Weird finding out your girlfriend is a fish person?" Erika asked jabbing playfully.

"She's my best friend, not my girlfriend, okay?" Tyler said giving her a cold stare.

Erika muffled her laugh now nearing Jon's house. "That one really gets to you, huh? Okay, sorry. I'll come up with another way to mess with you."

I'm sure you'll have little trouble doing so. But she was right. "Yeah . . . it *was* kinda weird. Wasn't expecting that."

"Does it bother you that she's a Mermaid?" Erika asked stopping Tyler for a moment to let him vent.

"No, not at all. In fact, it's kinda cool! What bothers me is . . . who else?"

"Who else are Merfolk?"

"No . . . well yeah, kinda. More like, who else do I know that's not human."

"Not sure. Only time will tell I guess," Erika said throwing her hands in the air.

Tyler whispered as he opened the front gate, "I guess, at least we . . ."

Both Tyler and Erika froze. Now safe within Jon's property, the two peered up the pathway to find Jon staring back down at them from his stoop. Emotionless at first, Jon's eyes showed only a glimpse of the rage welling up inside him.

"Out for a midnight stroll?"

The night had gone from bad to worse in a matter of seconds. Nothing about tonight went well, and now any notion that sneaking out would be fine was wrong and very apparent.

Tyler timidly answered, "We were—"

"Don't speak," Jon interrupted as he shook with fury.

This was now the most uncomfortable Tyler had felt all night. There was no hope of escaping Jon's wrath. Behind him, Penelope and Charlie stared back at Tyler. Penelope appeared just as angry as Jon but also concerned how Jon may react if Tyler wasn't careful with his words.

"Nothing! I repeat, *nothing* gives you permission to leave this property until your training is finished! Do you have any idea what manner of creatures Ezekiel has at his disposal?"

"Well, little black-eyed demon children for starters," Tyler said, unsure what compelled him to speak. He covered his mouth as though trying to shut himself up. Erika turned to Tyler, mortified.

"I . . . I didn't say that! Well, I did, but it just came out."

"Pretty neat, isn't it? That's my ten o'clock Curfew Enchantment at work. It makes you tell the truth for one hour after you return," Jon said outlining his property line with his finger.

"Had to use it on Mom a lot?" Tyler blurted out unable to control himself.

"Semi-daily, often with this one by her side." Jon peered down and shot Penelope a glare.

Erika stepped forward knowing Jon couldn't care less about her. "Since you haven't bewitched me, how about you ask me the questions."

Jon's knuckles cracked. His hands shook. He didn't like Erika already, and now they were sneaking out.

Jon corrected Erika. "Enchanted not bewitched, and as far as I am concerned—"

"Jon . . ." Charlie interrupted before Jon could say something he couldn't take back.

Tyler stepped forward to defend his Adjutor. "It was all my idea. Erika just followed along to make sure I was safe. If it wasn't for her, they would've overrun me. Be mad at me, not her."

Jon stared Tyler up and down. A part of him admired Tyler's honesty and owning up to his misguided decision. This was not the enchantment, but rather Tyler willingly admitting his fault. He could feel it in his gut. Nonetheless, Jon's cold and infuriated stare hid these thoughts.

Breaking the silence, Charlie pulled at Jon's arm. "Jon, patience. For Miel."

Hearing his oldest friend's words cut through his overwhelming anger, Jon pointed to Tyler. "You're all that's

162

left of her. If you . . ." He paused and shook his head as though clearing a dreadful thought. "Don't you ever leave this house without my permission again! Do you understand me?"

"Yes," Tyler answered frozen in place.

"I was never good with this parental stuff, Tyler. Don't make this harder on me than it needs to be."

"I understand, it won't happen again."

Jon turned to Erika as an unpleasant compliment surfaced. "Ezekiel wouldn't send a small group to hunt Tyler. You fought and brought your Scribe back safe." Jon held out his hand. "Well done, Adjutor."

Erika reached out and shook Jon's hand. "How's that taste coming out of your mouth?"

"Like arsenic," Jon scoffed.

Erika smiled knowing she'd feel the same complimenting Jon. "Well, thanks, old man. But I didn't handle them all. Tyler here is a natural magic wielder."

"What?" Jon peered at Tyler. "How? I haven't taught you any Latin, or how to manifest and gather the magic around you."

Tyler answered unsure if Jon was surprised, angry or both. "I looked up Latin on my phone, then I did what you said."

Jon tilted his head, pleasantly surprised. He turned to Erika and asked, "He used magic?"

"Quite well actually. He flung those creeps like ragdolls."

"Hmm, didn't expect that out of him. Makes up for his sword skills progressing at a glacial pace," Jon said bluntly.

"Gee thanks, Gramps."

"I'm all out of compliments for tonight," Jon said as he pushed the front door open. "Now. Bed. The both of you!"

Tyler and Erika quickly made their way into the warm house, leaving Jon and the two smaller creatures standing outside.

Charlie walked in soon after. "Good night, Master."

Jon nodded to his friend, then took a long drawn out sigh of relief before turning to find Penelope still at his side. "Okay, what? What did I screw up this time?"

Penelope ignored his sarcastic assumption. "Nothing. That was nice, Jon. Miel would be proud of you."

Jon was surprised by the compliment. "God, I wish she was here, Penelope. I don't know what the hell I'm doing with this kid."

"Do you think he wouldn't have snuck out if she was here? Miel would still be fuming! She would've done the exact same thing, except maybe swat his behind ... probably in front of Erika too."

The pair chuckled as Jon said, "Oh, my Miel was a sweet woman. But such a hard-ass."

Amanda

Hey, how're you doing?

> Hey, I'm doing ok. Sorry about earlier
> I was just curious, my bad. =(

No, it's ok, I'm sorry I snapped

164

at you like that. I was just really
embarrassed it came out like that
>_<

I'm sorry I had to keep it
from you this whole time :/

                It's ok, I get it now, don't
              want to end up on National
              Geographic or a lab table.

Haha, yeah I'd rather not. But hey, I guess
you know everything about me now

              Yep guess so, and now you know
                what's going on in my life.

So... we're good?

                        Totally <3
            Now I get to see you race, right?

Glad to hear it <3
Ha! Well, I guess you already know...
So the other girls may not mind.
Might make them swim faster having an
eligible bachelor watching them lol ;)

              Haha! Ok, let me know
                when's the next race.
              That is if I can go out
              Gramps caught me

Yikes! =/
I'll let you know
Jailbird

So, are you coming
back to school?

                              No, kinda have a "job" now

Any benefits?

                              Um free travel and vacations lol

That's pretty nice
You finally get to travel
like you've always wanted ^_^

                              Yeah, just wish my life
                              didn't implode to get it

I'm so sorry about your mom ='(
If you ever need to vent or anything
I'm here, okay?

                              Thanks, just keep texting me
                              Not sure where this life
                              will take me now

You got it
But it's getting late
Here, since you're curious

An attachment came through between their text message. It
took Tyler a moment to register what he was seeing, but

then he realized it was Amanda's Mermaid tail. The photo cut out just below her belly button to show off her normal human skin before harmonizing with her scaly lower body. Her legs, from hip to tailfin, had melded together into one drawn out mass. Her captivating rich aquamarine scales shimmered under the ceiling lamp.

Wow! Beautiful color!

Thank you ^_^
First and last time I'm ever
showing off my tail to you hehe

Hahaha don't flatter yourself
Talk to you tomorrow?

;)
Yeah for sure
G'night, love ya!

Love ya too
Night!

CHAPTER 19
MAKING GOOD ON A BET

Tyler tossed and turned all night as nightmares clouded any chance of a restful night's sleep. Most of these terrors were short and in segments. Cruelly, they seemed connected to one another, but they visited him out of order. Luckily for his sanity, he forgot most of what he dreamed of that night. Except for the final nightmare.

Tyler was face down in a riverbed; a few more inches closer to the running water and he probably would have drowned. *H-how did I get here?* That's when he felt an agonizing pain stemming from his leg. He knew the feeling all too well. His leg was broken.

No, not my leg. Someone else's. He started painfully crawling up the side of the gradual cliff he'd fallen from. He looked down at his hands and one look confirmed that they were not his own.

He slowly managed his way up the hill, grunting and moaning each time his broken leg snagged on a rock. Pausing, pulling strength from seemingly nowhere, his hand reached over his broken leg and he muttered, "*Sana.*" Instantly, his leg was mended. *Sana? Whoever this is knows magic.* With his leg fixed, the crawl to the road above was much easier, but the sight at the summit was horrifying.

Tyler mentally phased away for a moment, too horrified to look upon what his nightmare was showing him, trying to force himself awake. When he phased back, the deceased young woman who had been hung and burned alive was now resting on the ground with a cloth covering her body. The sign hanging from above was also taken down. It read, "Witch".

Tyler's mind was flooded with emotions, many of them foreign to him. He did not know this woman, nor the man he saw her through, but still he retched in overwhelming sorrow, so much that his stomach felt like it was full of fire ants.

This woman was a friend, a good and old friend. Someone he truly loved and cared about, murdered! It was as if Tyler had lost Amanda. *This poor woman . . . this poor man. Wake up! The pain, it's almost too much to bear!*

Instead, Tyler rose to his feet. He looked down the road. Tyler had never seen this place before, and yet knew exactly where the people responsible for this woman's murder resided. Anger surged through Tyler like a wildfire, erratic and completely out of control. *Is this how he feels?* It was like nothing he had ever felt before, but the emotion behind it felt familiar. And in that moment, only two names came to mind.

Marshall . . . Ezekiel.

The next thing Tyler knew he was standing over a small village, a sea of flames engulfing everything it touched. Men, women and children fled the all-consuming fires. Although the sight terrorized Tyler, he could see the man extending his arms – no, *their* arms – to intensify the flames.

Swooping down onto the village like a bat in the night, Tyler was now a passenger in his own nightmare. As the civilians ran in terror all around him, the man walked through the village as though seeking something or someone out. When he finally found it, Tyler was once again gifted with knowledge he couldn't have possibly known on his own. It was a man, an ordinary man, trapped under a log which had blown on top of him during the initial ignition. Red hair, portly, middle-aged, nothing special. *This man . . . he was one of the men who killed that woman! How do I know this?*

A voice echoed in Tyler's head, "Because *I* know this, Tyler."

Tyler could see the terror in the trapped man's eyes as he approached. "Y-you?"

For the first time, Tyler heard the man whose vision he was seeing speak. "Do you remember my name?"

The man shook his head, fear dripping from his face. "N-n-no . . ."

Tyler watched as he pulled out a dagger from his pocket and raised it over his head. Then he heard the man's voice speak again. "Ezekiel! My name is Ezekiel!"

As Tyler registered everything, Ezekiel plunged the dagger towards the trapped man's neck. But before the dagger cut through his jugular, Tyler jolted forward in his bed, gasping deeply for air as his heart nearly beat out of his chest. His back was covered in a thick mat of sweat and a ringing in his ear drowned out all other noises. And then, suddenly, there was sickening silence.

Was that . . . "No, just a nightmare," he whispered to himself, looking over at Erika to make sure she hadn't awoken. He wiped a sheen of sweat from his forehead. *Just a nightmare . . .*

✷✷

It had been two months since Tyler started his Magi training and his skills had flourished under Jon. Unlike his two years in high school Spanish, Tyler picked up Latin much easier and could soon carry out a simple conversation. Already demonstrating raw talent, Tyler could manipulate magic to do most tasks Jon gave him.

If anything, Tyler needed to learn to restrain his magic. A simple request to light a candle would result in a raging inferno atop the candlestick. However, Jon wasn't the least bit concerned about teaching Tyler to dial back his magic. He was just thankful it wasn't the other way around.

"You're a natural. Almost as gifted as your mom," Jon praised Tyler as he became stronger with each passing day. *He'd give Charlotte a run for her money.*

Tyler's swordsman skills, on the other hand, were lackluster at best. While he was no longer a punching bag during training, it didn't take Jon long to diagnose his problem. Tyler found it hard to take an aggressive charge. He felt more comfortable taking a defensive stance and holding off for the right moment.

He's not that kind of fighter, Jon. Beating it into him for months won't change it. So, Jon altered Tyler's training. If Tyler wasn't going to become a flurry on the battlefield, he would become an impenetrable brick wall. He would have to wait out his opponent for the right moment to strike. And sometimes that strike was magic. *He's not an ace like his mom, but this is better.*

"You're becoming a better swordsman," he told Tyler one day after lambasting him for over a month on his poor form and accuracy. Tyler's ears perked, but that was before Jon hit him with the bad news. "Still, your striking and confidence with the sword is terrible. Some moments require immediate action, and when those times come, you can't hesitate. You must act."

"How will I know those moments when I see one?" Tyler asked, shoulders sagging.

"Your gut will tell you. When it does, act on it."

✳✳

It was a cool November Saturday morning when Jon and Charlie left the house on a day-long errand run. This was the first day off Tyler had since starting his training. At six o'clock, Tyler was wide awake while Erika softly slumbered. *Wish my brain would let me sleep in too.*

Erika woke as Tyler pulled his sheets aside. She looked at him for a moment before falling back to sleep. *How does she never have bedhead? It's like she never tosses or turns!* Tyler thought as he played with his disastrous messy hair. *She's just as pretty waking up as going to bed . . . huh . . . pretty?*

After a quick breakfast, Tyler started his day in the library hosting his own private Latin lesson. Penelope woke soon after and sat alongside him drinking her cup of tea. Although Penelope kept to herself while Tyler read, she couldn't help but reminisce about sitting in this very library with Charlotte when she was learning Latin.

Lost in the text, the clock suddenly chimed four in the afternoon. *Hmm, I should start making dinner. Erika should be home soon.* That's when Tyler realized now was an opportunity to make good on the bet he'd lost to Erika months earlier. Tyler knew several recipes, but if he was going to cook a bet-settling meal, it had to be his father's Chicken Piccata.

With Charlie out of the kitchen, Tyler had free range to cook without bumping into anyone. *Bit out of practice, but it'll come back to me.* After an hour of cooking and cleaning, Tyler peered down at the two finished plates. *I think this is the best I've ever made dad's Chicken Piccata.* Tyler listened as the front door opened. *Oh! Perfect timing!*

Erika stepped into the kitchen gleefully humming a tune in her head. She turned to find Tyler already in the kitchen. "Hey! How're you doing?"

"Doing great! Just finished dinner. Take a seat," Tyler said as he garnished the dishes.

"Dinner? You cook?" Erika asked as she hung her purse on the chair.

"A bit," Tyler answered placing dinner on the table. "Also, I owe you dinner from our bet."

"Better than seafood or Chinese?" Erika asked as the meal's aroma wafted into her nose.

"Better than any you've had," Tyler said passing a garlic roll across the table.

"Feeling pretty good about this, huh, mister? You know I've been eating Chinese and seafood for a couple millennia, right?"

Tyler said nothing. Instead, he just waited patiently for Erika to take a bite. She took a fork full as she cut through the tender chicken. As he had hoped, Tyler watched as Erika's face lit up.

"Oh . . . wow! This is really good, kiddo."

"Better than seafood or Chinese?" Tyler asked cutting into his own meal.

Erika rolled her eyes but grinned the whole time. "I don't know about that. But definitely the best Italian I've had, and that's saying something."

"Does it satisfy the bet?" Tyler asked enjoying a bite of his creation.

"Definitely!" Erika said wiping her lips.

As he took another bite, Erika glanced back at Tyler. *He doesn't look much like a chef. But this meal's fantastic. I mean . . . I've been to Italy. This is just as good!* Erika shrugged a thought as she took another bite.

"So how is that roommate of yours . . . what was her name?"

"Lydia, and yeah she's doing well."

Tyler glanced at his backpack, then back to Erika. "I checked the Codex, I have Naga filled, but not Lamia. Think she'd mind an interview?"

"Well she's my roommate, so I think I can swing it for you. But just warning you now, she's fifty-percent crazy, fifty-percent sexual innuendos, one-hundred percent telling you the god-honest truth."

"What? Is she gonna come on to me or something?" Tyler asked putting down his water.

"Oh, if getting hit on is all she does, she went easy on you," Erika said chuckling.

174

"Is that a Lamia thing?"

"More of a Lydia thing."

The conversation went quiet for a moment as both enjoyed their dinner. Out of curiosity, Erika looked up from her plate. "That is unless you'd like me to play matchmaker."

"No no, I'm quite alright being single. Don't need to add 'dated a snake-person' to this year's achievements."

"Awww I would've guessed that's right up your alley. Ex is a Succubus, best friend's a Mermaid, Adjutor's a Siren. Why not?" Erika quipped.

He found the truth humorous, but ended it simply saying, "I'm good, thank you."

"Suit yourself. She'd probably be all over you and those guns you've been building under your sleeves."

"Gramps' disgusting milkshake works wonders," Tyler said having noticed his body toning with each passing day.

"How's your Ancori looking?" Erika asked seeing Tyler fiddle with his palm.

Tyler held his palm out showing Erika. "Coming along, what do you think?"

"I can't see it, remember? What's it look like?"

"Hmm . . . Well, the top kinda looks like the base of a triangle. The bottom is pretty rough but wide."

"Huh? That's interesting. Wonder how it'll finish."

"Me too," Tyler said picking up his fork and knife. Waiting for the conversation to grow quiet, Tyler peered across the table again. "Hey, I've been meaning to . . . can I ask you something? It may be a sore topic."

"Shoot."

Tyler nervously rubbed the handle of his fork as he motioned to the Codex. "I did a little reading on Sirens. I'm just curious, not finding someone . . . was it intentional?"

"Are you referring to what falling in love means for a Siren?" Erika's mood immediately dropped.

Tyler nodded. "Yeah, I'm sorry, I never . . ."

Erika waved off Tyler's premature apology. "It's okay, really. You're supposed to learn about mythical creatures after all." Erika took a breath. "A Siren remains immortal indefinitely. However, should a Siren fall in love, and truly feels it, they lose their immortality. Aging every year like humans. I don't know about you, but to me 'love' sounds like a pretty raw deal."

"Seems like a pretty big give up," Tyler said nodding.

"But yeah, I can totally set up an interview with Lydia, I'm sure she wouldn't mind."

"Hey," Tyler murmured bringing Erika's eyes back to his own. "Not sure how much a consolation it is, but you'll always have a friend in me."

The sincerity of his sweet gesture brought the smile back to Erika's face even though part of her knew their relationship would end with Tyler's mortality.

"Sounds pretty good to me," she said giving him a wink as she took another bite.

"So, changing topics, where should we go first after the exam?" Tyler asked.

"I think we should focus on your final exam first."

Tyler sat back finishing his meal. "Never mind that for now. Come on, where do you wanna go?"

Erika sat back in her chair thinking aloud. "Europe? Maybe Ireland to start?"

176

"Okay, I'm down to start there! Wouldn't mind getting off this continent."

Now more into the idea, Erika's mind kept rolling. "Yeah, start in Ireland, maybe cross into England, then France, Germany, Austria, Italy—"

"Start a European road trip."

"Always down for a road trip, though this will be more walking than driving."

Tyler got up and cleared the dishes. "Glad you enjoyed."

"Thank you! I've gotta make bets with you more often."

"Hey, Erika, I have another question for you," Tyler said, his thoughts turning back to his readings on Werewolves. "Do you know who Marshall is?"

"Huh?"

"I've already told you about my mom's Adjutor, Marshall. And you've travelled. Been out in the magical world. Have you ever come across a Werewolf by the name Marshall? Or where I might find him?"

Erika sighed. "Penelope still worries you're gonna go after him."

"She's right. At some point I will find him," Tyler said, his voice brimming with conviction. *And I'll be a Magi . . . he'll have a lot to worry about then.*

"I don't know who Marshall is, nor where you can find him. But I know people who might be able to help us track him down," Erika said leaning up against the kitchen counter.

"When the time is right, can you ask them? Will you help me?"

177

Erika scratched her head. "I go where you go. So of course I'll help you. Bastard has it coming to 'em."

Finally, someone who sees it like I do. "Okay then. When the times right."

CHAPTER 20
THE FINAL EXAM

The sun rose on the morning of Tyler's final exam, and the wake-up call was at six like every other morning. Tyler and Erika could hear Jon's footsteps nearing. *He's coming to wake us.* The pair turned to one another, waiting for Jon to knock on their door. *I've been up most of the night . . . we both have.* Each gave the other a timid smile. *Great! She looks nervous for me too . . .* Jon's footsteps came to an abrupt halt just outside their door. *Here it comes.* But Jon just stood there. It was as though all three were aware of each other's presence, but no one dared disturb the silence.

"Tyler . . . Erika . . . It's six."

"We'll be out in a minute," Tyler answered.

Jon said nothing as he turned and walked back down the hallway.

After months of training, today's the day. If he passed, he was ready to start his journey as a Codex Scribe. If he didn't, more months of training, and that's only if Jon allowed it. Tyler turned to Erika and grabbed his clothing. "I'll go so you can catch a few more Z's."

Erika got up and grabbed her own clothing. "No. I'll go first. You . . . collect your thoughts."

Tyler sat on the bed with his clothing folded in his lap as Erika left the room. *I'm ready. I've been waiting for this day for weeks now, and I'll finally be able to leave and find him . . .* He tried to push the thought of revenge from his mind, looking for a different motive. *Everyone's counting on you. You can't train forever. The journey needs to start!* Then he looked outside. *But that's also it. As soon as I step out of this house, the real danger begins. Ezekiel is out there, and he wants me dead.* After a moment, Erika stepped back into their room wearing her Adjutor robes.

"Your robes?" Tyler asked looking her up and down.

"A special day calls for a special ugly change in wardrobe," Erika answered rubbing his shoulder as though trying to encourage him through friction.

"Thanks for the gesture."

Erika could see Tyler's insecurities surfacing as his smile faded away. "Hey! You've got this! Okay?"

"But what if I don't?"

Erika gripped Tyler's shoulders bringing his wandering eyes back to her own. "You're ready! I know you are! But . . . in the off chance that things don't go well today. It just means our journey starts next year and we start training again. It's not the end of the world."

"That's if Gramps gives me another shot. If I screw this up . . ."

"If it comes to that, he will. You gotta give him a bit more credit, kiddo."

Tyler laughed. "That's rich coming from you."

She just shrugged. "Just because we don't see eye to eye doesn't mean I don't respect him. He might be a surly old bastard, but he sees the same potential in you that I do."

180

Tyler gave a short nod. "Yeah, plus he probably can't wait for us to fly the coop."

"Actually, he'd rather you stay and train more, pass or fail."

"Really? But he said it himself. There's nothing more to teach."

"Every master, even the old man, always feels as though they could've taught their student more. He's just as nervous too, whether he admits it or not."

Gramps? Nervous? "When did you two have a heart to heart?" Tyler asked cracking a smile.

"Every day. Now, get dressed! You've got an exam to ace," Erika said ushering him out the door.

After a quick breakfast shake, Jon led Tyler and Erika up to his own private library on the second floor.

"Where's Charlie and Penelope?" Tyler asked hoping to see them before his exam.

"I told them to stay in their rooms. They're both too sentimental. I don't need them getting you emotional before the exam," Jon answered as he opened the library door.

With the curtains drawn, the room was full and bright despite the overcast autumn morning. The bookshelves were not as full as the larger library but contained Jon's personal collection of books and documents. There was no grand table or chairs to sit in; the only furniture was Jon's antique wooden desk and an old armoire. A portable nightstand was set up with a single violet teardrop shaped flask on it.

"Erika, you can sit at the desk. Tyler, over here," Jon said pointed at the armoire. Tyler tossed and turned as he tried to find a comfortable position. *I guess they didn't care about comfort in the 1920's.*

"Comfortable, princess?" Jon asked with a hint of annoyance in his voice.

"Actually, I could use a pillow, have any?" Tyler jabbed.

Jon scoffed, "Sorry, must've misplaced them, smartass. Now, in the time you've been here, you've learned the ways of the sword and the tongue. So I must ask you, Tyler Grayson: Do you wish for me to administer your final exam?"

"I'm ready."

Jon took the flask in hand and rubbed his thumb over the clover-shaped cork. "The following test will determine just how well equipped you are for the outer world. Pass, and you will be a Magi. Fail, and you will need further training. Do you understand?"

Tyler gave the thumbs up as he eyed the glimmering violet flask. "What's with the psychedelic Kool-Aid?"

"This little devil is called 'Verumpotious' or truth potion. Created by yours truly." Jon swirled the potion in his hand as he uncorked the vial with a distinct *pop* sound.

Tyler remained transfixed on the glimmering elixir. "You mean you brewed it, or you were the first to develop it?"

"Both," Jon said staring at his crowning gem as a Magi. "Before this, Masters needed to come up with elaborate ways to test their trainees. Simply put, drink this and you'll fall asleep. Once asleep, the potion will tap into your greatest fears and insecurities, using them against you to create a world in your mind. Survive the scenario, and you pass. Don't, and you'll wake up, but fail the exam. Still with me?"

"I can't die for real, right?"

"No. But be advised, you'll feel everything. Every bite, every cut, every broken bone, everything. It's the most realistic nightmare you'll ever have."

I don't know . . . I've had some pretty realistic nightmares. "I gotta say, Gramps, you sound like you were a little sadistic back in the day," Tyler said as Jon handed him the flask.

"Were?" Jon corrected him trying to ease the tension.

"How'll you know if I passed or not?" Tyler asked as he put the lip of the flask to his mouth.

"I will monitor everything from here. Anything you see, I'll see."

Erika was already giving him the thumbs up when he turned her way. Not interested in how it tasted, Tyler knocked the potion back in one large gulp, and Tyler immediately started feeling the effects of Verumpotious as he gave the empty vial to Jon. Before he had time to look back at Erika, Tyler's eyes slammed shut and he drifted off into a white bloom of light.

Tyler fell forward, catching himself before falling flat on his face. *I'm . . . I'm home. My home. Clean, tidy, and full of unpacked boxes just like I left it.*

"Tyler? Are you home, sweetie?" The voice came from the kitchen. *Mom!?*

Overjoyed, Tyler ran into the kitchen. However, the joy was short-lived as he came around the kitchen wall to find his mother face down, motionless. Then, as though booming right next to his ear, Tyler heard a distinct gunshot. He turned, but there was no one there.

"I'm dreaming," Tyler murmured to himself.

"Are you sure about that?" A second familiar voice took him by surprise. His mother's body disappeared without notice as Vanessa strolled into the kitchen.

"Like what you see?" she asked already in her demonic form.

Tyler remained still. *What insecurities are the potion trying to surface?* Drawing his sword, Tyler held it out in a threatening manner. "Everyone around me said you were trouble, and I couldn't see the obvious signs."

"Me? Trouble?" Vanessa asked with a false innocence as she fiddled with her locks of hair.

Tyler didn't falter for a second. "I read up on Succubi. You were seducing me. You had me in a trance, demon."

Vanessa's blackened nails clinked together as she playfully clapped her hands in applause. "Very good, you figured me out. But you still haven't learned, silly boy."

In mid-sentence, Vanessa lunged at Tyler but was immediately propelled against the wall behind her. Vanessa coughed and gagged as she struggled to escape from what felt like an invisible hand around her throat. She peered up at Tyler to find his other hand held out and mirroring the invisible hand wrapped around her neck.

"Do it . . . she deserves it!" A voice whispered into Tyler's ear. It sounded familiar, yet he couldn't pinpoint who it was. "If you don't . . . she'll *kill* you. Make it quick, or . . . watch her squirm a little."

As the voice continued to egg him on, Tyler's grasp around Vanessa's neck tightened and her eyes bulged as she

184

gasped for air. *She's just as guilty! She's on their side. She does deserve it!*

Vanessa hissed in a burst of victorious laughter. "You don't have the guts! You won't kill me, even in your head."

"DO IT!" the voice screamed.

Tyler shouted, forgetting Vanessa was his mind's manifestation. "Everything you did was for nothing! I have the Codex and I'm going to finish my family's work."

"Nothing? Mommy's dead, sugar . . ."

Vanessa had more venom to inject, but Tyler wasn't having any more of her bile. In one fluid motion, Tyler hovered Vanessa midair before throwing her through the kitchen window.

A fiery explosion tore through the house like an atom bomb. Windows blew out. Doors ripped clean off their hinges. Tyler was knocked onto his hands and knees before he could regain his footing from throwing Vanessa out. When he got his footing, Tyler realized he was now standing in his father's office building. It was engulfed in a raging inferno.

This isn't real. It's just Verumpotious at work, Tyler thought to himself as he made his way slowly through the fiery labyrinth.

"Tyler? Tyler! Help!" a voice echoed out through the choking black smoke.

This isn't real! You gotta get out of here! Tyler said ignoring his mind's imitating cries for help. But they only grew more desperate and realistic as he circled through the maze. *Please! Stop calling me, please!* Tyler begged, still unable to find the exit. He wiped soot and sweat from his brow as he heard his father's voice grow weaker. *This is a mistake! This is a mistake!* Tyler turned and ran in the direction of his father's voice with his sword at the ready.

Flames shot out from a cubicle taking Tyler by surprise. The flames swirled and twisted until it formed into some kind of living reptilian fire creature. Tyler jumped back as the creature's flaming arm reached out to pull him into the inferno. The hissing beast lunged forward snapping its jaws as Tyler swung his sword, but the two were forced to step back into a jockey for footing in the narrow, collapsing passageway. Tyler took a mighty swing at the creature, but it bit down on his blade, wrestling with Tyler as it tried to pull the sword from his hands. He could feel the flames licking at his arms, singeing his arm hairs.

Tyler extended his other hand as the blade began to turn red hot. "Dis!" The creature was propelled deep into the office, collapsing through cindered walls as it smashed through them.

Waving his hand over the sword, Tyler cooled the blade before placing it back in its sheath. *A second or two longer and I could've burnt my hands on this.* Tyler heard a guttural hiss in the distance. *I don't want a rematch.* Tyler made his way down another passageway only to feel the floor beneath him give way.

The scene had abruptly changed again. It was pitch black, darker than he had ever experienced growing up in the city. Darker than a moonless night out in the middle of nowhere. Tyler couldn't see his own nose in front of him. All he could do was feel. And the only thing he could feel was the cold and sterile metallic floor.

Okay, they're tapping into my fear of the dark. But I can do this. That's when Tyler heard the distinct tapping sound of claws running around him. They were far away, but close enough to feel each step's vibration. Then it got worse, and soon there were a second set of claws, followed by a third and then a fourth. Soon there were too many sets to distinguish how many creatures there were. They were everywhere and nowhere.

"Little boy, it's not the dark you should fear. It's the horrors shrouded within you should dread," a voice hissed into his ears.

Standing up, Tyler listened as the movement came to a sudden halt. He had a sinking feeling in his stomach. The hairs on the back of his neck stood on end as the tapping grew more violent and clearly heading in his direction.

Tyler screamed half to intimidate and half in fear, "LUX!"

Casting his hand out like a flashlight, the room illuminated with a blinding light that devoured any shred of the shadow it once concealed. It was so powerful even Tyler squinted in pain from the light's radiance. Tyler opened his eyes to find several horrifying creatures hissing at him as they backed away from the light. Too distracted to accurately identify them, Tyler realized they looked like reanimated skeletal humanoids. The only flesh hanging from them were their mummified faces and sunken yellow eyeballs.

They hate the light, huh? Tyler lunged forward causing the hissing creatures to retreat down the narrowing hallway. *There it is! An exit door at the end of the hallway. Only one problem of course. They're standing in my way.* Tyler swirled his hand around like he was about to throw the creatures a curveball.

Focusing on the light coming from his hand, Tyler flared it out one last time before throwing it directly at one of the creatures at the back of the pack. The unfortunate beast writhed in pain as it stumbled about trying to get the ball of light out of its skull. With the light no longer in front of them, the majority of the creatures could see Tyler standing in front of them defenseless. As predicted, each of them charged Tyler except for the one struck by the ball of light.

"*Mutare loca!*" Tyler shouted when the creatures were only feet away from ripping through him.

Tyler instantly swapped positions with the staggering skeletal creature. This left him only a few feet from the rusted door while the creatures tackled their struggling and squirming brethren. While most immediately sheltered their eyes from the light, a couple managed to face away and see Tyler frantically wrestling with the door handle. They raced towards him just as it finally turned, and he pulled it open, leaped through the opening, turned and closed the door. A screaming mummified face nearly squeezed through before Tyler slammed the door on its face with a sickening squish.

The next thing Tyler knew, he was face down in the dirt and leaves, surrounded by trees. It was cold and dark, and he was vaguely able to make out his own frosted breath. Tyler scrambled to his feet when he heard spells whizzing and popping out in the distance. The forest strobed as spells snapped and crashed into trees, leading him closer to the action. When he got closer, Tyler ducked down and viewed the scene playing out before him.

188

Bunch of Magis over there ... and their all firing in the same direction. Then Tyler got a good look at their target. *It's Mom! She's behind that tree. Who's that she's with?* Tyler had a hunch who the silhouette was crouching down beside his mother, but it wasn't until Charlotte spoke that Tyler knew for sure.

"I had to, Marshall. I just hope he doesn't notice before I get back," Charlotte said just barely loud enough for Tyler to hear.

This is it ... this is when he ... NO! Tyler broke out into a full-blown sprint and barreled towards Charlotte and Marshall, ready to stop what he knew, in his heart, had already happened. He watched as his mother started a lasso motion with her hands as she readied her spell.

"3 ..."

Faster!

"2 ..."

He's pulling his gun!

"1 ..."

"I'm sorry," Marshall muttered raising his gun to Charlotte's back.

But before Marshall could pull the trigger, Tyler tackled him to the ground, saving his mother's life. Atop his mother's would-be assassin, Tyler immediately noticed a small dagger resting on the floor beside him. With Marshall kicking and struggling to push Tyler off him, he made a split-second decision. Taking the dagger in hand, Tyler drew it over-head and plunged it down at Marshall's throat, but then the scene changed again, and the dagger disintegrated as its tip drove into the white marbled floor beneath him.

Tyler was suddenly alone. The eerie whistle of complete silence was only interrupted when his clothes moved with him. Everywhere he looked was white as far as the eye could see, even the sky. *I think this room goes on forever.*

"Correct," the voice answered his thoughts, but this time it was much closer. This time, it was followed by a single man's round of applause. The sudden presence of another caused Tyler to jump back away as he turned to face the man.

"Who are you!?" Tyler shouted. *What are you supposed to represent?*

"Tyler Grayson, I presume. It is *so* good to finally meet you. Albeit in your head."

"Who are you!?" Tyler demanded again, this time holding up his right hand ready to fire off a spell.

The well-dressed man flashed his steel blue eyes and his pearly whites. "I'm the reason you know about our magical world. Ezekiel Godfrey," Ezekiel said holding out his hand.

Tyler immediately sprung to action, conjuring a fire spell. But before the flames could even spark from his fingertips, Ezekiel waved his hand in a smothering motion, extinguishing the spell.

"I'm on a bit of a tight schedule," Ezekiel said as a black blade materialized into his hand. Tyler reached for his sword, but it was gone! He turned back as Ezekiel neared.

All I've got is magic . . . Thinking fast, Tyler held is palm up and fired an orangey brown plasmatic spell. Ezekiel backhanded the spell away, not even a sign of distress or singed marks. Attempting to stall the fiend's march, Tyler let loose several more plasmatic spells, each of which were deflected off to the side by Ezekiel, except for the last one which he redirected back towards Tyler. Jumping out of the way by a hair, Tyler winced as the heat of his own spell careening passed him seared part of his forearm.

Ezekiel continued his march forward unimpeded. "Stop struggling, Tyler. I'll make it quick and . . . relatively painless. Just like your mother."

Tyler's eyes locked into a cold stare-off with Ezekiel. Nothing had changed, and yet the fear in his eyes had vanished. Energy surged through him. It started as a tingle in his feet and then coursed through his body causing his hairs to stand on end. Raising his hand, Tyler took aim.

"You haven't learned, have you?" Ezekiel asked.

As an electrical discharge sparked in his hand, a soft gust of wind started feathering through Tyler's hair. Digging one foot back and leaning into his other, Tyler let loose one last attack.

"HAAA!" Tyler roared as his plasmatic spell shot from his palm. But with so much energy and focus directed at his enemy, it didn't come out as a single shot, but rather a constant flowing beam.

Taken by surprise, Ezekiel dropped his sword and shielded himself from the blast. Crossing his forearms like an X, Ezekiel dug one foot and a knee into the ground as Tyler's plasmatic beam pummeled the invisible shield protecting him. Ezekiel could feel himself slowly sliding across the marbled floor from the force behind Tyler's attack. The soft gust of wind was now a raging torrent whipping Tyler's hair and clothes back and away from the destructive beam.

It was now a battle to see who could hold out longer. Would Tyler give into exhaustion and extinguish his spell, or would a crack in Ezekiel's shield leave the demon defenseless? It was a question Jon couldn't afford to find out. Without warning, taking both Tyler and Ezekiel by surprise, the scene desynchronized and was engulfed in a bloom of white light.

Opening his eyes, Tyler was welcomed back with an unpleasant nausea-inducing triple vision. His hearing was muffled, and every source of light scorched his retinas. It felt like his body was asleep but his mind was away, somewhere distant, trying to pull him away into the nether. Then he heard his grandfather's muted voice speaking over him as Jon forced Tyler's mouth open. Pouring a tasteless liquid down his throat, Tyler took a deep gasp of air before his senses stabilized and returned to normal.

"Am I dead?" Tyler quipped.

"No . . . luckily," Jon said helping prop Tyler upright.

"I thought you said I couldn't die while under?"

Jon ignored Tyler's question. "Have you ever met Ezekiel?"

"No."

"Ever seen a picture of him?"

"No! Why?"

"That wasn't your mind's imagination at work. Somehow, some way, Ezekiel found a way in."

"A way in? You mean that really was Ezekiel?"

"Yes . . . and I shudder to think what could've happened if he reached you before I pulled you out."

Tyler felt a knot in his stomach. "Wait! Is he still inside my mind?"

"No, Tyler. That much I am sure of."

Tyler breathed a sigh of relief. "So, wait, did I pass my exam? I survived all the scenarios."

Jon peered over to Erika and then back to Tyler. "Yes . . . but I don't like what I saw."

"What do you mean? I handled Nessa, defeated the fire salamander and escaped, I outsmarted the zombie things, and I saved my mom. Besides Ezekiel's interference, I thought I did well."

"I heard Ezekiel's voice too. He was there from the start, though I thought it was your imagination until he appeared," Jon said peering into Tyler's eyes. "I told you to let Marshall go!"

"I was saving—"

"You knew it was only a dream. Ezekiel played you! If he dangled Marshall out on a line, would you bite?"

Tyler hung his head low. *I thought I had done so well . . .* "So I passed, but you don't think I'm ready?"

Jon stood there statuesque. He knew how much Tyler wanted this. And he wanted this for him too. But he was also afraid what Tyler might do on his own. Jon just nodded. "Correct."

Tyler took a deep disappointed sigh. "Okay then." *I don't like it. But I accept it.*

The room grew silent as a distinct cracking noise filled their ears. Everyone turned to Tyler as he opened his right hand to reveal his Ancori. It had chipped again, but unlike before, this time the cut was complete.

Erika perked up and asked, "What happened? I can't see."

"It cut on its own again," Tyler answered.

"How much?"

"It's . . . I think it's finished . . ."

"What? All of it? How?" Erika turned to Jon. "I thought an Ancori's final cut happens only after a Master's approval."

"It would appear not." Jon glared down at the hourglass Ancori. *I was afraid of this.*

"What does this mean?" Tyler asked.

"It means you're a Magi now, with or without my approval."

CHAPTER 21
UNWELCOME VISITORS

It had been two weeks since Tyler passed his final exam. More importantly, everyone had gathered around the kitchen table to celebrate Thanksgiving. Charlie had been laboring away all day to prepare a holiday feast to remember with turkey, stuffing, mashed potatoes, the whole works, really. He wanted it to be perfect, especially for Tyler. Not only was this his first holiday without both parents, but it was his birthday, his eighteenth.

"As always you've outdone yourself, Charlie," Jon said as he sat back after finishing his plate.

"Thank you. Hope everyone saved room for cake!"

Thanksgiving cake? Tyler thought. "Not sure I do. I'm stuffed, Charlie."

"There's always room for cake," Charlie reassured Tyler. "Especially you, birthday boy."

"Oh . . . didn't think anyone knew."

"Of course we knew. Don't be ridiculous," Jon said sternly from across the table.

"Shall I get the cake?" Charlie asked.

Everyone turned to Tyler waiting for an answer. "Sure . . ." *Not really in a celebratory mood. But I'm not gonna bring everyone else down with me.*

Just then, there was a pounding coming from the front door. Jon looked at Tyler, then at Erika, eyebrows raised. A few seconds later and there was more pounding.

"Tyler Grayson! Come out!" a deep and unfamiliar voice shouted.

Tyler turned to Jon, unsure who knew he was living here. Jon sprung to his feet saying, "Stay here! I know who it is."

"Is it him?" Tyler asked jumping to his feet.

"No. Stay here like I asked."

Tyler remained standing in the kitchen as everyone listened quietly.

"Where's the boy!"

"It's Thanksgiving, Kroll. Think you could give us this day?"

"I didn't call for you, did I? Tyler Grayson!"

"Save your breath, he's not here."

"That's funny, because I'm looking right at him," Kroll snarled as he pointed into the house.

Jon turned to find Tyler peering down the hallway from the kitchen. He shot Tyler daggers with his eyes.

"Tyler Grayson! My master sends his warmest regards. You're a man now, aren't you?"

Standing deep inside Jon's home, Tyler walked out from behind the kitchen wall. "What do you want? Why are you here?"

A deep throaty chuckle rumbled from the towering demon. "Straight to the point, huh? My master wants to offer you a trade."

"I'm not interested."

He ignored him. "Lord Ezekiel is offering you and your friends clemency in exchange for the Codex."

"We can handle ourselves, thank you," he said, feeling his Ancori grow warm in his palm. "No deal."

Kroll chuckled. "He said you'd say that. That's why he told me to sweeten the deal. On top of that, he'll give you the Werewolf."

This caught Tyler's immediate attention. "Marshall?"

Kroll grinned eerily. "All wrapped up and bound . . . heck, we'll even throw in a bow if you want."

Tyler slowly walked closer to the front door. "I don't believe you, or anything your master says."

Kroll turned his head, peering at his underlings waiting for his command outside the property gate. "Seeing is believing then?" Kroll asked snapping his fingers.

Two smaller, but no less threatening, demons walked up the pathway towards their leader. In their arms they carried a bound and bagged body, and as they reached the step, the two dropped the defenseless man at Kroll's feet.

"I give to you your mother's Adjutor . . . her betrayer!"

Jon looked his daughter's murderer up and down before turning back to Tyler who had made his way to Jon's side. He could see his grandson's blood boiling beneath his skin. His eyes were locked onto Marshall. It was as though the rest of the world disappeared.

"Marshall?" Tyler asked in a stern voice.

The man turned his bagged head to face the direction his name was called from. *It's him! He's the reason she's dead! He's the reason she's not here today celebrating Thanksgiving, seeing me turn eighteen.*

197

"What do you say, Mr. Grayson? Do we now have a deal?" Kroll asked, grinning down at him.

"No . . ."

Kroll's smile disappeared. "What?"

Even Jon was surprised by Tyler's immediate answer. His grandson's eyes shifted back to Kroll. "I will avenge my mother one day. But on my terms, not on Zeke's."

"Ezekiel! Show my master respect or I'll gut you!" Kroll shouted in outrage.

"When that day comes, I'll have my revenge *and* the Codex. Tell your master that!"

Kroll bared his teeth like a dog ready to snap. "Watch your tone, boy! I'm not as merciful as my master. But he did give me one last instruction, should you refuse." Kicking Marshall over face-first towards Tyler, Kroll said, "A gift . . . Lord Ezekiel wishes you a happy birthday."

What? Why would he just hand over his leverage? Tyler stared down at the man now knowing he could have his revenge and give nothing for it. By now Penelope and Charlie were watching everything unfold from behind the kitchen wall while Erika swiftly made her way to Tyler's side. Despite both Penelope and Jon telling him to find a way to let go, despite them both watching him hover over Marshall, a part of Tyler wanted justice now.

Tyler raised his hand holding it out over Marshall. He knew several spells that would do the trick, but could he actually do it? Turning to Erika, he saw an unsure and unsettled look on her face. Turning to Jon, all he received was a cold stare off.

He deserves it! He shouldn't be allowed to . . .

198

He wanted justice for his mother, but he knew this wasn't the right way to get it, and it frightened him. It wasn't so much that he had come so close to committing the act, it was that he couldn't carry through. *No . . . not like this.*

All he had to do was pull his hand back, and yet somehow that was the hardest part. Closing his eyes, Tyler took a deep breath. Misunderstanding this, Jon thought Tyler was about to kill him, so he leaned in and batted Tyler's hand to the sky.

"*Secare!*" Jon shouted while waving his hand in a slicing motion. Instantly, the bound man was cleaved clean in half. Erika and Tyler took a surprised step back, and Penelope gasped as Charlie covered her eyes.

He did it . . . Gramps killed him. Tyler stood in disbelief. His campaign for vengeance was over before it started. But as both Jon and Tyler stared down at the body, they realized there was no blood. No grunting, no carnage, nothing. The body evaporated into thin air, leaving behind a severed cloak. It was an illusion.

Ezekiel wanted to see if I'd do it when the time came. He's testing me! Relief and frustration rushed into Tyler's head. Relief that his grandfather did not commit murder on his behalf, but frustration knowing Marshall was still out there. Vengeance was still on the table.

"You! That was not for you to do!" Kroll roared at Jon. "I think we'll settle the score!" Kroll raged as he and his two followers faded into living shadows, disappearing before their eyes. Suddenly, they all heard a disturbance coming from the backyard.

"Master!" Charlie cried to Jon as he peered out the back window.

Everyone rushed to Charlie's side and watched as the three demons reappeared at the back wall near the fountain and garden. Seconds later, an explosion shook the house as Charlotte and Miel's memorial erupted into flames. The fountain shattered as cement shrapnel flew everywhere, some small pieces flying through the house windows. Charlotte's Whengid's Glory was stomped under Kroll's hooves and wilted as it caught fire. In their rage, both Jon and Tyler stormed the backyard, followed soon after by Erika.

"Jon! No-no-no-no!" Charlie called out to him, but it was too late.

Before anyone could react, Jon flung Kroll into the back wall with all his might. The lumbering beast smashed into the concrete, leveling most of the wall with him.

"No . . ." Charlie gasped, looking at Penelope.

"Does this mean –?" Penelope said, backing away from the window.

Jon had attack Kroll, and by extension Ezekiel. The Oath which had safeguarded his home for years was broken.

"Fine work, old fool . . ." Kroll muttered from the rubble as blood ran down his chin in thick rivulets. "Attack!"

The two other demons let loose two red plasmatic spells at Jon, but Tyler blocked them by uprooting the earth and creating a wall of his own. The damp sod smothered the spells, and before they could send another flurry, Jon held out his hand and made the flames engulfing the memorial tidal wave down upon the demons. One leaped out of the way, but the other was consumed by the fire, dead instantly. Metal crashed with metal behind Tyler.

Erika was covering his six as she blocked and parried another demon's blade. *Wait! Where did that one come from?*

200

His question was answered as more demons flooded the backyard, then a violent explosion erupted from the second story library causing glass and singed books to rain down upon them. Even in the face of overwhelming numbers, Erika held the backline while Tyler and Jon continued bombarding the intruders with spells.

"Get close to me!" Jon shouted to Tyler. Grabbing Erika and clinging to Jon's side, Tyler watched as his grandfather turned every stone, shard of glass, and rubble into a swirling storm of mayhem surrounding them. Penelope and Charlie ducked back into the crumbling house as Jon unleashed his destruction upon the demons. But even after culling their numbers, more demons swarmed the backyard. Worse yet, all three turned when they heard a furious roar. It was Kroll and he was standing, bruised and bloodied, but alive and enraged.

Jon knew full well just how dangerous Kroll was. Even by his side, Tyler and Erika were not safe. He had seen the demon wreak havoc countless times, whether with sword, spells or even tearing Magi apart with his bare hands. Kroll had to be Jon's primary target.

At least he would have been if the invasion wasn't suddenly called off.

The three stood back to back at the ready while the demon's surrounding them stood their ground. Watching the sea part, Jon murmured to Erika and Tyler, "Heads up . . . it's him." Tyler and Erika turned around just as the demons parted for Ezekiel. He entered the circle.

"Well I must admit. I could have never imagined this turning out so well. I mean, I thought I might be able to goad Tyler into attacking my illusion. But Jon, giving up your safehouse? Is it Thanksgiving or Christmas?" He then turned to Tyler. "Happy birthday. How's the arm?"

"Aces . . ." Tyler muttered.

"Truly, I'm glad to hear it."

"I'm not giving you the Codex."

Ezekiel laughed, queuing the demons surrounding them to snicker. "I don't think you realize the precarious position you're in, boy. How about we all just calm down and have a little chat? Maybe find some common ground?"

"Unlikely."

"I wouldn't be so sure. I just want what's best for our people. And so do you."

"Your people don't belong here. Your people would—"

Ezekiel interrupted. "My people? What do you think I am?"

What's he getting at?

With his sword still sheathed, Ezekiel strolled towards Tyler. "You have been misinformed. I'm only half demon, my mother's side. My father was a human. I am what you would call a Cambion."

"Hard to believe people would allow that kind of breeding."

"You're correct. Outlawed by death to all three involved. But my father was high ranking, so I was conceived."

Tyler turned to Jon as though asking if this was true, but Jon remained still. "That doesn't change the fact you want the Codex to release a floodgate of demons into this world."

202

Ezekiel nodded. "You're not wrong about that, but that's only because it is owed to them."

"Owed to them?"

"Our human side hasn't always been the most honorable species. Demons were, long ago, promised land and power on this world in exchange for their military aid in a war long forgotten. But when the job was done, rather than receiving their reward, they were forced back into the darkness."

"And now you wish to flip the roles?"

Ezekiel scoffed and his blue eyes flashed red, but only for a moment. "You aren't listening to me! Despite the bad seeds I have encountered, I believe humanity is redeemable. I just wish to give my other half the land they deserve. Both can co-exist together."

"I think you're wrong."

"You *think*, do you?" Ezekiel asked. "Well I *know*. With the Codex and its powers, I would bring harmony between the sides and keep the peace. Imagine that? Peace on Earth . . . finally!"

"Demons would never allow it. It's in their nature to destroy!" Jon snapped, pointing at Charlotte and Miel's memorial. "There would be no peace. I'm no fool Ezekiel, and I didn't take you for one either."

"Don't you think they deserve a chance to prove otherwise?"

Neither Jon nor Tyler said anything.

"Earth's belonged to humans for so long and what have they brought? Slavery . . . genocide . . . even two worldwide wars! The bar is not set very high."

"And with the Codex in hand, completed, you would keep the balance and peace? Whether it be man or demon threatening it?" Tyler asked.

Ezekiel's eyes lit up, this time with excitement. "Yes! Now you see!"

"I don't believe you," Tyler said backing away.

The demon smirked and shook his head. "I'd consider you a fool if you flipped so easily. That's why I'm willing to make you another offer. An Oath."

Tyler turned to both Erika and Jon unsure what to think. "Go on."

"I will grant you all safety. Give me the Codex and join me for a week. If after a week you don't see things my way, I will give you the Codex back and give you all a day's head start to run."

Tyler shook his head. "I don't trust you'll keep you're end of the bargain."

"It's an *Oath*, Mr. Grayson. If made, I must oblige. It's risk free. No buyer's remorse. Give me a week, and we will see things eye to eye. And if we do, I will grant everyone here safety, and exalted positions in our new world to help me maintain the peace."

Jon interjected. "You keep reminding us that you'll need to keep the peace. You already know how messy things will become."

"You already knew my plan, Jon. I am hurt to hear you've misled your own grandson." Ezekiel said with a snarl. "People hate change, Tyler. Of course, initially there will be issues. But think long term! All you have to do is take my hand and see for yourself."

Ezekiel stretched out his hand for Tyler to shake. It was not forceful or rushed. He wanted Tyler to make his own decision and although Tyler could not trust him, a part of him understood Ezekiel's position. He even sympathized with it.

But can I trust him? This could all just be a lie. Demons are supposed to be very persuasive. But I can't help but wonder...

"Just take my hand, Tyler, and I will show you there are no villains in our presence."

Jon peered at Charlie in the distance and gave him a nod. Turning back, he interrupted Tyler's thoughts. "Ezekiel, I've already fallen for your poison. I won't let you do the same to my daughter's only son. Our Scribe." Before anyone, including Ezekiel, could react, Jon grabbed both Tyler and Erika by the collars and Jumped.

"DAMN HIM!" Ezekiel shouted, trembling with power and rage. The demons around him recoiled. Even Kroll winced for a second before regaining his stone-cold composure.

"Lord Ezekiel, what will you have us do?" Ezekiel's eyes burned red and the ground beneath him shook, daring his minions to flee. None did. "My Lord, we could always ..."

"No!" he snapped, teeth bared. "We accomplished a lot more than I hoped for today. The seed has been planted in Grayson's mind. Give him the night . . . to *think*. Call everyone back to base."

"Fall out!" Kroll roared. "My Lord, what of the home?"

Ezekiel snapped his fingers, causing the second story to collapse inward, leveling most of the house. "What home?"

✻✻

A thunderclap echoed through the barren desert as Jon landed with both Tyler and Erika in hand. Once safely on the ground, Jon let go, allowing Tyler to stagger about and walk off the Jump sickness.

"What happened? You Jumped us?"

"Yes, I couldn't let him keep spewing his bile."

"We have to go back! Charlie! Penelope! They're in danger!" Tyler demanded.

"They're fine. Charlie and I have been through tighter situations, and so has Penelope."

Erika surveyed their surroundings, unsure where they were. "All our stuff too."

"Yeah, we don't have any of our supplies. Heck, I don't even have my wallet to buy new ones." Tyler gasped. *No! How could I forget!* "The Codex! It's—"

Jon held out the massive book. "You mean this?"

Tyler took the Codex, relieved to see it was not left behind. "H-how? I . . . Thank you."

"When the demons are gone, I'll retrieve your belongings and find our little friends. But for now, you have to go."

Erika and Tyler looked at one another. "Go?" Tyler asked.

"Yes. There's no safehouse anymore. Things are more dangerous than ever before. I'm sorry, but I can't hide you any longer. I too must go into hiding. It's time you started your journey, Scribe."

"I thought you said I wasn't ready? Isn't that why I stayed with you even after I passed?"

206

Jon put a hand on Tyler's shoulder. "I did, but maybe you are now. You resisted killing who you thought was Marshall . . . I only wish I had waited to watch you do the right thing. But now, whether you're ready or not, you *must* go. Now! Go!"

Feeling Erika grab his hand, Tyler turned to her. "You ready to Jump?"

"Ready when you are, kiddo."

"See ya soon, Gramps. Thank you . . . for everything." And in the blink of an eye, they were gone.

CHAPTER 22
A PRIVATE CONCERT

Keeping along the United States West Coast, Tyler and Erika Jumped up to Eureka, California. *Boise Creek Campgrounds. I knew I could find it again. Hasn't changed a bit,* Tyler thought as he led Erika into the heavily wooded area. The two planned to sleep tonight, then Jump to Ireland early tomorrow so they'd arrive in the evening.

"You've been here before?" Erika asked looking around the unpopulated campgrounds.

"Yeah, Dad used to take me and Mom up here every other summer. I think it reminded him of his college days up here."

"Well guess no one's up here for the Thanksgiving holiday, so we own the campgrounds tonight."

Finding a covered campsite out of the elements, the pair spent the next hour clearing and making their overnight stay more comfortable. While Erika made their sleeping arrangements, Tyler took the time to put up several protective spells. Before long, night fell over the forest, leaving them in the dark if not for Tyler.

"Lux!"

"Umm . . . isn't that gonna draw attention? We kinda snuck in here, remember?"

Tyler pointed to their surroundings saying, "I put up a light dampening spell. No light can escape our little campsite."

"Oh! Clever."

It wasn't much, not the most comfortable way to spend a night, but the pair had a place to sleep. And thanks to Tyler's protective spells, their camp was warm, lit, bug free and invisible to anyone outside their defensive bubble.

After a quick trip to the campsite's bathroom, Erika walked back into their campsite humming along to her MP3 player. "You're up, kiddo."

"Good, you're back! Time for a little fun." Erika raised an eyebrow.

Without warning, Tyler's phone erupted with music, but the little phone's speakers had been magically modified to sound like stadium amps. To say the phone was loud would have been an understatement – anyone within a square mile of them could have heard it.

The musical outburst startled Erika. It took her a second to register what was happening. *Is he nuts!?* Tyler stood in the middle of their campsite, not the least bit worried about how loud he was being, just feeling the rhythm of the song.

Erika lunged forward grabbing the phone out of Tyler's hands and smashed her finger down on the pause button. "What the heck is wrong with you? No one can see us, but they'll hear us!"

Tyler grinned and wove it off. "Relax, you honestly think I'd do something like this if it meant getting caught?"

"Nooo?" Erika cautiously answered. *Not sure what exactly he's planning.*

Tyler walked to the nearby edge of his protective shield and tapped at it. "I took the liberty of sound-proofing our camp too. Full of surprises, aren't I?" He grinned.

Erika hesitantly handed Tyler his phone back. "You mean, no one can hear us?"

"Nope!" he yelled, arms outstretched. "No one can hear us! No matter how loud we are. No noise, thuds, vibrations or anything is leaving this circle tonight."

Erika laughed with a furrowed brow. "Oh really? Better not get any funny ideas."

"I want it." Tyler inched closer as he stared into Erika's eyes.

"E . . . excuse me?" Erika stepped back wide-eyed.

"Your MP3." Tyler grinned as he pointed to the MP3 clutched in her hands. "Hand it over."

Ha! He got me.

"Nothing funny, just fun." Tyler promptly laid her MP3 against another log. "We need to end today on a good note. Let's dance."

The music blared almost louder than before. This time Erika was ready for it. Putting his phone down next to her MP3, Tyler sang along with the unapologetic lyrics to the MC5's "Kick Out the Jams" as loud as he could.

Erika gently swayed back and forth to the music. *What? He just wants to dance?*

Taking her by the hand, Tyler was barely audible over the music. "Come on! Sing and dance with me!"

"You know I can't do that!" Erika screamed while shaking her head.

"What!? I can hardly hear you! Just sing!"

Oh well, she thought as she started singing along to the song with Tyler. It was only after completing the first verse that Erika realized Tyler was still singing and dancing alongside her. *He's still singing? By now I thought he'd be all over me.* Erika's heart fluttered as Tyler belted out the next high note to the best of his ability. *He's still singing!*

Erika's mood immediately improved feeling the beat and getting into the song. She was singing a song right next to someone, and they were singing right there beside her.

That ended too soon, Erika thought with a frown as the song wrapped up. But her frown immediately disappeared when the Arctic Monkeys' "Do I Wanna Know?" played afterward.

"You made a playlist?"

Tyler nodded as he clapped rhythmically.

The two went on singing and dancing well into the night. By two in the morning, both were exhausted, hoarse, with their ears ringing and bodies drenched in sweat. Turning the volume down to a listening level, the two laid on their makeshift bed, flipping through the songs he put into the playlist. Although he flavored the playlist with mostly alternative and classic rock, he threw in some funk and motown. He couldn't bring himself to add any jazz, a genre he often heard Erika playing.

With their eyes growing heavy, and contagious yawns ping-ponging between them, Erika blurted out, "You deserve a kiss for all this. But you're like a baby, so you get a 'thank you' instead."

"That's a pile of honesty followed by an immediate brick wall." Tyler busted up laughing in his overly tired state.

"I say things when I'm this tired. But seriously, thank you. No one's ever done something like that for me . . . just because."

"Was gonna do this at Gramps', but as you know, can't anymore. Probably would've been a little nicer there."

"No! This was perfect. And I didn't know you were a dancer! You've got some moves."

"Thanks! Started a couple years back after Dad passed. It really helped. So, I guess tonight was equally therapeutic for me too."

"Well, if you ever need a dance partner, I'll be your gal," she said with a wink.

"Sounds good, and you can make the next playlist."

"Consider it done," Erika said curling up onto his chest. "Oops, the left side of my face just fell asleep. Gonna crash here."

"Okay, want me to skooch over?" Tyler offered.

"No, you're warm . . . and everything's comfy." Erika gently shook her head with both eyes closed.

Tenebris. Tyler waved a hand overhead killing the lights. "Okay, Erika, good night."

Erika could only murmur a fading "good night" before swiftly drifting off to sleep.

CHAPTER 23
WELCOME TO IRELAND

After a late night of dancing and singing, Tyler and Erika happily took the opportunity to sleep in. Even the sun blazing through the foliage didn't rouse the pair. They would have slept well past noon if they could have, but then there was Jon.

"Um . . . morning . . ." Jon said standing cross-armed over the two of them.

Tyler and Erika sprung from their deep sleep, at first thinking they had been caught trespassing by a camp worker. Both took a sigh of relief when they saw it was only Jon.

"Did I disturb you two? I only left you yesterday, and already I find you two—"

"Ha! No, you got it wrong, old man," Erika said.

"Mhm . . . And my grandson's chest was the best pillow you could find?" He turned to Tyler. "You know how to use magic and you decided to sleep on the dirt? Softener spell? Levitation?"

"I, uh . . ."

"Never mind, I come baring your stuff," Jon said pointing to a neatly stacked pile of their belongings.

"You already went back? Penelope? Charlie? Are they okay?" Tyler asked.

Jon motioned for Tyler to calm down. "They're both fine. They send their love and well wishes. They also sent you this." Jon held out a professional business pen with Tyler's full name etched in gold. "Lynnle's Scribes pen. Your mother used the same kind of pen from the same shop. Virtually indestructible and the ink never dries or runs. It even works upside-down."

Tyler took the pen in hand and marveled at the simple but genuine gift. "Tell them I said thank you! I'll never lose it."

Erika shouted with glee, "Jon! You found them too! Thank you!" Now sporting a thick jacket, Erika held out her hands to give Tyler a silky-smooth blanket and a small crystal ball. "Happy Birthday, kiddo!"

"Wait, more gifts?"

"We were gonna give them to you after your cake, but yeah . . ."

Tyler rubbed the smooth blanket against his face. "Thank you! It's so soft."

Jon smiled and nodded. "A Dreammite silk blanket, quite the gift. Rain, snow, heat or wind, you'll always be the right personal temperature. They're worth a pretty penny."

Erika tapped on the crystal ball. "I think you'll like this too. It's called a Memorystone. Give this baby a rub and it'll record past or present memories. Rub and hold it to watch your memories again."

"That's awesome! I love them both, thank you!" Tyler leaned over and embraced her, and Erika gave him a light peck on the forehead.

When the two parted, Tyler turned to find Jon standing beside him holding a sword. He tilted the green, strapped handle towards Tyler. The sword was three feet long with two sharp bladed cross guards and a vivid steel-blue tint to its blade. As the sword's weight fell from Jon's hands to Tyler's, he was surprised to feel just how light it felt in his hands.

"You're our Scribe, and you need a sword. I've had Charlemagne since before I was your age. It's Elvish and reinforced with Dragon Steel, nearly impossible to break. This sword, it's seen a lot, just with me alone. And now, it'll see much more . . . with you."

"It's so light," Tyler said, turning it in his hands.

Jon grinned warmly. "I remember when it felt light in my hands too. Charlemagne weighs lighter or heavier in your hands depending on your morality. To someone like Ezekiel, it'd feel like a boulder."

Tyler was at a loss for words as he motioned through a drawn-out swing. "Thank you! Are you sure?"

Jon nodded confidently. "It's a great sword and it'll serve you well. Help fill in your rough edges a little. Treat it well."

"Thank you, Gramps. I will!"

"Well then, this is where I leave you," Jon said wrapping an arm around Tyler with a loud thudding hug. "You're up against a lot. But you're not alone." He turned to Erika. "Same goes for you."

"Thanks, Gramps."

"Thanks, old man."

"Good luck," Jon said backing away, and with a nod Jumped back to Los Angeles.

Dressed and with their belongings packed and ready for travel, Erika handed Tyler his backpack saying, "Well, I think we'd better get going. It'll be dark soon in Dublin."

"Yeah, we should get going. This instant time changing is going to mess with my mind."

"Well, we can take one calmer day before we hit the monster hunting trail. Get you acclimated. Besides, I want to celebrate your birthday with a couple rounds. Drinking age is eighteen in Ireland, you know."

Tyler slung his backpack around with a smile. "Hmm . . . I could go for that. Have a little more fun before we get down to business."

Erika took his hand and readied to Jump. "To Dublin!"

***

Seconds later, they were standing in The Fair City. It took Tyler a moment to catch his stomach, but even nauseous as he was, Tyler couldn't wipe the grin from his face. *Ireland! I've always wanted to come here. And what a perfect spot for a Jump,* Tyler thought, hidden amongst a thick cluster of brush and trees in Phoenix Park. Having an eight-hour time difference between the two points, Tyler and Erika arrived in Ireland a little past six in the evening. At the waning end of November, not only was the temperature significantly colder but it was dark out. Not dusk. Not twilight. It was night.

Tyler shivered in the cool night air. "Jesus it's cold out!"

"Ha! This is cold for you?" Erika laughed arriving fully-dressed for the cooler weather.

"A cold day in LA is fifty degrees, so yeah." Tyler reached into his backpack and pulled out a thick jacket.

"You wanna migrate south for the winter?"

"I'll be fine. Now, I think we're . . . huh? Umm, we should go this way," Tyler said pointing as he gripped his backpack strap tightly, scanning for landmarks.

Erika pushed Tyler's arm further to point him in the right direction. "Come on, let's go just in case locals heard us and get curious." After leading Tyler down the damp streets of Dublin, Erika pointed ahead as her chilled breath drifted in the air. "There it is! The Belching Banshee."

At first, Tyler couldn't tell exactly where Erika was pointing. The narrow and curved street made the slender building blend into the surrounding buildings. But as they neared Tyler could see a coal-colored sign with gold lettering hanging from the rain gutter. *Huh? Odd shaped building. It's got a chimney though. I hope it's warm inside.*

Tyler held the door for an elderly couple before turning to Erika. "After you."

Stepping through the foyer, any doubts Tyler had about the small pub were dashed. It was a busy Friday night. Both beer and food were flying around the pub to happy patrons. It had a splash of old Irish architecture mixed with a more modernized bar. Old timey streetlamps adorned the walls alongside black and white pictures.

Tyler was jolted back to reality as Erika grabbed his arm. "Come on. Let's get a drink."

"Erika? Erika Dems! They still let ya in here?" the bartender shouted with glee as he pulled out a glass for her.

"So long as I keep paying the tab."

"Usual I presume?"

"Yes, and a Banshee flight for my friend here."

The man peered at Tyler then back to Erika. "Seems young. Is he of age?"

The sly grin on her face said it all. "Leo, come on! It's me!"

Leo started mixing Erika's drink laughing. "Hey, just askin'. Not your job on the line, is it?"

Erika put an arm around Tyler's shoulder saying, "You're fine, he just turned yesterday."

"Ha, lookin' for much younger men now, huh?" Leo joked a winking grin.

She immediately created space between herself and Tyler. "Very funny. Just friends. In business together actually."

Leo handed Erika her Irish Blackout before starting on Tyler's flight. "Oh, what kinda business?"

"He's a Scribe," Erika whispered as she leaned forward.

"Scribe?" Leo turned to Tyler with a concerned look on his face. "Forget flight glasses. Best get ya pints. Upcharge is on me."

"Um ... thanks, but you really don't have to—"

Leo interrupted, "No, kid. You're gonna need it." His manner and tone was as though he was talking to a dead man.

Erika raised her glass to Leo. "As always, an expert confidence booster." Once again taking Tyler by the shoulder, she led them away to an empty table.

Leo called out to her. "A tab a take it?"

Erika just winked.

"You're gonna help me with these, right?" Tyler asked as he juggled the oversized flight.

"I think I can help."

In what seemed like the blink of an eye, two hours passed. Then another two. Between beers, stories, drunken outbursts of drinking songs, and more beers, both lost track of time. Before long, the hour hand was flirting with midnight. By now, most of the crowd had long left for home. Only the regulars and youngsters remained.

Tyler played with one of his empty glasses as he concluded his story. "Serious though, ask Amanda, she'll tell you the exact same story, I swear. She's even got the same scar on her shoulder."

Erika leaned back with a giddy smile having had several drinks too many. "I believe you, I did far stupider in my younger years."

Putting his glass down, Tyler let his head roll back and forth. *Perhaps we had one or two too many.* "Safe to walk outside?"

"Large city, but I'd say no worse than LA. At least in my experience."

He peered down to see Erika's glass was empty. "Want to walk around?"

Erika pulled out her wallet. "Sure, let me pay the tab and we're off." Tyler motioned for his wallet but was immediately shot down. "Nope! Tonight's on me. Birthday gift, remember?"

"You sure?"

"Absolutely, just relax, I'll be right back," Erika said straightening her jacket.

Even bundled up she looks . . . ah! Stop it, Tyler thought to himself as he watched Erika walk up to the bar counter. *You have to stay focused! And it's not gonna happen. But . . . she does.* Tyler sat back and took a deep relaxed breath. That's when he noticed a man sitting across the room staring at him. Tyler turned away but watched the man through an angled mirror on the wall. *He's giving me the creeps. Eyes open, Grayson. I've got a bad feeling.*

The man's eyes shifted away only for a second before leering back at Tyler. *Wish the dizziness would stop! I'm either being paranoid . . . or watched.* Tyler shifted uncomfortably in his seat as he glanced over at Erika. *She's still taking care of the tab. I should let her know.* But as he got up, Tyler noticed the man giving a sudden nod. Tyler watched another man approach the window from outside. *He's standing right behind me.* It was difficult to see him through the mirror, but then Tyler saw the man pull something from his pocket.

"DIS!" Tyler shouted as he turned around with both hands extended. With one hand pushing the gun aside and the other pushing the man back, Tyler watched as his would-be assassin flew back across the street and gun fired up into the pub ceiling away from patrons. Inebriated, Tyler's magic pushed out everything in front of him including a large portion of the pub's wall. He then turned back just in time to narrowly dodge a blue plasmatic spell coming from the man across the room, but then he knocked over his table and fired another.

"Clipeus!" Tyler screamed, putting up a shield before countering, *"Congelo!"* The ground quaked as the man's muscles froze and sent him falling off to the side. The remaining patrons tried to flee the pub, but everyone hit the

deck as the other windows blew in followed by three hooded men. The air filled with confused screams as the three men murmured something incoherent under their breaths before a line of thick and crackling blue sped towards Tyler.

Repercutio! Tyler slapped the hostile spells aside.

One drew its sword to meet Erika's blade crashing down upon them while the other two hissed in unison, "Give us the Codex, Tyler Grayson!"

"Shove off! *Dis!*" But his spell missed his targets, belting a glass of beer into the wall beside Leo the barman seeking cover.

Before Tyler could react, he was hit by a quick-moving *Revincio* immediately anchoring his right hand to the table. The spell felt like a mix between his hand falling asleep and trying to lift an absurd weight. *I swear, if I get out of this alive, I quit alcohol!*

"Let's gut this pig!" The pair pulled knives from their pockets.

"Lucem magnam!" Tyler shouted, his instincts kicking in.

Before anyone in the bar could prepare themselves, Erika included, a blinding brilliant light flooded the room like a flash grenade. All three hunched over covering their eyes for relief. *Now!* Tyler motioned as though clearing a table *"Dis!"* and threw all three out of the pub and rolling across the street.

Breaking free of the binding spell, Tyler ran to Erika and led her out of the pub. Her eyesight slowly returned to her as the cool night air kissed her face.

"You okay?" Tyler asked seeing Erika holding her arm.

Erika winced as he pulled her hand aside to reveal a gaping wound she received in the scuffle. "Yeah . . . I'm fine. New plan, no more cities! Those weren't your average demons. I think Ezekiel is done talking."

"Sana," Tyler murmured holding his hand over Erika's arm. She flinched but then realized her wound had sealed and the pain subsided. "Come on! Let's get out of here."

The two fled from the pub looking for a safe place to Jump. But as they fled, they saw a young man whimpering in pain as he dragged himself away from the pub. He withdrew towards a nearby wall, afraid.

He's out of danger . . . but I can't just leave him here! Tyler kneeled beside him asking, "You okay?"

"My leg! I think it's broke," he said as a thick stream of sweat poured down his face. He was going into shock.

Tyler reached down and grabbed the man's leg. "Where? By the knee?"

"Gah! Yes! Stop! It hurts! Don't touch m –"

"What's your name, sir?" Tyler cut him off as he murmured something under his breath.

"M–Malcolm? Why?"

"You okay, Malcolm?" Tyler repeated himself as he massaged Malcolm's leg.

Malcolm thought he was talking to a crazy, deaf sadist. "What? No! I'm . . . I'm actually feeling kinda better. Huh? My leg doesn't hurt anymore!"

Tyler got up, patting Malcolm's leg. "Glad to hear it, Malcolm. Must have been the shock. Have a safe night!" Malcolm watched as the pair marched out of sight down the street into the shadows. Then to his surprise, a roar of thunder echoed down the Dublin streets. Strange thing was there was no lightning, nor a cloud in the sky.

CHAPTER 24
TYLER'S FIRST ENTRY

He was running frantically through a downpour. This village was his home, and yet he ran through it as though he was a criminal, nearly slipping on the muddy road several times. Reaching a house, he opened the door and threw himself inside weeping.

"Ezekiel? My son, what's wrong?" a man said coming from the other room.

Ezekiel answered, "Father . . . I am in trouble. I was with the council, and they attacked me! In my anger I lost control, and I . . . they're gone. All of them."

He looked up at Ezekiel, nodding his head. "They grew frightened of your power, of your half-breed nature."

"I didn't want to, father. But why did they betray me? Am I not the bridge between my people? Is it all lies?"

There was a sorrowful tone in his father's voice. "Perhaps, Ezekiel, the world isn't ready yet."

And without warning, a portal opened to Ezekiel's side, revealing a hellish landscape awaiting on the other side. The outer edges of the gateway spun wildly like a miller's saw, ready to suck all passersby into its gaping maw. Ezekiel turned back to face his father, confused, when he felt himself thrust into the portal. But much to their surprise, when he reached the opening, his shoulder slammed into its edge, unwilling to accept him.

Tyler heard Ezekiel's frantic thoughts. *I've seen this before, long ago. He did this to my mother when . . .* He pushed the thought from his mind. *It's a return portal. To seal someone back from whence they came, to never return.* Ezekiel continued to struggle against the portal while his father desperately continued his efforts to push him through it. *But I am not from the underworld. I am born of the Earth!*

"I tried, son. We all did. But I'm afraid you are not made for this world," his father said, and this time he pushed harder as Ezekiel tried to struggle past him. But his father was strong, and as he took a strong grip on Ezekiel's chin, he pushed his face into the spinning outer edges of the portal.

"Ahhhhh!" Ezekiel screamed in anguish as the portal's rim sliced through his bare flesh like a saw. *"Dis!"* he shouted with all of his force behind it, and he felt it break his father's grip if only for a moment. Bent over and traumatized, Ezekiel held his face expecting to feel blood running down his fingertips. Instead, the large wound had cauterized shut, and it ran from under his chin up and through his right ear lobe.

Anger poured over him, and as the nightmare grew foggier and harder to see, Tyler watched as Ezekiel's father rose off the ground at Ezekiel's will. He could feel the betrayal, the hurt and the loss. Then, in a burst of magical outrage, the man obliterated into a flash of light. Ash fell to the ground, no single piece larger than a blade of grass.

"What have I done?"

Tyler opened his eyes. He was back to reality. The pair had nestled underneath the shade of a lush autumn tree, and a creek trickled off in the distance while a choir of birds chirped all around them, almost lulling him back to sleep. *No, no more nightmares . . .* Tyler's eyes flickered open to a postcard-worthy scene. He glanced down at Erika sleeping softly against his shoulder as a strand of her tangled hair tickled his nose. *Guess I wasn't the only one tossing and turning last night.*

With the dreammite silk blanket stretched over them, Tyler looked around before the temptation to fall back to sleep crossed his mind. *Maybe just a little more. Everything bumps in the night out here . . . How does Erika find it so easy?* She squinted for a moment before waking.

"It's breathtaking, isn't it?" she asked watching Tyler as he took in the beautiful forest around them.

"Sure is. I wish every morning could start like this." Tyler pulled Erika's arm out from underneath the blanket as he inspected her scar. "A little scarring. How's it feel?"

Erika stretched her fingers. "Feels fine. Thanks, Dr. Grayson."

"I still can't believe it."

"What?"

Tyler gently let go of her arm. "The second you stepped away, they attacked. They must've been watching us for some time. They're like vultures waiting for their opportunity to feed."

"Maybe more like jungle cats stalking their prey," she said flippantly.

"And how about knowing where we were . . . twice! First the mall, now the pub. They must have eyes on us. Or they're tracking us somehow."

Erika turned from him. "Maybe we should hide out somewhere for a little while? I doubt things are going to get any easier."

Tyler froze. "We just started, and I have a job to do. "

"It'd be safer. You'd be safer."

"Hey, stop that! None of this was your fault!" Tyler said grabbing hold of her hand. He could see her concern as their eyes met. "Erika, we'll be fine. Don't get cold feet on me now."

"I'm not."

"Good, 'cause I can't do it without you," he said letting go of her hand. "Breakfast then we're off?"

Erika corrected him. "How about breakfast, enjoy the view a little longer, then we're off?"

After a quick and easy breakfast, Tyler and Erika started their hike through the forest. The two only had a vague idea where they were as they journeyed deeper into the trees. *Hopefully exploring off the beaten path is safer and fruitful.* With only the crunching of dirt and twigs beneath them and a wide array of birds all around them, the jarring text message tone of Tyler's cell startled him out of nature's simple embrace.

Tyler peered down at his phone. "It's Amanda." *Huh? She went out of town to visit family for Thanksgiving. I thought she said she wouldn't have cell signal?*

"How's she doing?" Erika asked as she took a gulp from her water bottle.

"Fine . . . I think," he said staring down at the text message as a news article linked.

Amanda

"Dublin Night Skies Light Up. Authorities Rule Out Terrorist Attack."

Please tell me you weren't there! =(

Showing Erika the text, she laughed nervously. "Looks like our shenanigans made the front page."

> Yeah, we were there
> We're ok though

Thank God you're ok!
We drove into town
and this is what I find
on my newsfeed

> So sorry to interrupt your
> regular newsfeed

>=(
Be careful please!!!
<3

> I'll try <3

Tyler sighed in frustration as he put his phone away. "Well, bushwhacking it from now on, I guess. Too many witnesses in cities."

228

Erika nodded as she handed Tyler the water. "Yeah, probably for the best."

Taking the Codex out, Tyler peered down unable to find a single glowing page. *Hmm nothing.* Then he had a thought. It was as though someone was instructing him what to do, yet there were no voices.

Putting his hand over the Codex's cover, Tyler called out to the tome, "Find me a creature!"

A sudden small downdraft of wind circled around Tyler for a moment, disturbing the red and orange leaves scattered around his feet. Then, without any further instruction, Tyler turned to Erika after tucking the Codex into his backpack. "Alright, this way."

"What? That worked? How do you know where you're going?"

"I just feel it. It's like the Codex is telling me which way to go. It's calling to me. This way, come on."

The two traveled down a small and uncharted pathway around a formidable rock formation. It was just as beautiful and scenic as before. A waterfall cascaded down into a small pool which trickled off into a river, and with more autumn colored trees lining and littering the small pond's shoreline, Tyler led Erika up a gradual ledge approaching the waterfall. Tyler held out his arm and brought them both to a standstill.

"Led us to a waterfall?" Erika asked.

"No . . . I don't think so. Not *to*, but maybe through?" Tyler wondered aloud. Stretching out his hand, Tyler directed the winds to channel into and through the waterfall, parting it down the middle. To both their surprise, when the water parted, a carved-out passageway hidden behind the raging waters was revealed.

Wasting no time, the pair walked carefully over the slippery wet rocks and through the discovered opening. The passage was tunneled out by someone or something large, uniform and plowed clear of stones. The journey through was an even slope downwards, and as they neared a bright exit, they were still able to see their entrance. Tyler and Erika were surprised when they emerged at a stone base above a hidden ravine, and when the winds at the tunnel entrance stopped, the waterfall covered the opening and created a steady creek that ran down the tunnel and meandered through the wild hidden garden. Before them was a forest like above, but this one was hidden away as though nature wanted this bit of land to itself.

Erika patted Tyler on the shoulder. "Well done! Now we just need to—"

She was cut off by a distant animal call. It sounded like the throaty roar of a bear but more nasally, then as the howls branched out through the treetops above, it sounded more like an ape. It called out once for a second or two before stopping, and the rest of the forest seemingly held its breath. Holding still, Tyler and Erika looked around, not making a sound. Then it called out again, letting out three howls before stopping. *It moved closer!* Tyler thought.

Still feeling the Codex's call, Tyler motioned to Erika. "This way."

As the beast bellowed again, Erika's hand darted out for Tyler's as she pulled him back. "Stop, stop, stop."

"What? What is it?"

230

"Don't you hear it?" Her eyes shifted back and forth as she scanned the sky for anything moving.

He listened as the animal called out again. "Yes, it's really close."

Erika tugged Tyler as he pulled away. "No, not that. Listen to its call. It's in distress ... probably injured."

Oh great! It's probably pissed off then. Tyler listened to the howl once again. "How do you know?"

"You'll eventually pick up on sudden pitches. Trust me, that thing isn't happy! We really shouldn't bother it."

Just then Tyler's backpack started to glow pink. Eagerly whipping his backpack around him, he fumbled around with the zipper. "It's a new one! We found one!" Erika only gave a nervous half-smile. Tyler took out the Codex and opened it to the glowing pink page. "Ever heard of a Knucker before?"

"What? How hasn't that been documented yet?"

"I take it that's a yes."

Erika peered down at the book and swore under her breath. "Yeah ... what a first find. The book led you to a bloody water dragon."

Tyler tucked the book away. "Sweet! Let's go log it!"

With her sword at the ready, Erika kept one step ahead of Tyler. The terrain was rough and filled with potholes and stones. Erika stepped over a half-buried root but heard Tyler's shoe scuff against it. Turning just in time, she caught him before he hit the ground.

"Smooth ..." she quipped pulling him upright.

As the path narrowed, the creek formed into a repulsively unpleasant musky bog. Tyler and Erika crept from behind a downed tree to see the beast laying on the opposite shoreline, and his knees almost buckled with a mixture of fear and excitement as it came into full view.

Before them was a large dragon-like creature with thick weathered pink scales and a softer yellow underbelly – a Knucker. The monster had jagged black front and back claws that could easily rip through its prey, and it's thin but large wings erupted from its back as it thrashed around trying to free itself. A large metallic harpoon and chain sunk into a rear claw.

"Sons of Eric, this is their work. Monster hunters," said Erika, scanning the area.

"They harpooned it? Why?"

Erika nodded. "Fanatics who modelled their Order around Eric the Undying's work, but they took it a step further. Instead of logging Codex entries like your great granddaddy, their goal is to rid the world of all strange and dangerous creatures."

"And they just left the poor beast like this?"

"No . . . They'd have finished the job if they could."

That's horrible. Hopefully they aren't nearby. "Can it breathe fire?" Tyler whispered as he slowly crept out from cover.

Erika snuck alongside him. "Pretty sure. Let's back off."

Tyler stared at Erika tilting his head. "What? No way! We have to log this."

"This thing's dangerous . . . you could get seriously hurt!"

"Okay, Grandma. Come on."

Erika scoffed. "What's the plan then, tough guy?"

"Get closer."

232

The Knucker jolted around catching them in the corner of its eye. Its mouth hung ajar as it let out a rumbling warning hiss. The barbaric harpoon holding the beast in place only made the exchange tenser, and the dragon beat its powerful tail into the ground as though continuing to warn the pair to back off.

"It's okay, I'm not gonna hurt you," Tyler said gently raising his hand.

The ground quaked as the Knucker let out an ear-deafening roar. Small flames billowed from its mouth into the sky, a very clear sign it was giving him one last chance to back away.

I can't leave it like this, plus there will never be a better chance to get this entry. Tyler held his hands up as though retreating. "Okay, change of plans . . . Congelo!"

The Knucker shrieked in panic and rage as its muscles tensed and became rigid, and then the great beast fell. Tyler held out his hands to gently guide the creature to the ground, and once it was resting on the shore, its fiery, slit eyes followed Tyler as he neared. He waved to Erika for help.

"Yeesh, the Sons of Eric really did a number on this guy," she said, shaking her head.

Tyler cringed at the carnage the harpoon caused to the poor beast. "What kind of trap is this?"

With her sword at the ready, unsure how long his magic would work, Erika examined the trap. "Yep! It's a Sons hunting trap, alright. It sets a spear through the foot, working kinda like a Chinese finger trap, but deadlier."

"Think you can free it?" Tyler asked petting the Knucker's injured leg to ease its pain.

"He can't move, right?" Erika watched as the beast's chest rose then fell.

"He'll be fine, I'll reapply it again if his muscles start warming."

Putting her weapon down, Erika moved in closer and took hold of the long harpoon. In one fluid motion, she pushed the trap inwards before cleanly pulling it out. The Knucker's eyes flared before realizing it was free.

Tyler quickly stopped the bleeding with his magic, and with a great effort, he mended the wounds. *You'll be okay now. All just a bad memory.* The Knucker's muscles loosened as the pair carefully backed away over murky waterlogged soil.

Now at a safe distance, Tyler and Erika watched as the great lizard shook off Tyler's spell. It stretched like a dog after a long nap while whipping its tail side to side. The Knucker searched for a moment before finding Tyler and Erika, and it stared at them, motionless except for the tip of its tail slowly rising and falling against the soft, wet floor. It flinched nervously as it tested its back claw, and once the Knucker knew it was safe to step on its leg, the beast gave Tyler a slight but clearly intelligent nod before returning to its grazing.

Tyler pulled out his Codex, taking his eyes off the Knucker. "Still have your sword out?"

Erika tightened her grip but held the sword tip down so as not to appear threatening. "Just finish the entry."

He wrote:

'A large fire-breathing, dragon-like creature, it seems to have some form of intelligence or at least a sense of gratitude when

helped. *This Knucker has all the traits of a carnivore: sharp teeth, large front and back claws . . .'*

Just then, the Knucker rolled over an enormous tree stuck in the muck and used it to trap a large fish in the shallows before eating it.

'And strength, apparently. They can identify useful tools in their environment to aid their hunt; like a downed tree. Again, I feel this creature is smarter than people probably give credit. Its wings seem strong enough for flight. Due to its size, I'd imagine a Knucker's diet must consist of larger prey. They would probably jump at the opportunity for livestock if it could do so safely.'

Seeing another fish swim by, Tyler waved his hand over the water and murmured another stunning spell. *I wonder . . .* He waited for the limp fish to surface before snatching it up. Tyler held his prize in the air, earning the Knucker's attention.

Erika stared wide-eyed. "Umm . . . what the hell do you think you're doing?"

"I think I can feed it," Tyler said inching closer.

"And if you're wrong?"

"You'll save me," Tyler answered not wavering from his path.

"I don't exactly have the best track record, remember?"

Tyler stopped only a moment before continuing. "You're right. I'll just save myself."

Quickly but cautiously, Erika followed up behind him bridging the gap between the two. "If the old man was here, he'd tell you how stupid you're being."

Shrugging off Erika's comment, Tyler held the fish out to the Knucker. "You like fish, right? Want it?"

The Knucker stood its ground. Its tail swept from side to side again resembling more of a dog than a large serpentine creature. Moving closer, but at a constant and cautious pace, Tyler realized he had moved much closer than he probably should have.

"Okay . . . here you go." Swinging the fish back and forth, Tyler tossed it underhand, and the dragon snatched it gleefully out of the air before coming back down with a muddy thud.

The Knucker was convinced. After Tyler had freed it, tended to its wounds, and now fed it, the Knucker's face made an unmistakable dragonic smile. Lowering its head and giving Tyler a lick with its forked tongue, the tension and the fear of the unknown vanished.

"Told ya," Tyler said turning to Erika as he pet its rough, scaly nose.

Erika's grip loosened. "No way."

"Come on. Give 'em a pet. He's friendly." The Knucker enjoyed the attention as it let out a low guttural purr.

A weak, nervous laugh escaped Erika. "I'd rather not."

"Come on, trust me."

"I don't like this." Erika sheepishly walked to Tyler's side and reached out gently for the Knucker's snout.

Warming up to the newcomer, the Knucker turned and gave Erika her own lick.

Tyler rubbed under its jaw. "See! He likes you."

236

Erika agreed with a nervous cringe across her face, frozen in fear except for her arm. "Yep, sure does. Do I taste good?"

"Why are you so tense? It would've attacked by now if it was gonna."

"Not a fan of scaly, slimy, slithering things," Erika said cautiously. She pushed the Knucker's tongue away all the while petting the towering beast.

"Aww, he's not slimy. All those amazing scores and this big ol' puppy dog scares you?" Sensing her fear, the Knucker left her alone, walking back into the muck.

"I've had my own experiences with dragons . . . got everything you need?"

"Think I do." He turned to the Knucker who had already started hunting another fish. "Thanks, buddy." Seeing Tyler wave, the Knucker gave a definite bow before returning to its newly caught meal.

'As I thought, the Knucker isn't a ruthless monster. While it is easy to see why some people would feel threatened or afraid, if you show this creature respect, and perhaps even a kind heart, it will treat you with the same respect; maybe even let you pet it!'

Closing the Codex, the page now glowing a brilliant blue, Erika handed it back to Tyler. "Your first entry . . . well done! Though I'm sure most of history will disagree with your findings."

"Yeah, well—" Tyler was interrupted by the rustling of footsteps.

"This way! The brute is over here!" a man with a heavy Irish accent shouted as he rushed in Tyler and Erika's direction.

The Knucker hissed and reared up, trying to intimidate its hunters, unaware they would not waver from their mission to see the dragon dead.

"Go! Get out of here!" Tyler cried to the Knucker waving his arms to prompt the beast to take flight.

Listening to its new friend, the Knucker bowed before turning and ramping up for flight. With a couple quick steps and its powerful wings flapping, the Knucker lifted off the ground. But just as it did, a man sporting another deadly harpoon slogged through the muddy water, cocking back and threw it at the retreating dragon.

Aimed square in the back, the harpoon would have hit and killed its target if not for Tyler batting the harpoon away with a quick *"Dis!"* sending it harmlessly into a rock wall twenty feet off target.

With the Knucker now out of range, all any of them could do was watch the dragon fly off into the treetop horizon. With his sword drawn, the man pointed his blade at Tyler's chest. "You cost me my prey! I oughta stick you instead."

Erika drew her own sword and held it against the man's throat. "You can try."

"Careful, sweetie. You don't know who you're dealin' with," the man said, surprised by the speed and control Erika carried with her blade.

"Seems we have that in common," Erika answered as she tilted her head in Tyler's direction.

Just then, two other monster hunters stepped into the muck with their swords drawn. All three of them were dressed the same in black camouflage, with short flat top haircuts, clean-shaven faces, and jacked after years of training.

"And who might you be?" the man asked, unconcerned even with Erika's blade still hovering at his neck.

"Tyler Grayson, the Codex Scribe."

All three men's eyes widened. The Irishman asked, "Wait? You're the Scribe? Well then that means Charlotte's . . ."

"You knew my mom?"

"Yes, I've met her. We know every Scribe. First to last, last to first. Except you, of course."

"Are we okay then? We can all lower our weapons?" Tyler asked.

The man shifted his eyes to Erika. "Boys, lower your weapons." At their leader's command, they lowered their weapons, prompting Erika to lower her own. "That said, you denied me my kill. You let a dangerous creature free on this day, boy."

"That dragon wasn't dangerous! I just finished logging and petting it."

"Just like his mother . . . too compassionate! You're fortunate it didn't rip your arm off, kid. Get in my way again, and the Sons of Eric will have more than just dragon on the menu, got it?"

"Is that a threat?" Erika asked.

"No, it's a promise. Don't make enemies with us." Picking up his harpoon, the man joined his squad saying, "Until next time, Grayson."

"What's your name?" Tyler asked before they could leave.

"You can call me Foxtrot. You don't need to know my men's names," he answered over his shoulder as they moved up the slope and disappeared from view.

CHAPTER 25
A TRAVELER LIKE ME

Tucked away deep into the forest, under the eroding roots of an oak, Tyler and Erika unpacked their sleeping gear. With the sun's rays peeking out over the mountain through the thick autumn foliage, there was only enough light to see outlines, but this too faded into darkness moments later. Tyler hummed almost hymn-like as he cast seamless and invisible protective barriers around their temporary campground.

Lux! Tyler waved his hand out over his head before asking Erika, "Too bright?"

"Maybe a little, but it's fine," she said sitting on her rolled out sleeping bag as she polished her blade on a small red cloth.

Tyler waved his hand in the opposite direction, stopping halfway through the arch. "No problem."

With the light dimmed, Tyler kicked off his shoes and got into his sleeping bag. Erika put her sword down beside her and did the same. Throwing his dreammite blanket over both of them, Tyler adjusted to make sure the footing of both sleeping bags were covered.

Erika asked, "Aren't you cold? You should tuck yourself in with it."

241

Budded up to keep each other warm, Tyler pulled the blanket to their chins. "You kidding? We're sharing it."

After bathing in a chilly creek earlier, Erika was happy to hear Tyler insist. "Thanks."

The pair laid there silently as the forest once again came to life with creatures of the night. It felt almost enchanted as the twinkle of fireflies danced near and far. Seeing the colorful insects light up the night sky made Tyler pause for a moment before nature once again captured his attention. Soon, other not-so-mythical creatures began foraging for food in front of them. Their invisible bubble gave Tyler and Erika a front row view to uninterrupted nature. It was peaceful, calming and simple; a relaxing way to end a successful day.

Tyler glanced down at Erika. Her eyes flickering as she tried to keep herself awake. "No music tonight?"

"Too sleepy," she yawned, snuggling closer as she surrendered to slumber.

"Mind if I listen before bed?"

She reached over and handed Tyler the MP3. "Knock yourself out. Night."

"Good night," he whispered as he waved his hand to extinguish the light overhead.

Tyler scrolled through her playlist options hoping to find a 60's playlist. But as he passed through her playlists, he found one titled "Tyler's Playlist." Tyler thumbed through it. *It's all the songs I compiled for our private concert. Every single one . . . in exact order! She must've made it earlier today . . . from memory!*

"Nice playlist," Tyler said flashing the screen towards her.

Erika peeked her eyes open. She only gave Tyler a smile before rolling back to sleep.

Finding a 60's playlist, Tyler relaxed and listened. The blur of music and nature coming together created a chaotic but tranquil mood. Try as he might, soon Tyler also found himself nodding off. He wanted this moment to last as long as he could. He closed his eyes only for a moment. But when he opened his eyes again, three hours had passed.

Taking the earpieces out, Tyler reached over Erika and tucked them back into the mouth of her bag. He peered out into the forest to find everything still. *Even the fireflies must've fallen asleep.* Tyler sat upright for a moment looking at Erika. *Two nights in a row . . . her hair's so wild and unruly . . .* Unzipping his sleeping bag and kicking off the blanket, Tyler slipped on his shoes. *Hmm, gotta find a tree or bush nearby. Call of nature.* Laying the blanket gently over Erika, Tyler walked out from the protection of their camp.

The only noise were the leaves crunching beneath his feet as he walked up a slight hill. Tyler reached the foot of a tall tree standing at the outer rim of a cluster, but before Tyler could even reach down for his zipper, he found himself bucked back downhill. Stunned and the wind knocked out of him, Tyler gazed up to see the tree was no ordinary tree. The tree twisted and snapped until it took on an almost humanoid form.

What in the hell is that! The dried tree bark softened until it was made flesh, and slowly the tree turned into a giant elderly man. *Holy hell! He's huge . . . and jacked!* His long, greying hair and beard were covered in damp moss. Only freckled notches of wood and branches jutting out from his legs hinted at the creature's true nature.

"Haven't you demons done enough to this forest! Now you've come to piss on it for good measure?" the man shouted down at Tyler, his voice booming.

Tyler backed up. "I'm not a—"

The creature nearly flung Tyler through the air as it batted his hand at him, but he dove out of the way just in time, earning him another earful. "SILENCE FOUL FIEND! I will make an example out of you!"

"Adducere Charlemagne!" Tyler cried as he held his hand out. The twang of steel grew louder until Charlemagne charged out from the camp. Tyler grasped the sword in hand before falling back into his learned defensive stance.

The tree beast roared, "You think that little toothpick will save you, demon? BEHOLD THE MIGHT OF THE FOREST!"

The earth trembled beneath the creature's anger. The outrage in his voice pushed Tyler back, and he almost lost his footing. The giant reached down, but this time Tyler was ready. Sidestepping the colossal hand pummeling the ground where he once stood, Tyler took a quick upswing with his sword, slicing into the fleshy backhand of the creature.

Tyler watched as the giant took a step back, snarled and held his bloodied hand. "Please listen! I'm not a demon!" Tyler said, taking a step back himself.

The tree-man paused for a moment, then lunged forward yelling, "Your lies will not trick me!"

Tyler held his hand out and yelled, *"Dis!"*, successfully pushing back one of the giant man's hands. But before he could launch another spell, Tyler grunted as the beast wrapped its fingers around him, squeezing him tightly.

244

"Suffer my wrath!" the man roared, pinning Tyler to a nearby tree. Tyler watched as the man reached for his stomach before his huge finger rubbed up and down. At first, Tyler was terrified and confused. But then he realized what the creature was doing.

"Haha, stop it! Hahaha, what are you . . . are you tickling me?"

"Yes! Death by tickle, fiend! Suffer!"

Pinned against the tree, Tyler was almost at a loss. *Is he honestly trying to tickle me to death? . . . Is that even possible?* Much to his surprise, this outlandish idea started to become more frightening as time went on. Tyler laughed uncontrollably at first, but soon his sides began to hurt, and he could hardly breathe as he laughed more and more.

"Haha! Ha! Ah! Stop! Ah!"

The man had no intentions of stopping. But before he could torture Tyler anymore, both heard the resonation of a sword chopping through wood.

Surprised by the stabbing pain at the arch of his feet, the tree man dropped Tyler, giving him the time and space he needed. *"Dis!"*

The spell hit the giant in the chest. It sailed through the air into another tree. Bending it but not breaking. Tyler hit the ground and rolled after falling several feet. *Lucky I didn't break anything.*

"What the hell were you thinking going off on your own?" Erika yelled as she handed him his sword and backpack.

Boy am I happy to see her! Even as angry as she looks. Tyler took his sword. "I had to whiz."

"So you have a little demoness too, I see!" the two heard as they turned to find the man leering down at them with sap dripping from his roots.

Erika held her hands up. "Leshy, we mean you no harm. Please let us go."

Without another word, the Leshy charged, this time his intent to inflict a quick death.

Tyler shot out another pushing spell, but for the first time, Tyler watched as the Leshy batted away the spell. Only a bright flash of light flickered as the spell hit the back of the Leshy's hand.

"Stay here!" Erika shouted to Tyler, pushing him out of the way.

Sword at the ready, Erika dove between the Leshy's feet before the creature had a chance to crush her, and as she slid, her blade sliced deeper into the Leshy's roots. With tree sap covering her blade and shirt, Erika quickly climbed up the back of the Leshy using its vine loincloth and overgrown hair to ascend. The Leshy tried to swing her off but couldn't reach Erika at the angle she climbed. Anytime he came close, he was met with the searing sharp pain of Erika's sword stabbing into his hand. Then Erika saw her target as she reached halfway up its back. A small notch of wood stuck out amongst his fleshy skin, and using the hilt of her sword, she struck his weak spot, sending the Leshy stumbling forward to his knees.

He reeled in agony. "Oomf! Ow ow ow! Gaaah!" the Leshy cried with a labored billow. It glared at Erika as she stood at Tyler's side.

"You toy with me, demoness? Do you like to play with your prey before running them through?"

Erika sheathed her sword but kept her hand at the ready. "We told you! We're not demons."

"In fact, I think we have a mutual enemy," Tyler added, taking a step forward.

The Leshy's eyes lightened, but only for a moment before shouting, "Prove it!"

Tyler reached into his backpack and pulled out the Codex as another pink page glowed. "I am—"

"The Codex of Creatures!" The Leshy's eyes widened as they locked onto the small glowing book. "You . . . you are the Scribe?"

Tyler peered over to Erika, making sure she was ready just in case the Leshy didn't like his answer. "Yes. My name is Tyler Grayson."

The Leshy stood, still gritting his teeth while pain sweats streaked down his face. "I . . . I am sorry. I did not know. Nothing like you has stepped through these woods for many many years. What are you two?"

Tyler answered, "I'm a human."

Erika raised a hand, "Siren." Sharply turning her head, Erika peered out into the darkness unsure if the shadows themselves were moving. She gripped the hilt of her sheathed sword as she stood watch.

The Leshy appeared as though he was searching the depths of his memories trying to make sense of Tyler's answer. "Human? Hu-man?" Then something sparked his memory. "Man! I haven't seen mankind in ages. My name is Pesci. But my friends call me Mossy."

Pesci the Leshy? No wonder he goes by a nickname, Tyler thought, still unsure how Mossy felt about him. "So, you like Scribes?"

Mossy rubbed his thick beard. "Well, you are no demon. So that much is good. Now, being a Scribe, that can also be good . . . or . . ."

"How can that be a bad thing?"

Mossy pointed to the Codex. "That book holds a lot more power than I think you know, boy. Power corrupts both Man and Demon. Tell me, do you oppose the Cambion? The one called Ezekiel?"

"Yes! We're here to—"

Mossy eagerly asked with a growing smile, "You wish to end the reign of Ezekiel?"

"Yes, that's why we're finishing the Codex."

"Umm, kiddo!" Erika whispered with urgency, still staring out into the shadows.

Tyler glanced back to Erika and then out to the forest. The shadows appeared darker than before. With the way the moon crept through the treetops, the sudden cloud of black shadows seemed eerily out of place. It grew darker by the second.

"We need to go, now!" Erika said drawing her sword.

Mossy leered out into the shadows squinting an eye. "Your friend is right, young Mr. Grayson. I can sense foul creatures heading this way. Lapdogs of Ezekiel! Hurry, we must go."

Without warning, Mossy snatched up his two new friends and placed them on his shoulders.

Erika spoke into Mossy's ear, "All of our supplies. We can't leave our camp behind."

Mossy peered where Erika pointed but couldn't see their camp until Tyler broke the protective bubble. Once he saw their belongings, Mossy pinched his lips into a whistle. "No, we cannot have that!"

Suddenly, the forest came to life as all manner of animals emerged from their homes. Predator and prey all stood ready for Mossy's command. Tyler and Erika watched as the animals turned and ran to their campsite, and each grabbed something with their mouths or paws. In a matter of seconds, their camp had been disassembled.

Watching the animals scurry below him, Mossy turned and led his woodland friends deeper into the forest. He carefully marched alongside them before letting out a deep throaty roar. Whatever tracks the band of creatures left behind, however small, were brushed away by a flurry of leaves carried like a broom through the wind.

Mossy stepped over and under trees and rock formations as he led his tiny friends to safety. As a single migrating herd, the woodland creatures marched onwards carrying Tyler and Erika's belongings. It was the furthest any human had delved into the forest in many years.

"Where are you taking us?" Tyler gently spoke into Mossy's colossal ear.

"You need to fill the Codex. I think we can help you with that." Mossy trudged through a fast-moving creek. He lifted a large downed tree across the water, building a bridge for his herd.

"How?" Tyler asked as he glanced over to Erika.

Mossy smiled. A chuckle never surfaced, but his body trembled. "Let's just say, I have a way of convening the creatures of the forest when I see fit. Creatures that may help you fill in that book. Now, rest little one. As I vaguely recall, you humans need to hibernate at night."

Try as he might, between each lumbering step Mossy took and his rumbling arrhythmic humming, there was no way Tyler was going to get any more rest tonight. Erika had also given up on sleep as she rested shoulder to shoulder with him. Uncomfortable and paranoid, Erika kept peering over her shoulder while blasting her MP3.

She looks stressed out.

Tyler mouthed to her, "You okay?"

Erika just nodded.

Glancing down from time to time, Tyler would watch the tiny animals scurrying around Mossy's roots carrying their supplies. Occasionally, one of the smaller critters would get stuck on a rock or branch, but one of the other larger creatures would come to their aid.

Pulling out the Codex and turning to the glowing Leshy page, Tyler started filling in the page with the information he had gathered. *Hmm . . . still rosy pink. He'd help me, right?*

Tyler tapped on Mossy's shoulder to get his attention. "Mind if I ask you a few questions?"

"Ask away, Mr. Grayson."

"Hmm, alright. Let's start with where you're from."

Mossy thought for a moment, having been away from his homeland for centuries. "My people and I hail from Russia. I was born many years ago on the Russian-Latvian border."

"Are there female Leshies?"

250

Mossy grinned. "Oh yes! Large! Rrrobust maidens! As beautiful as they are intimidating. Not quite as fair as your feisty little mate, but brutishly elegant."

Tyler corrected him, "She's not my mate."

Tilting his head just enough to look at Erika, Mossy turned back to Tyler. "Hmm . . . do humans no longer bother with ceremonial partnerships?"

"No, we do! We're just not partners. We're friends . . . co-workers."

Mossy squinted with a puzzled face. "Something off-putting about her?"

Tyler glanced over at Erika, who was oblivious to their conversation. "No, not really."

"Could do a lot worse," Mossy said smiling as he saw the way Tyler looked at her.

"You have no idea." Tyler chuckled under his breath.

"Oh, but I do," Mossy said. "In my youth, I once courted a squirrel."

With a furrowed brow, Tyler could only mumble, "O . . . ooh?"

Mossy continued as he stepped through the thinning forests. "Oh yes. It was nice at the start. She'd run through my branches. Sleep atop my head. It was pleasant." Then his tone changed. "But then I started finding nuts hidden in my beard, scratch marks all over my trunk, and then I saw it. That treacherous little squirrel was nestled atop my best friend's head!"

"That's . . . horrible. I'm sorry."

Mossy calmly composed himself and shrugged. "It's okay, I won in the end. Over eight-hundred years later, I'm still here and she's not . . . she's very dead."

Withdrawing his own experience, Tyler only said, "Oh? Well, I guess mine wasn't as—"

The forest continued to thin until Mossy and his herd came into a clearing. The land was dead. The sounds of nature absent as though any and all life fled long ago. Uprooted stumps of trees littered the clearing, and Mossy sighed in despair, as though seeing the carnage dug deep into his heart. A small, winding depression in the land, once filled with life-giving water, was now dry and cracking. Pollutant residue coated the fractured waterway. Even the overturned dirt seemed void of life. It was bleached by some unnatural force.

"Where are we?" Tyler asked. "We aren't stopping here, right?"

Mossy snorted as he marched along the outskirts of the clearing. "No . . . no. We will not be stopping here. But perhaps it is best for you to see this place. This was once a beautiful haven for life. A place we once called 'Erch-ma-din'."

Tyler peered down at the animals running along the forest floor. *They seem restless and disturbed.*

"What happened here?" Tyler asked.

Anger welled in Mossy like a fire raging out of a furnace. "Ezekiel forsook this land, turning it into the foul sight you see before you. The woods, metals, stones and anything he and his ilk could get their cretinous hands on. They murdered this land! It will take many many years before nature licks this wound, perhaps long after I have passed on."

252

Erika's mouth hung wide open seeing the devastation. Tyler peered out into the wasteland. "Where did they take everything?"

Mossy pointed out and away from the ruins of Erchmadin. "There . . . far from this place. He made an outpost, guarded by demons and all manner of dark creatures he has recruited. As I am told, it is just one of many hives he has created, all of them tainting the lands they stand upon."

"And what is this place called?" Erika asked adjusting herself on Mossy's shoulder.

Mossy grumbled as he ground his back teeth together. "My people call it 'Gol-mesh-ka'." He turned and stared Tyler in the eye. "Throne of Corruption, in your language. I will help you fill your book with knowledge. But you must promise that you too will not forsake this land."

"I won't," Tyler promised with the herd disappearing back into the forest.

"Good!" Mossy said leaning his head back. "You two may wish to cover your ears." Then taking a deep breath, Mossy howled with all the might he could muster. It sounded like a bellowing warhorn.

"What was that?" Tyler asked.

"The Call."

CHAPTER 26
A WELCOME SIGHT

Sleeping silently in the comfort of his sleeping bag, Tyler rolled over, digging his face into his arms as the warm rays of the sun peeking through the leaves above shimmered into his eyes.

"Hmm, doesn't look like much of a Scribe to me."

"Yaah, tiny Scribe. Chicken arms."

"Now now, you two. What he lacks in size, he may make up with wit?"

Tyler's nose squinted, waking softly from the chatter.

"You sure this is a real Scribe, Mossy? Look's nothing like Eric . . ."

"Or Paris . . ."

"Or Damian . . ."

"Or—"

Unmuffled, Mossy interrupted. "Mr. Grayson here may be small, but he is *our* Scribe. When he wakes, we shall—Ah, he awakes! Good morning, Mr. Grayson!"

Opening his eyes, Tyler jolted back into his bag. Mossy stared him down, his frame well into Tyler's personal space. But as the shock cleared and Tyler sat up, he was greeted to the sight of several creatures sizing him up while more mythical beasts piled into Mossy's campground by the minute.

"Where are we?" Tyler asked as he kicked the bag out from under his feet.

"Why, don't you remember us setting up camp last night?"

"Kinda," said Tyler. *The lack of sleep's catching up to me.*

"Hmm . . . you need proper hibernation tonight. Need to keep your mind sharp. Mr. Grayson, welcome to the deep forest. You are safe now."

On his feet, Tyler stared at all the creatures surrounding him. All eyes were on him. Tyler smiled as he pulled out the Codex. *There's so many pink pages!* Looking up from the Codex, Tyler could see the once doubtful faces replaced with a look of awe.

One of the nearby Satyrs hugged another and rejoiced! "We have a champion! The forest has a voice again!"

"My my my! You have quite the cup to fill, Mr. Grayson," Mossy said before turning to the gathering crowd. "We must help our new friend with his quest! Please stay, become comfortable, and rest in my grove."

While most dispersed to unwind and make themselves feel at home, a handful of creatures stayed put, ready for Tyler to start his interviews.

Erika came up from behind, resting an arm on his shoulder as she handed him a peach she picked off a nearby tree. "Morning, kiddo. You've attracted quite a crowd."

"Thanks," he said, taking the peach. "Check out the Codex."

"Wow! Guess Scribes haven't hit this area before."

"Guess Ireland was a good first choice," Tyler said nudging her.

Erika's smiled. "I've been known to have a good idea every now and then."

Tyler thought of a playful sarcastic remark, but said, "More often than not, actually."

"Well, I'll leave you to your scribing."

With Erika merging into the crowd, Tyler took a seat on a stump placed there just for him. "Okay, who's first?"

A hysterical outcry of squeaks came from three tiny winged creatures. "Mee me-me-me!"

"Okay, you three can go first—"

"Yay!" they echoed as they fluttered and danced around him.

"Alright, so what are you three?"

The teeniest and most child-like in appearance darted up to Tyler. "Hello! I'm Cheryl, I'm a Fairy! That one with the short hair is Lizzie, she's a Pixie! And the one with the butterfly wings, that's Crystal, but she just goes by Chris, and she's a Forest Nymph!"

"Okay, so let's start with Cheryl first," Tyler said as he flipped through to find her page.

Tyler wrote down everything each of them had to say no matter how nonsensical the fact. By the time each individual page had turned blue, Tyler wasn't sure if there were any significant differences between the three. Their real differences were in their behaviors.

While interviewing both Cheryl and Crystal, Lizzie couldn't help her Pixie tendencies. She found great amusement in causing trouble, and although it was nothing sinister, it was rather annoying, especially when she would hide his pen.

Of all three interviews, Crystal's was the hardest to control. She was a Forest Nymph. Emphasis forest. Emphasis nymph. She was intrigued by only two things: the forest . . . and men. Being a man, Tyler needed to redirect the conversation a handful of times. He dodged her hungry eyes long enough to fill in the Codex before thanking her quickly and calling for the next creature.

Gonna need to sleep with one eye open around that girl—woah! Tyler peered up as a large hulking bear creature walked over on his two legs. He slowly backed up to a stump and sat with a thunderous bounce.

"Hey," the bear said making himself comfortable.

Not noticing or feeling her land on his shoulders, Cheryl watched as Tyler conducted his interview.

"Hey," Tyler mirrored as he took in the beast's massive size. "What's your name?"

The bear stretched out a cramp. "Oh, sorry! Long walk . . . big bear. My name is Jari. I am an Otso." He pointed out to a smaller bear and her cubs. "That beauty over there is my wife, Annikki. Honey! Honey! Wave to the nice human boy. Yep, that's her. And those little ankle biters are our cubs. Niko, Eero, and Eeva."

Tyler turned and waved to them, catching sight of Cheryl mimicking Jari on his shoulder. "Pleasure to meet you, Jari. Where are you from?"

Jari pointed with his snout as he leaned back. "We're from Finland."

Putting the country of origin into the Codex, Tyler made a cringing smile. "Wow! That's a long walk with three cubs."

"Oh no, it's okay. We were actually on holiday in England when we heard good ol' Mossy's call."

"Still a long hike, but I'm glad to have you here. Can you tell me a little about Otsos?"

Jari scratched his big bear head with a claw. "Not much to say about us. Pretty much like other bears. Hmm, except for the talking . . . that's different I suppose."

Annikki called out from afar, "Tell him about your job, honey."

"Oh yeah!" Jari's face lit up. "We're forest guardians. All Otso males watch over lost human boys, like yourself. All Otso females watch over lost human girls."

After writing this into the Codex, the pink page turned blue. "Wow? That's it?" Tyler was dumbfounded.

Jari stood and stretched his cracking back. "Yep, not surprised by that. Just your average guardian angel forest bear."

"Well thank you for coming here while on your vacation," Tyler said, extending his hand.

Jari stared at Tyler's hand with a confused expression. Not use to the custom of shaking hands, Jari shook Tyler's in jolts with an uncomfortably tight grip. "Our pleasure. If you want to meet the family or listen to some unbearably pun-y bear jokes, we'll be around."

The sun soon stood at high noon, and Tyler still had a lot more pages to fill. Sitting around a campfire with Erika and several other creatures he had met, Tyler sipped at the vegetable soup being passed around to everyone. He sat back and watched everyone enjoying each other's company while Cheryl napped on his shoulder and Mossy, with some of his closest friends, stood laughing off in the distance. He gripped a large wooden pipe between his lips, biting down on it between puffs.

Meanwhile, some of the more musically gifted creatures played together, filling the entire grove with music. As soon as the music started playing, Erika took off her earpieces and listened.

"Beautiful, right?" She nudged Tyler as they leaned against each other.

"Yeah, it's perfect."

Erika yawned while closing her eyes. "This was the kind of music I use to listen to when I was a little girl."

Catching Erika's contagious yawn, Tyler's eyes grew heavy. *A nap sounds good right about now.*

"Hey! Hey, wake up," Cheryl yelled, clapping her tiny hands against Tyler's cheeks.

"I'm tired, Cheryl. I haven't slept well for a couple days," Tyler groaned.

The fairy giggled. "A couple days? You just need to visit the Fey! Few hours of sleep in there and you won't need to sleep for weeks! Wanna go!?"

Erika interrupted her invitation. "Tyler's gonna be pretty busy finishing the Codex. But maybe in another decade."

"Yay!" Cheryl cheerfully sped off into camp. "I'll go get things ready! I'll be right back!"

"Thanks, Erika. She's adorable, but she's been attached to my hip all day." Tyler leaned back as though a weight had been lifted.

"More like your shoulder."

"She mentioned the 'Fey' before. Where is it?" Tyler asked.

"Another world, on a different plane of existence. All I know is nothing makes sense there, and magic goes a little . . . wacky."

"That explains the bizarre behavior."

Erika pulled herself off the ground and held out her hand. "Come on, let's spar."

Tyler's brow furrowed. *We're both exhausted and she wants to spar?* "Now? Why?"

She reached out further. "Just come on."

Taking Erika's hand, Tyler rose with a bounce and followed her out into a clearing.

The last thing either heard coming from the inner camp was another one of Jari's jokes. "Why did the mermaid wear seashells? Because she grew out of her B shells!"

Tyler chuckled under his breath. "Hold on. I've gotta text Amanda that one."

Just outside the inner camp of Mossy's Grove was an open meadow. The grass was untamed but kept short by roaming herbivores. The sun shined into the clearing unrestricted by any tall trees. It was the warmest the two had felt thus far in Ireland.

As Tyler put away his phone, Erika pointed to Charlemagne. "Okay, sword out."

"And you?" Tyler asked as he unsheathed and gave it a rolling twirl.

"This lesson is all about you, kiddo. I think I figured a few things out."

260

A small crowd gathered behind him from afar. "I'm all ears."

"First, Ezekiel knows you favor your magical abilities by now."

"He does?" Tyler asked with concern.

She nodded and paced. "Yes, after Dublin I would think so, and if he's been taking good tabs on you, he knows you prefer the pushing spell."

Dis . . . Tyler knew he was guilty of this. "So, what do I do?"

"Start using more spells. He's probably told his minions to watch for a pushing spell. That's when you hit them with something else!"

"So be unpredictable."

"Exactly!" Erika emphasized pointing at Tyler.

Tyler then realized. "Wait, but if he knows I'd rather fight with magic over swords, won't they key in on that too?"

"Correct. Changing up your magical arsenal isn't gonna be enough. We need you to be a better swordsman."

Tyler sighed in frustration. "But I'm not—"

"Stop it!" Erika interrupted. "You're not bad, okay? I've seen a whole lot worse."

"But 'not bad' isn't gonna cut it, is it?"

"No. You need to be a better sword fighter, and you need to be one before we leave."

She can't be serious! And . . . oh great! We gathered a crowd to watch my ass-kicking. "So what, you're gonna give me a crash course in two days? Something that Gramps didn't teach me?"

"Yup," Erika said, bridging the gap between them as she rested an arm on his shoulder. "Did the old man ever mention spellblading?"

"Spellblading?"

"I thought so." Erika backed away instructing him, "Point your sword at me." Tyler pointed Charlemagne as she asked. "Good. Now, I want you to let go, but keep it levitating with magic."

He'd never been too hot at levitation, so when Tyler let go of the blade and tried to float it midair, instead his reach grabbed a handful of Erika's hair and yanked upwards, while Charlemagne fell harmlessly to the ground.

Peering across to Tyler with a furrowed brow, Erika grit her teeth but kept silent.

"Sorry," Tyler said letting go.

"It's fine, try again. This time, start levitating it before you let go."

Tyler picked up his sword, rubbed the Ancori in his palm with his ring finger and closed his eyes. He was always too forceful, too erratic with his magic, and while it worked to push demons through plate-glass windows and stun water dragons, conquering this would require a different type of mindset. *It's just another mental exercise, like balancing the training staff on my lap. But this can be* easier *if I just focus.*

After a moment of concentration and deep breathing, Tyler let go of the blade. His eyes remained closed, and he envisioned its point facing Erika, even if he didn't see it. He could feel the weight of the sword disappear as his hands dropped to his side.

"Open your eyes, kiddo." He did so, and saw Charlemagne balancing in the air in front of him. A thin, almost invisible layer of magic surrounded it, glowing Citrine, the same as his Ancori. "Very good! Now, move it around. Control it, make it do what you want."

Tyler spun it around in place, haphazard at first. It felt awkward, sometimes over-rotating, sometimes jerking it one way too fast. But soon, Tyler had enough control and feel to turn and spin on command.

Erika smiled. "You could use a little more practice. But, you now know how to spellblade."

Emboldened, he gave his sword a ferocious spin, fast enough to cut a small tree in half. Tyler's doubt faded away. "Why didn't Gramps teach me this?"

"Spellblading's a lost art. It was popular back when I was younger. I doubt the old man's even heard of it."

This is amazing! Tyler sent his sword sailing safely passed Erika, stopped it, and commanded it to return, digging itself into the dirt beside him. "How could this fall out of popularity?"

"It's a very physically demanding method. Channeling your body's strength and mind's focus at once. Most Spellblading Magi could only fight short scrimmages."

Tyler frowned. "So even when I get better, I'll only be able to do this for a little while?"

Erika pulled his sword from the ground. "I said *most*." She strolled up to him before patting his pecks. "You're an athlete. You've conditioned your body better than the average bookworm Magi of the past." She handed him his blade. "Can you do this as long as magic or sword fighting?

No, probably not. But I think if anyone can revive the art, it's you."

Making the sword hover at his side, Tyler turned to find Erika's gently beautiful eyes staring into his own. "Think so?

"Know so."

She's never been so . . . Tyler smiled. "Alright . . . you want to spar then?"

Erika tilted her head with her own smile. "Ha! No, not yet at least. Still, one more thing I want you to try."

"Go on?"

"Another lost art. 'Ancient' actually. I've seen Magi use magic on everything around them, focusing on projecting magic outwards. But there's magic within you too. Rather than force it out, channel it and use it to enhance yourself."

"Enhance myself, how?"

Erika pointed to a tree out in the distance. "How long do you think it'd take you to run to that tree and back?"

Tyler stared at the tree for a moment before guessing, "I'd say about thirty seconds." He paused when he saw Erika's sly face. "I could run faster?"

Erika nodded. "Run faster, jump higher, swing harder, the list goes on. Jon trained you under Mera-su. This is Kena-su."

"Why didn't Gramps want to teach me this?" Tyler asked remembering Jon and Erika argue over it before.

"It's the most tiring of the Old Disciplines. Remember, he trained you to fight drawn out battles. Personally, I think you're more of a sprinter than a marathon runner. But maybe—with training, we can get you sprinting marathons."

264

"Let's give it a shot then." He drove his sword into the dirt.

Taking a runner's stance, Tyler could hear the crowd cheering him on. Starting off as a jog, Tyler picked up his pace until he was sprinting towards the tree. The air whistled through his hair and ears, and, at first, he didn't know what he was looking for. *What's the next gear?* But as he focused less on pushing his body and more on the familiar tingle of magic in and around him, Tyler felt it. Part of him knew this feeling had always been there. He commonly used it to cast spells, but in those instances he always pushed the feeling outwards, never inwards. *It feels like a fire raging in my stomach! My whole body is warm!* His arms and legs tingled as the trapped energy looked for a place to escape before retreating back into his body. Then Tyler tapped into the magic, but this time he didn't release it.

At first, Tyler didn't realize he had achieved Kena-su. It felt like he was still just jogging, but he looked up just in time to avoid smacking face-first into a tree branch. Tyler peered back at Erika as she gave him an encouraging nod. Digging into the dirt, Tyler shot himself up into the branches above him, and glanced down as he perched himself firmly atop a thick branch. *I'm like fifteen feet off the ground!* Jumping back down, easy as springing off a step, Tyler broke out into a sprint. He was at her side in five seconds flat.

"Had a good run?" Erika asked over a roaring applause. Some of the nymphs were buzzing around him, whistling and eyeing him down like a meal. Tyler blushed and started laughing. He felt amazing.

"Heck yeah. I . . . I've never run that fast before," Tyler gasped, trying to catch his breath.

Erika helped prop Tyler up to open his lungs. "So, how about a quick rest, then we spar?"

"No . . . let's start now."

"You sure? You look tired," Erika said taking out her sword and giving it a couple practice swings.

"Full contact or light?" Tyler asked gripping his sword from the ground.

"None of that powder puff crap. Full contact," Erika answered with a wink.

Tyler smiled as a thought crossed his mind for a moment. "Ladies first."

Springing forward, Erika charged Tyler, her blade clashing against his blade. Locked at the wrist guards, Erika pushed him away with a swift knee to the chest. Tyler stumbled backward, but never lost his footing. Waiting for the inevitable attack, Tyler surprised Erika when he jumped clear over her in a summersault, their blades clashing yet again while in midair. A collective astonishment combed over the crowd as he touched back down.

Erika readied her sword as they circled each other. "Acrobatics, huh?"

"I've got a couple other ideas," Tyler said playfully.

Every time Tyler swung Charlemagne, Erika cut him off and metallic twangs rang out into the crowd. Likewise, whenever Erika went in for a quick jab or swing, Tyler countered with a block followed by his own strike. His efficiency surprised even Erika.

As the match dragged on, Tyler began to doubt if he could best Erika. He was tired. Sweat stained his clothes dark, his muscles grew sore despite his training, and a burning sensation deep in his lungs told Tyler he couldn't last much longer at this rate. Spellblading and Kena-su had given Tyler a strategy to hold up against Erika's seasoned, near flawless sword skills. And even now it still wasn't enough. But then he saw something he needed to see at that moment.

He stared down Erika as her warrior eyes searched for a chink in Tyler's armor, when a single drop of sweat rolled down the side of her face, down her cheek, and fell to the floor. He looked closer. Erika was breathing heavy. Her clothes were damp with sweat, and her fast-paced fighting style had all but disappeared. *She's tired too! It's now or never!*

Tyler charged, igniting the crowd. The way he saw it, he was going to either win or lose the spar here and now. Drawing the fight out any longer would just favor Erika. But, sidestepping and batting Charlemagne away, Erika countered. Her sword nearly struck Tyler in the upper torso if not for a last-second dodge. Bringing his blade down, Tyler readied to surprise her before she blocked his attack, but before he could pull it off, Erika swung her feet around Tyler's and swept them out from underneath him. Swinging his body through the air, Tyler spun himself around and kicked her away onto her hands and knees.

Tyler hit the floor hard. This hurt, even with the invigoration of the Mera-su technique. *Get up! Get up!* Sore and exhausted, Tyler scrambled to pick himself up, but Erika threw herself atop him. With her knee pushed into his chest and her sword at his throat, Erika had won.

Damn . . . so close. Tyler sighed in defeat. And as he stared up at Erika, she smiled back at him. But it wasn't a gloating "I beat you" smile. It also wasn't a cocky "Nice try" smile. Without a word said, he knew it was an "I'm proud of you" smile. Her skin glistened with sweat. Her chest rose and fell, out of breath. Strands of soaked hair parted down her face. Tyler had given Erika a run for her money.

With Tyler dropping his sword in submission, Erika lowered her own. The two just stared into each other's eyes, and it took her a moment before she realized she should get off him. By then, some of their audience had already returned to camp to give them privacy.

Erika held her hand out and pulled him to his feet. "Sorry about tripping you. That sounded like it hurt."

Tyler stretched out his back. "We're practicing, don't worry about it."

"Yeah, I guess."

"No powder puff crap, right?" Tyler reminded her.

"Right."

"How's the hip? Sorry about the kick."

Erika chuckled softly. "Don't apologize for that. I'm impressed you even pulled that off. Didn't see it coming, and neither would anyone else." Wrapping an arm around his shoulders, the two walked back towards the inner camp with a tired limp in their step.

"But if you want to massage it for me, I won't argue," Erika added with a wink.

CHAPTER 27
XEAL

After another day in the safety of Mossy's grove, Tyler and Erika settled down for one last night with their new friends. While some needed to leave after Tyler filled in their page, most stayed, and even some gathered around a firepit enjoying each other's company and conversation as the day turned to night. The pair laid their heads against a log while Tyler stretched out his blanket over both of them.

Tyler pulled out his Memorystone and took in the moment.

"What're you recording?" Erika asked.

"This," Tyler said, smiling to himself.

"What? Lying around the campfire?"

Tyler nodded. "I wanna remember it, wouldn't you?"

"Yeah, I would," Erika said, snuggling up close. "Have any other memories?"

"Of course I do."

"What? What else do you have in there?"

"You wanna see?"

Erika held out her hands. "Yes, let's see it."

Tyler handed her the stone as he got up from his seat. "Here, check them out. I gotta go, well . . . you know."

"Do I need to follow you this time?" Erika said with a playful smirk.

"Ha! What? You wanna hold it for me too?" Erika rolled her eyes as Tyler added, "I'll be fine. Be right back."

As Tyler walked out of sight, Erika laid back and peered into the Memorystone. What she saw surprised her.

Tyler's first memory was Thanksgiving night in Eureka. Both of them dancing and singing, both of them having fun. *Must've recorded this later. What a wonderful night.*

The second memory was the next night. She watched them sit in the pub, enjoying a glass together, talking and laughing. *I don't think I've laughed that much in a long time.*

His third memory was the following day with both Tyler and Erika petting the Knucker. *His first entry.*

The fourth, and most beautiful memory to Erika, was of them huddled together under the blanket watching the fireflies dancing around them. *Aww, He . . . no! Stop, Erika! You can't . . .*

Tyler's fifth memory was taken from his point of view. Erika pinning him down, a sword at his throat, but a beaming smile on her face. *He really sees me this way? Beautiful?*

Then, of course, the sixth and final memory was the one Tyler took just moments before, once again the focal points being Erika and himself. She tucked her knees to her chest and checked to make sure no one was looking. Burying her face into her arms, Erika trembled as she wept.

Meanwhile, Tyler neared the edge of the grove as Mossy sat at the gateway taking a puff from his pipe.

He peered down at Tyler and asked, "Mr. Grayson, out for a little night stroll? Where's your lady friend?"

Tyler kept walking. "Just gonna relieve myself. Any other Leshies out there I should know about. Don't wanna accidentally—"

"You should be fine," he said cracking a smile while he held his pipe.

"Okay, I'll be back." Tyler entered the thicker tree line out of Mossy and the grove's sight.

Once he had relieved himself, Tyler turned and started the trek back to the campfire, the sound of leaves crunching beneath his feet echoing in the cool, windless evening. Then he saw something different. A glowing, lavender blue ball of light appeared from behind a tree. It was no larger than a baseball and the illuminated creature cautiously hovered closer and closer towards Tyler.

As Tyler stepped towards the tiny creature, its color turned dole and began retreating away from him timidly.

"I wonder if this is another creature missing from the Codex?" Tyler whispered to himself before gently holding out his hand. "It's okay, I'm not gonna hurt you."

The creature approached for a second before darting back further into the forest. Tyler followed it several yards before he noticed something in its behavior. Watching it, the tiny ball seemed to be running in all directions. *It's not running from me . . . what's it doing?* In what seemed like a desperate attempt to escape the forest, the ball of light shot straight up into the sky through the forest canopy and disappeared into the night sky. *What was that? It was so beautiful, but why was it so eager to leave?*

Tyler stood still as the hairs on the back of his neck stood on end. Out here alone, he heard the familiar crunch of footsteps. Turning in the direction they were coming from, Tyler watched as a tall man dressed in a professional business suit stepped out from behind the trees. He was now just as visible to Tyler as Tyler was to him. Tyler froze. *It's him!*

Ezekiel stepped closer with an eerie grin. "So good to see—"

As fast as his body could carry him, Tyler shouted, "Trahere!" A nearby fallen tree trunk lifted off the ground before ramming its sharp end through the demon.

Ezekiel let out a frustratingly calm sigh as he walked safely and unharmed from the trunk. "This is only a vision of me. A visual copy. A hologram. But I must say . . . This?" He peered at the stump Tyler tried to impale him with. "Well, that's not good manners."

"You're not getting the Codex! So what do you want?" Tyler demanded.

"That depends," Ezekiel smirked wickedly.

Tyler's eyes shifted trying to find an escape route. "On what?"

Ezekiel continued slowly walking towards Tyler. "I must admit. I don't know what to make of you. When I heard the next Scribe was a mere child, my first thought was to just find and kill you. Be done with it." He paused almost as though he was enthusiastically fantasizing the thought. "But you survived the Black-Eyed Children with one spell and no magical training. Then you managed to hold me off during your exam until Jon rescued you. No easy task. So, I tried to reason with you, bring you over. But my intel informed me

272

your conviction against my cause had only strengthened. So, back onto the kill list."

"Then you sent your agents to kill me in Dublin."

"Correct. And you bested them—drunk no less. And now, you've managed to gather a mass of creatures. You must be quite persuasive."

"Impressed?" Tyler quipped, still scanning for an exit.

"I was. But not as much after my 'agents' told me about your Ancori."

This caught Tyler's attention immediately. "What about it?"

"I've heard it has a peculiar shape. May I see it?" Tyler stood his ground flashing his Ancori to Ezekiel. "Hmph, it's true. All of it."

"You know what it means?" Tyler asked.

"It's called a Xeal cut. Very rare. Most people mistake its shape for an hourglass, but it's actually an 'X'."

Xeal? X? Can I honestly trust anything he says? Then again, he is older than Gramps. Maybe he's seen this before? "And what does it mean?" Tyler asked.

Ezekiel purred with a sly look in his eyes. "Its meaning is much like 'X' in a math equation. Do you know what 'X' is in math?"

Of course, it had to be math. Ugh, X? What is X in math? Wait . . . "It can be anything," Tyler answered.

"Infinite possibilities," Ezekiel said with a smug nod.

Tyler stared down at his Ancori. *Infinite possibilities.* "Wait, how do you even know this?"

"Because Tyler, the Ancori that resides in your palm was once my own."

No . . . "You can't unbind an Ancori. You're lying!"

"By myself? No, you're right, I could not. But the power over the Ancori is bestowed upon certain gifted Magi at birth, one of which is your grandfather. In exchange for him removing my old Ancori and binding me to my new one, I gave him an Oath that, until quite recently, stood for decades."

That would explain the nightmares . . . they were his memories? That would explain why Gramps was hiding it from me, and why it's so small compared to the other stones. Gramps must have doled the cut and kept it locked away.

"Before I fashioned myself an Ancori to grant me the strength I needed, your Ancori served me well. And I'm sure it will do the same for you. Which is why I had to come here."

"Why?" Tyler asked as he backed away.

"You aren't like many other Scribes," Ezekiel said licking his lips. "You're special. While I still question how much of your magical capabilities are your own, I'd imagine my old Ancori wouldn't simply bind with another so easily. You're a natural."

Tyler stood quietly as he watched Ezekiel's every move. "What are you getting at?"

Ezekiel advanced upon Tyler. "More than ever I am convinced. I could use someone like you. We could make an extraordinary team!"

"Piss off!" Tyler answered with an almost knee-jerk reaction. He could feel his blood boiling. While this man didn't kill his mother, he gave the order. Marshall and this Cambion would pay for what they did.

"So hostile for such a young boy. It's because of what happened with your mother, isn't it? And your father I suppose."

Tyler did not answer. His cold, expressionless stare said it all.

Ezekiel licked his lips as he savored Tyler's restraint. "Would you like to see them again?"

"What do you mean?" Tyler's face unclenched.

"We could bring them back. We *would* bring them back."

"How? Magic can't bring—" Tyler asked, but Ezekiel interrupted.

"With the Codex, we can do what magic alone cannot."

Tyler let his guard down. *I . . . I could see them again. Hear their voices and feel them near. I could tell them that I love them.* It stopped Tyler in his tracks.

"You're lying." Tyler's face grew stern again.

Ezekiel shook his head and smiled. "It's all possible, and I would do this for you, Tyler. All I need . . . is the Codex."

"You'd just kill me after."

"I'd make this all an oath magically binding my promise to you. If you give me the Codex. If you end this long drawn out chase. If you do this for me, I'll make you a favorable Oath that not even the fires of Hell could burn."

Ezekiel stood with his hand extended. Tyler realized, at this moment, Ezekiel was offering him a way out. Unlike every Scribe before him, Tyler could actually have a long and full life. *I'd still have magic. I could travel. Have adventures. Most important, Mom and Dad would be alive. And he couldn't touch us!*

"Do you fancy a woman?" Ezekiel asked trying to sweeten the deal. Tyler didn't say a word, but Ezekiel could tell just looking into his eyes. "Ah . . . there is a woman, isn't there? She could be yours."

Could the Codex keep her immortal?

"You can have power, Tyler. The world can be ours. We could rule not as servant and master, but as equals. I believe fate has brought us together, and all you need to do is take my hand." At this moment, Ezekiel's hand seemed to phase through. It was physical and possible for Tyler to grab.

"And what's in it for you?" Tyler asked.

"I've already told you my plans, Tyler. To allow both my people to thrive in this world—"

Tyler interrupted. "There's more, I know there is. No one is completely benevolent."

"Would it be so wrong to be rewarded for my service by granting myself immortality and the power to reign and keep peace?"

There's more. I can feel it. "What about the girl? Is bringing her back a part of your reward? The 'witch'."

Ezekiel froze as a panic ran over his face. He didn't say a word, but Tyler knew his mind was scrambling, trying to figure out how Tyler knew about the girl he had never mentioned to anyone else. He threw a hateful glare at his old Ancori and answered, "Never mind what you think you know about me." Ezekiel thrusted his hand back out. "My offer stands."

"What about this forest?"

Surprised, Ezekiel stared with a furrowed brow. "What of it?"

"What happens to this forest? What happens to everyone else? My friends, the creatures in the Codex. What about them?"

276

Ezekiel pondered his answer. "Our great empire must have a foundation, Tyler. It cannot be without servants to build it," he said coldly. "Those who comply will live happily. Those who don't, well we wouldn't have a place for them in our world, would we?"

Snapping back to reality, Tyler batted Ezekiel's hand away. "Even if you're truthful about your new world, someone else suffers, and I won't be a part of that. I think I'll take my chances, thanks."

Ezekiel sneered with a mix of outrage and a giddy euphoria. "Your mother said the same. You understand though . . . this doesn't end with you finishing the Codex. I won't just roll over and bow down to you, boy. The path you're taking, it ends with one of us killing the other. Can you stomach that? Your mother had the chance once, long ago, and she never took it."

Tyler said nothing. He knew he could do what his mother couldn't, but Ezekiel didn't need to know that. It was more than that though. He *wanted* to kill him.

"It's too bad really, I was hoping we could end this mindless circle. Tell me, Tyler . . . do you feel alone?"

The question struck Tyler as odd and out of place until he saw something out the corner of his eye. Not making any sudden movements, Tyler glanced over to see an immense quadruped beast standing motionless only fifteen yards away from him. *How did that thing get so close without me noticing?* It was too dark for Tyler to see the behemoth with any detail, but he could make out long quill-like fur cascading down its back and a long skeletal snout. Its jaws were gaped open, ready to strike.

"When my pet is finished, I'm going to pry the Codex off your cold dead corpse, Scribe."

"Too bad I don't have it on me," Tyler said stretching his fingers, readying himself.

"It doesn't matter," Ezekiel snickered. "The Codex *will* be mine." He turned to his pet as an intimidating hiss escaped past its jagged, putrid canines.

The beast recoiled like a cat, but before the monster could launch itself off the soft leaf-covered ground, a clean metallic ring silenced the creature's hiss. A sword was stuck clear through the beast's head, and a second later Tyler saw Erika ruthlessly pull her sword from the slain creature as it fell on its side, its lifeless eyes reflecting the faint moonlight above.

"Run!" Erika yelled as she grabbed Tyler by the hand and rushed him back to camp.

"Kill them!" Ezekiel exclaimed as the shadows lurking in the forest behind them erupted into dark savage monsters. They raced towards the pair, jaws drooling and snapping wildly.

"Move it!" Erika panicked as the creatures gained ground. There was no way they would make it all the way back into the inner camp. But as they crossed back into the outer grove, they watched as Mossy's fist swung overhead and crushed one of the beasts, snapping its back in two.

The pack of snarling devilish canines came to a halt and hissed and howled up at Mossy.

"Not in my GROVE!" he roared angrily as they circled him.

Flinching for a moment under the torrential winds, the fiendish hounds launched themselves at Mossy. *More just keep coming!* Tyler thought to himself as Jari suddenly charged past him, leapt into the air and crushed one under his weight before tackling another as it lunged for Mossy's throat. The ground thundered beneath Tyler as a wave of defenders came to their aid at the Leshy's call. The battle was here and now.

Over the roar of battle, Jari cried out, "Annikki! Get the cubs out of here!" Gathering her young from the sudden maelstrom, the mother bear led them and several other smaller creatures away from the fray.

Charlemagne soared through the air towards Tyler and he turned to face the brawl, gripping the hilt and summoning his magic. Throwing his hand forward, Charlemagne flew from his hand and sliced straight through a gaunt mummified creature. With a flick of the wrist, Tyler tossed the lifeless being to the ground and called his blade back to his hand.

He stumbled backward as a skeletal hand drove through the earth and tried to drag him under. Acting quickly, Erika came to his aid and severed the hand at the wrist before spinning and cleaving another foul canine lunging at her. It tumbled toward her, and she fell under the slain hound's weight.

Pulling Erika off the ground, Tyler heard a chorus of giggles from overhead. A trio of glowing Sprites shot down from the canopy above, shooting fire from their hands that exploded into a torrent of flames upon contact. They giggled gleefully as defenders dove for cover.

"Stop! The forest! Please!" Tyler heard Cheryl cry out somewhere behind him as she tried to get the devilish Sprites to turn away.

Their giggles turned maniacal as they chanted, "Burn the fairy, burn the fairy!" All three cast another round of fire from their hands, this time aimed directly at defenseless Cheryl. But before the fireballs connected, Tyler pulled the swirling balls of fire out of the sky, wound up like he was pitching a fastball and then hurled the fireballs back at the Fire Sprites. He watched them fall out of the sky in a nosedive.

Soon the ground turned red with the bodies of Ezekiel's dark allies and Tyler's slain defenders. Incensed by all the senseless death, Tyler used a combination of magic and spellblading to cleave his way through advancing beasts, but as the battle dragged on, Tyler grew tired.

Erika pulled Tyler under her wing with a demanding tune. "Rest! We're gonna need you to Jump us out of here!"

The battle's nowhere near finished! "Jump? They need us!" Tyler shouted over the raging carnage.

Erika tripped and stabbed a demon charging them. "No, they need you alive!"

Catching her sight just in time, Erika raised her sword to bat away the monstrous sword of a demon bearing down on Tyler. But it wasn't just any ordinary demon. It was Kroll, blood-covered and grinning, and the beast had Tyler in his crosshairs. Worse yet, Erika was barely able to hold her sword, and Tyler was in even worse shape. Kroll showed no signs of tiring.

"Duck!" Jari shouted from behind them. Hitting the dirt, Tyler and Erika watched the guardian bear soar overtop of them, pawing aside Kroll's weapon before tackling the monstrous demon to the ground. Jari went in for the quick kill, but Kroll snatched the bear by the jaw and violently

280

threw him to the side. Jari scrambled to all fours and blew past Kroll's lumbering strike before latching onto his arm, but Kroll gouged at his eyes with his long and cracked fingernails, and Jari roared as he let go and reset himself, one eye red and bleeding.

"No . . . Erika, he can't see!" Tyler said, lunging forward, but Erika pulled him back.

Shaking off the wound, Jari crouched low and launched at the demon again, but his aim wasn't true, and he was met with a concussive strike to the side of the head from Kroll's tree-trunk of a forearm. Tyler pulled himself away from Erika, but it was too late.

Kroll lunged for Jari's head, grabbed him by the throat and, with a sudden twist, there was a loud crack. The earth quaked as Jari fell to the floor, slain.

Jari! NO! Enraged, Tyler used what energy he had and flung his sword out like a spinning disc. Catching sight of the weapon soaring towards him, Kroll side-stepped, but was taken by surprise when Tyler adjusted its trajectory in midair. The beast howled in pain as Charlemagne sliced into the side of his chest before boomeranging back into Tyler's hand. Kroll put pressure over his gushing open wound, muttered a threat under his breath and Jumped from the battlefield.

"Coward!" Tyler screamed, scanning the trees for Ezekiel's lieutenant. He was gone.

Mossy called out to Tyler as he cleared a pathway through a clutter of Ezekiel's warriors with a single swing of his bloodied arm. "Mr. Grayson! Hurry! This way! Now!"

Grabbing Tyler, Erika pulled them through the battlefield towards Mossy, both clashing blades with zombified creatures before defenders came to their aid and mauled the corpses. Tyler peered at Mossy, his flesh covered with bloody slash marks, puncture wounds, and bruises. He could see the worry in the old Leshy's eyes.

"Mr. Grayson, you must leave now!"

Tyler shook his head. "I'm not leaving you here! They got Jari!" *His poor wife . . . And his cubs . . . they now have to live without their father . . . because of me.*

Mossy's face curled up into an ugly, angry sneer, and he grew as his rage welled in his chest. "Listen to me, boy! You must survive! Do as I say, hurry!"

"I don't think I can Jump us far," Tyler said as sweat dripped down his face.

"Then Jump as far as you can! You and your friend are no longer safe here."

Tyler turned to Erika, a concerned look on her face. "It'll take whatever I got left."

Erika knew once they Jumped, Tyler's life would be in her hands. "You're not leaving my side!"

Tyler turned back to Mossy. "Don't die on me."

"I will try," Mossy answered. "Now go!"

Taking Erika by the hand, Tyler chanted under his breath and in an instant, the two disappeared. The crackle of thunder rumbled through the grove, and its defenders shouted out in a battlecry, "For the Scribe!"

CHAPTER 28
BATTLE OF THE FOREST

The ground quaked with a thunderous roar as Tyler and Erika landed several miles outside Mossy's grove. Tyler reached out for a nearby log to hold himself upright. Exhausted, he breathed deeply while scanning the area for watchful eyes. Erika was hunched over gripping her head, her hair tossed about as she shook with a frustrated, painful expression.

"Erika . . . you okay?"

Erika reached out and pulled Tyler along as she massaged her splitting headache. "We need to go. Ezekiel already knows we—" The sound of demons marching through the forest interrupted her as one shouted, "This way!"

"Stick close." Erika drew her sword as they fled.

The two ran as hard and fast as their legs would take them. Erika helped pull Tyler along as he slowed. When the demons came too close, they hid under anything they could find. It took all their cunning and deception to throw the hunting party off their trail. Still reeling from her headache, Erika shook it off before grabbing Tyler and leading him away.

"Shh . . . they're close," Erika said peeking out from behind a cluster of trees. *If they come this way, I'll have to fight them all.* Her grip fastened around her blade. Luckily, the group turned and ran off as though responding to another search party. *Yes! Some luck for a change.* Her face lit up. Erika hurried Tyler down the road away from the hunting parties.

"We'll rest for a moment, Jump out of here, then link up with your grand—" Erika was interrupted by a sudden snapping noise coming up from behind them. They peered over their shoulders to find the road behind them suddenly gone, and a wicked wall of thorny bark grew out from the ground high into the canopy. Both were now in a full-blown sprint as the vines whipped out from the soil beneath them, thrashing and cutting at their legs.

Erika was only a foot ahead of Tyler, but a foot was all it took. Catching both off guard, a wall of wood and thorns shot up from the earth between the two. The impact sent Tyler crashing backward, while Erika tumbled forward.

"TYLER!" Erika's hysterical shouts were muffled through the bark. Grabbing her sword, Erika whaled away at the wall as chunks of wood and splinters flew out at her like shrapnel.

Tyler searched high and low trying to find an escape. But before he could find one, he heard a rustling of leaves behind him. He turned as a dust devil swirled and twisted around faster and faster. *It's him . . . he's coming.* The twister raged until finally Ezekiel stepped forward, revealing himself as he unsheathed his black-handled, curved sword. He severed a vine laying across the floor, killing the creature just to show Tyler it was truly him this time.

"It didn't need to be this way. I offered you a way out." Ezekiel threw a hand in the air as he paced back and forth.

"Guess there's no point in delaying this." Trying not to show his weakness, Tyler pulled his sword from its sheath as he walked out to meet the fiend. "It was gonna come to this someday."

"Mmm, that's the spirit. Let's end this."

Their blades screamed as they met the other. Ezekiel was fast and deadly accurate. It took all Tyler's focus and reserved energy just to defend himself. Tyler would spellblade to pick up the pace, but the fiend had a flawless form and left Tyler without an opportunity to counterstrike.

Ezekiel came in for a killing blow. He dodged to the side and, seeing a fleeting opening, he tried to thrust his blade into Ezekiel's belly, but only realized halfway through his strike that he was too tired to spellblade or push his body any further. Ezekiel brushed aside Charlemagne and, in one fluid motion, ran his blade across Tyler's shoulder. Tyler shot backward, muffling his screams of agony, clenching his shoulder as blood poured through the gaps in his fingers. It was a warm and wet burning sensation and his sleeve was soaked red.

Amused as he watched every nuance of Tyler's grimacing face, Ezekiel waved his hand over the young Scribe. Much to Tyler's surprise, the pain disappeared and his wound sealed. Still clinging to his shoulder, Tyler watched Ezekiel back away.

"I liked that . . . More."

Tyler returned to the ready position. He gripped his sword with shaking fingers, blood now staining the hilt. Determined, he swung his blade down with ferocity, but just like before, Ezekiel batted Tyler's sword aside and backhanded him away. Tyler recoiled, still holding his position. His face on fire, his nose writhing in numbed pain, Tyler spat dark crimson drool from his mouth.

Ignis! Tyler thought as he lifted his hand. Before the fireball could discharge from his palm, Ezekiel extinguished the source spark. Holding back his full power, Ezekiel pointed a single finger at Tyler and electricity surged through the air, striking him in the chest, sending him to the dirt in violent convulsions. He grunted through his tightly clenched jaw, squirming in pain as the spell coursed through him.

Ezekiel broke his spell. "You dare use magic against me? Get up!"

Shaken, shoulders limping, Tyler slowly picked himself up and pushed through it, holding his sword at the ready. Ezekiel opened with a flurry of swings and stabs. Tyler defended himself, but each swing came in faster and faster until Ezekiel pushed through his guard and drove his blade into Tyler's thigh. He grabbed Tyler's hand by the wrist, cocked his head back and crushed his forehead into Tyler's face. A loud cracking noise snapped through Tyler's ear, and his nose gushed blood and bent off to one side broken. He collapsed as Charlemagne fell from his fingers. Tyler had nothing left to give.

Ezekiel sighed and kicked Charlemagne aside. "I was hoping for a little more fight in you. Hmph! Our Scribe . . ."

"How 'bout one more?" Tyler asked with a still defiant look in his eyes.

"Hmm, I think not," Ezekiel said before sending his jagged blade into Tyler's other thigh.

286

Tyler gasped for air. The pain overwhelmed his senses as Ezekiel stuck his blade deeper. Blood stained the dirt beneath him. Tyler couldn't feel his leg, then Ezekiel gave the sword a twist, carving out more of Tyler's flesh. He screamed as Ezekiel tortured him and his leg spasmed uncontrollably. All he could taste was his own blood. All he could hear was his heart beating in his ears.

Firmly clasping his sword, Ezekiel slowly drew the blade from Tyler's leg. It was a painful relief from his torment but drawn out longer solely to torture Tyler. Centering himself over Tyler's broken body, Ezekiel hovered the blood-soaked tip of his blade over Tyler's chest. There was fear in Tyler's eyes. He was powerless to stop Ezekiel.

"Scared to fight another round?" Tyler shouted trying to goad Ezekiel into giving him another chance.

Ezekiel said nothing but smirked over his prey.

"Just one more?" Tyler asked.

"No . . . no more," Ezekiel said resting the sharp point of his blade against Tyler's chest.

Bringing his blade up, Ezekiel savored the look in Tyler's eyes one last time. But before he brought his sword down to pierce Tyler's chest, Ezekiel was blindsided. Erika threw them both to the ground in a full body tackle. Atop him, Erika balled her fist, winding up, and cracked Ezekiel across the face. She wound up for another but was thrown off him. She landed awkwardly on her side but immediately jumped to her feet. Erika readied her fists, for her blade laid shattered at the carved opening she made.

"Erika!" Tyler called out to her. Summoning what little strength he had left, he threw her Charlemagne. The sword wasn't heavy in Erika's hands, but it required her to grip it with both hands to swing properly.

Ezekiel spat blood as he wiped red from his face. "Is this how you wish to end it all?"

Taking a deep breath, Erika squared off with Ezekiel. "Just walk away."

"You had your chance," Ezekiel smirked. His sword raised ready to shed her blood.

Erika charged with Charlemagne in hand. Sparks flew as the two blades met. Ezekiel swung wide looking to slice her in half with a single strike. Instead, Erika ducked out of the way before carving her way towards him. Ezekiel was forced into a full retreat, but she lunged forward past his guard and crushed the hilt of Charlemagne into his chin. Erika jumped out of the way as Ezekiel fell backward and swung wildly in retaliation.

Ezekiel leered up from the ground, drooling red, his eyes ablaze. He launched himself forward, and a powerful sword-breaking swing battered Charlemagne, but the sword kept steady in Erika's hands. An ominous thunder rolled over them, for a moment drowning out the sound of sword meeting sword. Catching Ezekiel's blade by a cross guard, Erika locked blades and elbowed his face. She pulled back, but not before raking Charlemagne across his chest. "Ahh!" Ezekiel hissed as blood stained his shirt. Erika brought Charlemagne back and charged, ready to run its cold steel through the fiend.

Ezekiel screamed with a fiery, hell-raising fury, "Enough games!"

Erika collapsed to the ground, her head throbbing with a pain she had never felt in all her years. She grasped her head, squirming on the floor as the torture dug deeper. It felt like the blur of a wrenching tension headache mixed with the bombardment of a dull, merciless pounding. Erika groaned, gritting her teeth as the pain traveled through her body. Unable to bear it, she dropped Charlemagne to the cold ground beside her.

Ezekiel stood over her, and pulled Erika to her feet by her hair with his magic. He glared at her coldly, her life meaning nothing to him.

"You've got strings holding you down," Ezekiel mocked her. The pain was so intense she couldn't open her eyes to see his hate-filled gaze. He raised his sword and pulled it back, ready to impale it through her skull. Ezekiel didn't need to enjoy this kill. He just wanted it to be done.

"Wait!" Tyler called out to him.

Ezekiel turned to find Tyler standing on his bloodied feet with the Codex in hand.

Tyler held it out. "It's yours . . . just let her go and it's yours."

"Her? You really are oblivious, you foolish boy," Ezekiel scolded him.

"Let her go, and it's yours . . . and I won't come looking for it."

Ezekiel grinned, all the power in his hands. "Or, and this is the best part, or . . . I kill her, then I kill you, and then I take the Codex."

A voice boomed to everyone's surprise. "You'll do no such thing! Step away from my grandson!"

Startled, Ezekiel froze as he watched Jon step out from the shadows with his arms raised, ready to unleash an onslaught of magical devastation upon the fiend.

"Well, well, Jon! My dear, stupid old friend. I've been looking for you." Ezekiel pulled Erika closer as he held his blade to her throat.

"Put that away," Jon told Tyler pushing the Codex back at him. His cruel stare never broke from Ezekiel. "Let the Siren go, or I'll teach you just how spitefully inhuman I can be."

"Oh yes, just give you this little harlot and we can all go home happy, right?"

Jon remained still. "Don't test me. You of all people know what I am capable of."

Ezekiel laughed, enjoying the anger seething from Jon's face. "Go ahead, try it. I know you won't."

A fire sparked from Jon's fingers. "Betting on that?"

Pulling Erika closer, Ezekiel's blade kissed her flesh but did not draw blood. "Unless you wish to risk her life, I'd suggest you settle down."

"She means nothing to you, let her go."

Ezekiel mocked Jon. "Mmm mmm mmm. She means something to the boy, so she means something to me. Besides . . ." He rubbed her cheeks before giving it a pinch. "I have a bone to pick with this one."

"Ezekiel!" Jon yelled, taking a step forward.

"Here's what's happening. Erika is coming with me. You know where, don't you, Jon. Now, Tyler can come alone and give me the Codex, or he can choose not to and the game will continue on. But the Siren, she will not." He turned to Tyler. "Bring the Codex to me by eighteen-hundred hours tomorrow night or she dies."

Without a reason to say another word, the winds under Ezekiel's feet swirled, engulfing both of them. The last thing Tyler heard was Erika shouting to him over the raging winds, "Don't do it, Tyler!" Then the winds stopped. Ezekiel and Erika had vanished.

Tyler hobbled to Jon's side. "Where did he take her?"

"His outpost here in Ireland," Jon said tending to Tyler's bleeding wounds with tender hands.

Golmeshka . . . Tyler picked up his backpack and tried to find north to orientate himself.

Jon reached out for his grandson's shoulder, not finished healing his wounds. "Tyler . . . you have to let her go."

"Let her go? You mean just let her die? No way! Absolutely not!"

"She knew the risks in becoming your Adjutor."

Tyler refused, shaking his head. "No, I'm not leaving her—"

"So what's your plan?" Jon interrupted. "Give him the Codex and hope he doesn't kill you both? Or maybe you wanna try fighting him again? That seems to have worked so well for you."

He's right. What then? Tyler would be throwing himself into the belly of the beast with little to no chance of escaping. Erika's last words echoed hauntingly in his mind, only making it harder on him.

"I'd be dead if she didn't save me. I owe it to her to try," Tyler said meeting Jon's unwavering stare.

"And if things go south?" Jon asked.

Even if things go well . . . it's a real possibility. But it was a possibility Tyler accepted. "I'll teleport the Codex to you."

"You're a fool . . . Just like your mother!"

"Runs in the family."

"Fine." Jon took his grandson's hand. "If you're going to do this, you'll need a full night's rest."

"I don't think I can sleep this one off," Tyler said with his wounds still painfully twinging.

"Leave it to me." And with that, they disappeared.

CHAPTER 29
GOLMESHKA

Tyler woke springing forward in the bed Jon had prepared for him in the new hideout. Both his body and mind had been silent for hours. Peering around the dimly lit room, Tyler found Jon sitting at his bedside, his lack of sleep evident from his red bloodshot eyes and the dark baggy circles under them. With his grandson now awake, Jon got up and grabbed two large cups. One was just a glass of water for himself and the other was the all too familiar brown shake.

Tyler took the drink and downed it. "Thanks."

Penelope rushed into Tyler's arms. "Sweetie! Thank goodness you're okay!"

"It's good to see you too, Penelope."

Charlie peered into the room stirring a pot of steaming food. "Good to see you awake, sir. I'll have food ready in a moment."

"Hey, Charlie. Thanks, but how long have I been out?"

"A while," Jon said. "It's 9:00 AM, 5:00 PM in Ireland."

"I have to go," Tyler said springing to his feet.

"Please, Tyler. Reconsider. Erika wouldn't want you to risk your life for her," Penelope pleaded.

Tyler turned and stared each of them in the eye. "I'm going, so don't try to change my mind. It's happening. Best thing you can do is help me get back."

While Penelope rubbed her temples, Jon pushed him back onto his bed. "I know where it is. If you're still hell-bent on going forward with this stupid idea, I can help you Jump right outside the base. But, first, you'll need a plan." He handed Tyler two tiny pink pills and a cup of water. "These are Asudolor capsules. They'll help numb your current wounds and any you pick up in the next few hours."

"They're painkillers?" Tyler asked popping them into his mouth.

"In a way, but they're better than any painkiller out there. No side effects, and your body won't be sluggish and slow. Now, I want you to hold onto this and keep it on you."

A large brown pill fell into Tyler's hand. "What's this one?"

Jon closed Tyler's hand around the pill. "Adredium, also known as 'The Cure'. Just in case they inject or force you to take anything. It'll negate anything attacking your system. Takes thirty minutes to take full effect, so keep that in mind."

I'll tuck this into my pocket just in case they take my backpack. Tyler readied himself. "Okay, what's the plan?"

Jon walked back to Tyler holding two large, leather-bound books. "You can't beat him. But you might be able to outsmart him. This one," he said holding the book in his right hand, "is the Codex." He then held up the left book. "This one's a fake."

"Won't he tell right away?"

"Besides mending you last night, I've been focused on this copy, imbuing it with concentrated magic. It'll be

294

convincing, but you're right. Don't doddle . . . he'll figure it out sooner or later."

"What if I give him the wrong one? How will I know?"

Jon placed Tyler's hand over the real Codex, and a torrent of energy surged through his fingertips and into his body. It was cool and calming, but inspiring. It was like no adrenaline rush he had ever felt before. His eyesight strengthened, his hearing sharpened, and his sense of smell seemingly picked up everything in a two-mile radius.

"Think you'll mistake the two?"

"How? It's never felt like this before?" Tyler asked holding the Codex tightly in hand.

Jon helped pack the fake Codex into the backpack first, followed by the real Codex. "The Codex has taken in the full power of the creatures in the Leshy's grove," he said, before adding, "Also, a good night's sleep goes a long way."

Zipping his backpack, Tyler turned to face Jon possibly for the last time. "Any suggestions so he doesn't kill me on sight?"

"Tell him or his guards that you want to bargain with him. I have no doubt he's still holding out hope that you'll join him."

"Why?"

"Ezekiel likes to strike deals to get what he wants. He's a businessman first, and a ruthless killer second. You're not the first he's tried to convert."

"Hopefully the last," Tyler said with a fire growing in his eyes. "Will Marshall be there?"

Jon sighed. "There is much we don't know about what happened to your mother that night, Tyler. But if the Werewolf is there, you need to consider all possibilities.

Vengeance is a slope slick with blood, and most often, it's not just the victim's. You need to *focus*."

Tyler nodded. He was focused, but if Marshall was there and he could take his shot, he would.

"I don't like this . . ." Penelope said to Charlie.

"Neither do I," Charlie answered. He turned to Tyler. "You have to come back. None of us can bear to lose you too."

Tyler kneeled and extended his arms. "Not the plan. I'll be back with Erika before you have lunch ready."

Penelope and Charlie clung to Tyler. "Please come back, sweetheart," Penelope whispered into Tyler's ear.

Tyler stood and turned to Jon. Cupping his hands around Tyler's head, a jolt of energy passed into him. Jon glared into his eyes. "Do you see Golmeshka?"

He nodded.

With nothing else left to say, Jon held out his hand. "Come home."

Tyler pushed his grandfather's hand aside, bringing him into an embrace. "Thanks . . . just in case."

Jon was unable to speak, unsure what to say. Relenting, he wrapped an arm around Tyler and held him.

Stepping away from his grandfather, Tyler took a breath and vanished. The next thing he knew, Tyler was landing hard but safely onto solid compacted soil. The forest surrounding the outer walls of the large compound left Tyler completely exposed on the trampled dirt.

Standing off in the distance, Golmeshka was exactly as Tyler imagined it. *It looks like an old World War bunker from the history books.* Its walls were barricaded and reinforced with twisted steel and metal. A stony, concrete wall surrounded the menacing building's parameter. The air smelled like the ashy remains of a campfire, growing more nauseating by the second. Tucked away in a remote and desolate corner of Ireland, no one would ever find Golmeshka unless they knew exactly where to look.

A loud bang rifled out from the demon made walls. Tyler was not alone. Stepping out from the bunker's doorway, two "men" wearing military grade armor walked out towards Tyler. *Better idea if I let them come to me.* Tyler thought holding his ground. But as they neared, Tyler recognized one.

"Tyler Grayson, so good to see you again," Kroll said.

He killed Jari! While he's not expecting it, I could slit his throat. Carve him up! Stab . . . No! I have to resist. Erika's life depends on me keeping a cool head for now. Focus, Tyler! Focus! Tyler gave a nod. "How's the wound?"

Kroll just sneered and held his side. The wound was still fresh. Apparently, Ezekiel hadn't allowed his lieutenant to heal himself. *Or is he too weak?*

"He looks like her, doesn't he, Kroll?" the huskier demon hissed and laughed.

"Like who?" Tyler asked locking eyes with Vil, Kroll's companion.

"Your mommy, boy! I was there when she died with a hole in her back, begging! Hah!" he cackled.

In the blink of an eye, Tyler threw his hand out and magically grasped the fiend tightly by the skull. He lifted and squeezed him tightly, feeling his head concaving in midair. Tyler stared coldly as he drew Charlemagne and held it inches from piercing the frantic demon with bulging eyes.

To Tyler's surprise, Kroll just stood there laughing. "Come now, Grayson. Killing this cretin would start negotiations off on the wrong foot." Controlling his emotions, Tyler lowered Vil, but not before giving his skull one last squeeze. Any harder and his head would have popped like a watermelon. Vil recoiled as Kroll showed him the back of his hand. "Now, an important question. Do you have something valuable to use as a bargaining chip?"

"I think I have something your master wants." Tyler pulled his backpack around. He opened it and flashed the Codex.

Kroll stared into the bag until Tyler pulled it away. The demon's eyes locked with Tyler's, and then back to the bag, shifting between the two. He let out a laugh. "Clever, boy. Just this way. Our master will want to speak to you in person."

"I want to see Erika first," Tyler demanded as he followed.

Kroll laughed. "Your friend's fine. A little black and blue, but fine."

"I'm not meeting with Ezekiel until I know she is alive."

"Got the time, Vil?"

Vil flashed his watch as he rubbed his head. "17:18."

"She's alive. You'll just have to *trust* us."

With no other options, Tyler walked silently behind the two into the fortress, and he soon realized the bunker was like an iceberg. As he marched down the steep stairway, the labyrinth expanded outwards below the surface.

"Hah! The Scribe's here!" Tyler was greeted with hisses and jeers. Some even had the guts to spit at his feet. All the same, Tyler remained focused and kept a level head as he tapped the hilt of Charlemagne. *Now's not the time. Just keep walking.*

The demons entered a cold sterile and featureless steel room.

"Come on in," Kroll said turning and holding the door for Tyler.

Be on your guard. It could be a trap. Tyler stepped into the room.

Kroll kicked out a chair. "Have a seat."

Taking a seat, Tyler rested his arms on the table in front of him and watched as Vil walked into the room holding a glass of water.

"For you," he said handing Tyler the glass.

It looks like water. It smells like water. I bet it even tastes like water. But Tyler could tell in the way the demon handled the drink that this was not a kind gesture to ease tensions.

He pushed the glass away. "That's okay. I'm not thirsty, but thanks."

Kroll reached over Vil and stared Tyler in the eye. "No . . . this is for you," he said pushing it back to Tyler. "Now drink. The clock's ticking."

I don't have a choice, do I? Tyler gingerly took the water in hand and drank. Much to his surprise, it had a fruity, lemon flavor. When he finished, Tyler showed them the empty glass and dropped it onto the table, nearly shattering from the impact.

"Now?" Tyler asked already feeling light-headed and weaker.

The two smirked as they walked out of the room. "Lord Ezekiel will be with you in a moment," Kroll answered.

Alright ... here we go. Tyler fiddled his fingers, hardly noticeable to the camera watching him from above. An electrical current erupted from his fingertips, ran up the wall and then froze the camera, implanting the footage with the same image of him sitting still in the room. Tyler pulled the Adredium pill from his pocket and swallowed. He still felt light-headed and drained, but he could already feel The Cure working through his system.

Tyler opened the door and snuck out when he saw no one was coming. Creeping around corners, ducking in between gaps and behind tall fixtures, Tyler made his way through the bunker undetected, tampering with each camera along the way. Every now and then he would find himself trapped and unable to hide. But he had a spell for that too, and Tyler managed to camouflage into his surroundings then waited silently until the demons passed.

In these moments, Tyler also explored the passing demon's minds. He read long enough to slowly lead him to Erika's room, but never lingered long enough to alert them to his magic. After several demons, a handful of dead-ends, and too many close calls to count, Tyler peeked into another room and found her.

Erika faced away from the door, kneeling with a bag hung over her drooping head. *It's her! She's alive!*

CHAPTER 30
THE BARGAIN

Waving a hand over the door knob, Tyler disabled the room's camera before stepping inside. He ran to Erika's side, pulled the bag off her head and untied the cloth gag around her mouth.

"Erika! Thank God you're okay," Tyler said holding her in his hands.

But as he held her, she felt light and weak and could hardly hold herself upright. Tyler loosened his grip and looked her over. *She's all bruised up! What did they do to you?* Rage filled him as he stared at her wounds. *I'll kill them all!* He peered at her wrists and saw more bruising. *These chains have rubbed her raw! We need to get you out of this!*

"Erika . . . can you hear me?" She seemed hardly conscious. Her eyes were barely able to meet Tyler's before falling away.

"Lean back!" Tyler shouted winding his hand like a whip. *Dirrumpo!* He tried severing the chains holding her, but they remained firm.

"Magic won't work."

Tyler sprung to his feet as his eyes met Ezekiel's glaring at him from the entryway. Stepping forward and locking the door behind him, Ezekiel grinned.

"I must say, from the cameras to reading minds, you're truly resourceful. Though, so predictable."

"I'm here just like you wanted. Let her go," Tyler said holding out his backpack.

Ezekiel rolled his eyes with a sigh. "Sure, but I want to see it. Show it to me."

Digging into his backpack, Tyler flashed the Codex, then tucked it back in. Satisfied, Ezekiel pulled out a set of large iron keys from his pocket and threw it at Tyler. He turned to the camera and gave a nod.

Catching the keys mid-air, Tyler fiddled with her lock until a clear metallic click sounded and her chains fell to the floor. Tyler held her hand trying to rouse her, but her sedated trance persisted. If anything, it appeared to be getting worse.

"What've you done to her?"

Knowing he might find Tyler in this room, Ezekiel took the liberty of stocking a hidden shelf with a selection of his prized spirits and liquors. He pulled out a bottle of aged bourbon and poured two glasses. "I just gave her a nasty little concoction of mine. It helps loosen the mind, calms the nerves, slips the victim slowly into a vegetative state, and then . . . well, use your imagination."

Tyler rose to his feet and held out his hand. "You better have an antidote."

"Of course, I have one," Ezekiel smirked as he passed a glass of bourbon towards Tyler while the other glass kissed his lips. "Wouldn't be much of a bargaining chip if she was as good as dead, now would she?"

"The antidote." Tyler slid the glass back.

"Don't have a taste for fine spirits?"

"Not into drinking anymore, thank you very much. Now, I need the antidote, or you'll never get the Codex," Tyler demanded.

"I know your plan, Tyler," Ezekiel said coolly with an eerily calm smile. "It's simple. As soon as I give you the antidote, you'll grab her, Jump back to wherever your grandpa is hiding, and everyone goes home happy. That's your plan, right?"

"Came up with it all on my own last night," Tyler said sarcastically.

"Well, it sounds good in theory. But you have several obstacles in your way."

"Go on."

Ezekiel sat relaxed across the table from Tyler sipping his glass. "Well, first, my helpers gave you the same spiked drink Mommy Dearest drank just before my good pet, Marshall, put a bullet in her back. Could you Jump beyond my fortress's outer walls? Maybe, but I doubt much further, let alone back to America."

Tyler's fingernails bit into his palm, but he said nothing.

"Second, and most important, this fortress is now surrounded by a Fey Forcefield, making it impossible for anyone to use magic, myself included." He broke contact to stare at Tyler's backpack. "At least for now."

"No magic? Prove it."

"Prove it?" Ezekiel chuckled, unsheathing a dagger. "Tell you what . . ." He raised the dagger to his own throat and pressed the tip against his flesh. "I hear you are fond of using pushing spells. Go ahead, do it."

Hesitating at first, Tyler raised his hand. *Dis!* Nothing happened.

"Need I say more?" Ezekiel sheathed his dagger.

"Ok, no magic. Is that all?" Tyler asked bluffing in an unconcerned tune.

Amused, Ezekiel put his drink down and stood confidently. "Third. Even if I let you leave with the Codex, the antidote, and little Miss Erika, an everyone goes home happy scenario can't possibly exist."

What does he have up his sleeves? Tyler glared at Ezekiel. "Why not?"

"Oh, Tyler. You really are a naive fool, aren't you?" Ezekiel mocked him. "Tell me—honestly. Don't you find it, I don't know, odd? That the moment you step out of Jon's safety, to a mall of all places, I knew exactly where you were going?"

"You had sentries waiting outside his house."

Ezekiel grinned and then tried again. "Hmm, okay. Sentries . . . Then how did I know the exact Dublin pub you'd be in and the exact time you'd be there? Remember, after our first meeting at your grandfather's, I had no idea where you were, or where to instruct my 'sentries' to watch your movement."

Tyler once again said nothing. *What's he getting at?*

"Furthermore, where was Erika? Held up by five demon children? Paying the tab? Away . . . from you?"

Tyler said nothing. A sick twisting knot lumped in his throat. *Wait . . . No.*

Ezekiel pushed the glass of bourbon towards Tyler. "Let's face it. Like mother like son, your Adjutors betrayed you both."

304

No . . . s-she wouldn't! Tyler knelt beside Erika, holding her face, and stared into her eyes. *You didn't . . . please tell me you didn't!* But he could tell by the look in her watering eyes he'd been played.

After all this time! Tyler trembled, unsure what to feel. Betrayal? Heartbroken? Hurt? He felt lost. And then he felt anger.

"How could you!?" Tyler screamed, startling even Ezekiel. *My mom paid for trusting her Adjutor. And now here I am, risking mine for someone who's been betraying me from the start!*

Despite everything Tyler and everyone else told him, despite his failing efforts to let go, he wanted justice for his mother. No, he wanted revenge. Only Marshall's blood would do. He had not found Marshall yet, but now Tyler was face to face with his own betrayer. *It'd be all too easy. She can't even stand.* And for a moment, Tyler just stared at her with his hand caressing the hilt of his blade. *Look at me, Erika! Show me something! Show me it wasn't all a lie . . . please!* Then he remembered.

Tyler stood slow and defeated, turning to Ezekiel. "Let's make a deal."

"Go on." He tried to hold back his grin, but he was beyond pleased with himself.

"I'll give you the Codex, and I won't come looking for it. In exchange, you give me the antidote, drop the Fey Forcefield and let us Jump out of here, safely."

There was disappointment painted across Ezekiel's face. "I know how it feels to lose someone close. And I especially know what it feels like to be betrayed by someone you thought you could trust." He ran a finger across his scar.

Ezekiel held out his hand. "Join me, Tyler! I need someone as cunning, resourceful, and naturally gifted as you. Join my new world."

Tyler stepped away and held out his own hand. "My offer stands. You get the Codex, you lose an enemy, and get what you've always wanted. But heck, if you're feeling charitable, I'd take Marshall off your hands."

Ezekiel seethed angrily now, his offer shoved back into his face. He wouldn't gain an ally but he would have the Codex.

"Deal." Ezekiel thrust his hand into Tyler's.

Tyler felt a foreign strange energy flowing through his hand. It didn't feel dark or evil nor did it feel good. It just was. He pulled away with a jerk as the Oath's bite coursed through them both. They were now both magically obligated to their Oath.

"The Codex!" Ezekiel demanded holding out his hand. "Then you get the antidote."

Pulling the Codex from his backpack, the very book responsible for cursing his family for centuries, Tyler gave it to Ezekiel.

Triumphant and dominant, Ezekiel held the Codex high. He inspected the binding with his caress and a victorious smile on his face.

But it was all an act. Ezekiel shoved it back into Tyler's chest, nearly pushing Tyler off his feet.

"You thought you could fool me?"

Tyler froze for a moment.

Ezekiel's steel blue eyes flared a fiery red. "You think you can trick me with a fake? Better yet, you think my servants are so blind?"

"I don't know what you're—" Tyler said, but he was instantly interrupted.

"You practically paraded both books in front of Kroll! You thought my lieutenant wouldn't tell me immediately? Fool! I'll give you one last chance, boy. Give me the Codex or break your Oath and die!"

Tyler reached into his backpack and pulled out the Codex, confirming his guilt. "Take it." Nabbing the book from Tyler, Ezekiel held it closely like an infant. "You got the Codex. Now, give me the antidote, and let us Jump."

Ezekiel turned and gave the camera a nod. Reaching into his pocket, he pulled out a grey flask and handed it to Tyler. Popping the cork, Tyler bent over and helped Erika swallow the strange liquid. It took a moment for the antidote to take effect, but slowly Erika seemed less sedated and more in control of her body. Tyler helped her to her feet and slung her arm around his shoulder.

Erika didn't know where she was and how she had gotten there. Seeing Tyler, she immediately felt at ease. But the serenity was short-lived. She turned to find Ezekiel's threatening, mischievous smirk. Head still heavy, her eyes dropped and fixed themselves upon the Codex securely in Ezekiel's clutches. She lunged forward, but between Ezekiel pulling the Codex out of grasp and Tyler pulling her back, Erika couldn't even brush her fingertips along the binding.

Tyler anchored Erika to him as she desperately tugged. "No! Stop—let go! You can't give it to him!" Ezekiel chuckled under his breath, enjoying Erika's frenzy.

"A deal's a deal," Ezekiel boasted with a mocking stare. "Which reminds me. With this book, our deal's been met, Erika. I hold your Oath fulfilled. Begone, you filthy harpy!"

Winding up her fist, she would have dived at him again if not for Tyler pulling her back. "It's not worth it! Just let it go!"

"Are you insane?" Erika shouted.

Tyler grabbed her hand. "We're Jumping. Now!"

"Oh, and Tyler," Ezekiel said regaining his attention. "I'm feeling a bit generous . . . Marshall Dunn, your mother's Adjutor, he should be returning from an assignment any minute now. You might be able to catch him off guard while you're leaving."

Dunn! I've got his name! Marshall Dunn. "Until we meet again," Tyler said with a nod.

"Sooner than you know," Ezekiel said finishing the last of his glass with a victorious smile. And with that, Tyler Jumped himself and Erika out of the fortress, but only just.

Taking a seat once again, Ezekiel kicked out his feet and opened the Codex. He reached out and took Tyler's full glass. *Waste not.* Putting a hand over the Codex's open pages, he closed his eyes in an attempt to embrace the Codex's power. There was nothing. He tried again. And then again, each time his efforts doubling, each time his yearning more urgent. Standing in a smoldering fit of rage, Ezekiel threw the Codex at the wall as it burst into flames, quickly turning the fake Codex to ash.

"Kroll!!!" Ezekiel blared as his eyes festered with an unholy crimson blaze. "Rally the troops now! Find them!"

Kroll turned to gather Ezekiel's minions for an immediate Jump and asked, "Your orders, Master?"

"Kill the Siren!" Ezekiel answered stamping out the embers. "And bring the boy to me! Alive!"

CHAPTER 31
THE CHASE

Jumping to the treed outskirts of Golmeshka, Tyler and Erika stumbled forward using a giant pine to catch themselves. Tyler knew it would not be long before Ezekiel figured out he had tricked both him and his guards. He grabbed Erika's arm and led her away.

"We can't leave! He's got the Codex—" Erika shouted trying to pull him the other way.

"You mean this?" Tyler asked unzipping his backpack to reveal the real Codex.

"He doesn't have the Codex?"

Golmeshka burst to life. A high-pitched bell followed by an air raid siren deafened the surrounding forest sounds.

"And he knows it! Run!" Tyler threw Erika her purse. She pulled her extendable rapier from the pink bag, and then tucked it into her pocket as they fled the scene.

The ground shook as Ezekiel's minions poured from the bunker, led by the massive bulk of Kroll.

While the demons led by Kroll were far behind, a slender more agile monstrosity was sent out ahead like a hunter's hound. The pair ran as fast as their legs would carry them. Although they had a head start, they could hear the lone beast carving its way through the forest towards them.

"Don't look back!" Erika said pushing Tyler forward.

But no matter how fast they ran, or how hard they tried to mislead their pursuer, the monster found their trail. Then another creature pulled up alongside them in the distance. *Great! A second one!* After a moment, he turned and found the creature was still giving chase but had closed the gap. Although it had the physique of a demon, the way it moved and stalked Tyler through the thick forest was animalistic. *There's a clearing up ahead.*

"I'm gonna hit the demon to our right with a stunning spell when we reach the opening," Tyler murmured loud enough for Erika to hear.

Tyler and Erika whipped through the trees into the opening just as the other creature jumped out. He was already halfway through casting his spell when the creature's appearance stopped him dead in his tracks.

It's him! Marshall . . . Tyler was certain.

"Marshall? Marshall Dunn?"

"Tyler . . ."

Tyler couldn't hold back. "Murderer!"

Marshall stood his ground, his pistol clinched in his hand. Erika held her sword at the ready while Tyler readied to cast a spell. *He's disguising his face, morphed between human and Werewolf so I can't recognize him. Coward!* Tyler took a deep breath. *He's in my way now. There's no escaping it . . . I have to kill him!*

But, distracted by Marshall, the creeping beast behind them came close and launched itself at Tyler, teeth gnashing for his throat.

The thunderous bang of a revolver rumbled through the forest, and before anyone could react, the demon plummeted to the floor dead with a single bullet shot clean through its head. Marshall's gun was still smoking, and he raised it to the sky, then took four more shots to empty his gun. With one last bullet in the chamber, he lowered it and, with a reluctant determination, fired the bullet into his own leg, dropping him to the floor.

The pair stepped back in shock. Tyler stared unable to make sense of Marshall's actions. *What? What the hell is he doing?*

Grunting as he tossed his gun aside, Marshall peered back up at Tyler. "Run, boy! Now!"

Tyler could only stare at him, confused and conflicted.

"Tyler, we have to get out of here!" Erika said, pulling him along. Tyler took one last look at Marshall before he turned and continued their escape, leaving the Werewolf behind. Moments later, Kroll and his minions came upon the sight of the dead demon and Marshall holding his bloody leg, trying to stem the bleeding.

"What happened? Where did he go?" Kroll demanded, pulling Marshall off the ground by his scruff.

"We tried to stop him, but he pulled my fire into your freakshow over there. I tried to pull my hand back toward him, but he forced me to fire a bullet into my leg," Marshall lied, dragging out his answer as long as he could.

"Which way did he go? Smell him out!" Kroll shouted, throwing Marshall onto the ground.

Marshall snarled at the demon. "I can't smell him over the stench of your soldiers. But he went that way . . . I think."

"He's wrong! Tracks! This way! This way!" growled another demon.

312

Kroll turned back to Marshall. "Useless old mutt. I'd put you down if you weren't in Lord Ezekiel's favor." Kroll halted another demon from attending to Marshall. "He's a Werewolf. The dog will regenerate from his wounds . . . eventually. I need all of you! Charge forward! Jump and surround them!"

Trees parted as hundreds of demons and other fiendish creatures swarmed the forest. A barrage of thunderclaps and bursts of light turned the treetops and foliage into an uncoordinated firework display, and the roars of Ezekiel's minions sounded like a rock concert from the depths of hell.

Tyler and Erika zigged and zagged through the foliage away from the demons. Seeing a blue flash streaking towards them, Tyler pulled Erika and himself to the ground. A near hit. Tyler turned and launched the demon with breakneck speed before it could fire another spell.

"They're over here!" they heard a demon call out to their comrades.

Another spell soared towards them. Tyler grabbed Erika by the hand and Jumped them a few feet away, all he was capable of. Seeing an opening, they ducked through the tree line down a small hill. But as they scrambled through the darkness, another demon jumped out with its sword swinging at their waists. At the last possible moment, Erika drew her sword and blocked the attack before running it through the beast, but she stood there exposed as a bombardment of spells rained down from above. Tyler snatched her away with another short Jump.

No matter how fast they ran, no matter how hard they tried to evade their demonic pursuers, with each turn Tyler and Erika found another demon waiting for them. *There's so many of them! Come on! Kick in already!* His magic was still hindered by the polluted water. He could feel the Adredium pills at work, but the poison had burrowed deep, and with each labored Jump he used to escape, Tyler grew weaker. Then, as the two came into a small break in the forest, they found themselves surrounded. Demons were everywhere they looked. There was nowhere else to run.

"Orders! Remember the orders, boys! You can hurt him, but don't kill him," Kroll barked with a threatening snarl. With Erika too close to Tyler to unleash a hellfire of spells, the horde of foul creatures drew their swords as a single unit. "There's nowhere to run, boy! Give us the crafty bitch and we'll have that Codex." The sound of metal sliding against metal pierced miles through the forest. Drawing Charlemagne from its sheath, the two squared back to back, dancing in a circle as their attackers closed in on them.

"Tyler!" Erika shouted to him over the booming march.

"What?"

"If this doesn't turn out—"

"We're getting out of this!"

"If we don't . . . thank you."

"Let's give 'em hell then," Tyler said, squeezing Erika on the shoulder. "Everything we've got!"

Spinning his blade at his side like a propeller, Tyler watched as fear and uncertainty washed over the demons, then he pulled back his blade, let a row of them approach and then carved through them, cleaving several in half.

The rest lunged forward from all angles, but Tyler pulled Erika back a step and liquified the ground beneath the charging forces. Watching their allies swallowed whole, the next row of demons hesitated to charge in blindly.

Climbing over his fallen Incubi, a hulking brute swung its ax at Tyler's head. Ducking just in time, Tyler watched as the Incubus's weapon soared over before Erika's sword plunged through its chest. Catching a pair rushing Erika with her back turned, Tyler spellbladed Charlemagne through the air and sunk it into his chest.

"Ignis!" he said holding out his hand blasting the other into a fiery inferno.

Returning to Tyler's hand, Charlemagne clashed with another demon's blade. Crushing the hilt of the sword into the demon's face, Tyler raked Charlemagne across its throat before freezing another with, *"Congelo!"*

Tyler pushed back another demon and turned as four Incubi surrounded Erika. *I've gotta help her!* She cut down two and impaled another in the time it took for Tyler to react. *Never mind . . .* Another enormous beast charged him and wound up for a mighty swing. Tyler blitzed the brute, and as he was too far into his swing, all the beast could do was watch and howl in anguish as Tyler ran Charlemagne through his heart.

The winds blew through the forest as the battle raged on. It started small – hardly enough to overturn fallen leaves. But like a tidal wave passing through the forest, a powerful gale came down upon them threatening to uproot even the most robust trees. If not for its short duration, the battle may have come to a halt, and then the gust trampled deeper into the forest almost as if it hadn't happened at all.

An Incubus dove at Tyler, but he channeled the nimbleness of Kena-su and ducked out of the way faster than both thought humanly possible. Repositioning himself, Tyler strong-armed his hand into the demon's side. *Dis!*

The monstrous creature careened into his allies as Tyler added, *"Catena Fulgur!"*

Lightning discharged from Tyler's hand, electrifying the falling savage. The current whipped wildly, jumping from demon to demon, and their howls were only drowned out by the loud pops and snaps of lightning dancing violently through the forest. Grunting, Tyler was too focused holding the spell to notice Kroll bearing down on him.

Caught off guard, Tyler was knocked violently from his feet, winded and bruised. As he landed on his side, Kroll cleaved his massive, rusted warhammer upwards on the carry through. The familiar taste of blood kissed Tyler's lips. His vision doubled. He felt a wrenching in his gut as he tried to breathe. Even with Mera-su, Tyler found it difficult to ignore the throbbing blunt-force pummeling, and as he laid sprawled on the floor with all sense of direction and purpose smacked out of him, Tyler's eyes met Charlemagne stuck into the ground beside him.

Grasping the hilt, Tyler winced in pain as his hand was stamped into the ground beneath Kroll's metal boot. "Stop fighting, runt," he snapped. A swift kick to the face soon followed, and Tyler lost consciousness.

He woke seconds later with his lips kissing the dirt below. Peering up in a haze, he watched Kroll reach for his collar to drag him away. But before the fiend could carry him another step, Erika cleaved her sword across his face. Her sword bit through his metal helmet and cut deep into Kroll's pronounced forehead. The monster screamed with a hell-raising, disturbing roar before it stumbled backward and away, holding his face as blood poured from between his fingers and splattered the ground below.

"You okay?" Erika shouted as she stood over Tyler. Her sword drawn, she was ready to cut through the mob of demons. When Tyler did not respond, she peered down at him.

With blood running from his nose, his lips cut and swollen, Tyler struggled to lift himself. He made it to a knee, then collapsed to the floor in defeat. He tried again, but Erika pushed him back down as she held their ground.

"Stay low!"

"Kill the girl!" Kroll screamed, retreating from the center of the battle. The remaining demons marched forward, seeing Tyler was no longer a threat.

They stepped over and onto the bodies of their fallen comrades as they surrounded the pair. Erika needed to pull off a miracle, and even then, it might not have been enough. All her years of training, all her cunning, anything she had left in her, it was now nothing less than do or die. She took a quick glance at Tyler as he stared back. *There it is.* Erika found the motivation she needed. *I have to protect him! I'm his Adjutor!*

"Half of you will die before you land a finger on my Scribe! And you, Kroll. You'll be the first!" Erika screamed, crouched low with Tyler shielded behind.

The demons looked at each other, and most took a step back, not wanting to be a part of Erika's half. But Kroll roared, his face red with crimson blood. "Enough of this! Shoot them instead!"

"Them? But the Master, his orders–" The lone demon's voice was cut off by the sharp tip of Kroll's warhammer crashing into his throat.

"Damn the orders!"

"Shit ..." Erika whispered. She glanced down at Tyler. *I tried, kiddo.* She knew it was over.

There was only one last thing she could do for him. Dropping her sword, Erika dove over Tyler, covering him with her own body as a flurry of spells raced towards them.

Tyler stretched his hand to the sky as she fell over him. With the Codex in his other hand, he whispered one last spell, *"Repercutio."*

The Codex shimmered an intense pale red, lighting the surrounding area with its glow. A cascading paper-thin ray of light poured out from Tyler's hand, draping over the two like a bubble. A second later, the blue plasmatic spells collided into the shield and ricocheted wildly in all directions, some rebounding and killing their casters. The forest lit up like a firework display, both blinding and stunning everyone caught in the middle. Not one spell penetrated the Codex-empowered barrier.

When the shield dropped, Tyler grabbed his sword, reinvigorated. Both combed the floor blindly for Erika's sword as their vision slowly returned to them. But an overwhelming sense of dread filled them as they were pushed to the forest floor. Tyler was restrained by a demon holding each limb as his face was shoved into the ground. Not giving Erika the same treatment, all Tyler could hear was her crying out for him as she struggled with her captors. And then the wet sound of a sword slicing into flesh interweaved between her cries of agony.

318

Erika fell to the floor with a thud, her horrified eyes staring into Tyler's with her breath laboring. Despite holding pressure against her stomach, blood poured out between her fingers. The winds strolled back across the bloody battlefield, brushing leaves against Tyler and Erika.

"Leave her to bleed out and die! We got the boy," shouted Kroll victoriously.

Tyler could see her eyes fluttering on the edge of consciousness as blood pooled beneath her. His eyes grew intense. His breath deepened. And his heartbeat raced as Tyler was engulfed in a blood-boiling rage. He wanted to make them pay.

For Mom . . . For Dad . . . He stared at Erika as her breath grew shallow. *And for Erika!* If this was it, if this was how it ended, *he* was going to end it. He did not care if the rage and magic stirring inside tore him apart. *If we aren't gonna make it out alive . . . neither will they!*

"Alright, chain this pathetic little—AH!" a demon barked before he was interrupted. The ground trembled under their feet.

"Where is it coming fro-umph!" another demon started before he was tackled and crushed into the ground.

The demons holding Tyler's limbs turned frantically, scanning the area for hostiles. Tyler watched as a large blur of fur streaked over top of him, violently driving the demon atop him several feet away and into the ground.

With a quick flick of the jaw, Annikki snapped the demon's neck before letting out a fear-inspiring roar. Even the staunchest of the demons' blood ran cold. Turning their attention on the rogue Otso, the demons were taken completely by surprise when the trees parted and unleashed a mob of creatures out onto the battlefield.

With a brutal stroke of his giant mighty arm, Mossy swept over a dozen demons. "Clear this forest! Not one of these foul beasts escapes!"

Then Tyler heard another familiar voice, one he did not expect to hear. "Alright, Sons of Eric! Rise up! I want to mount our hall full of demon heads," Foxtrot shouted as his squad poured onto the battlefield.

Tyler's captors turned to face their attackers giving him the opportunity he needed. He blasted one away with a fireball while Annikki streaked through the rest. Crawling to her side, Tyler held his hand over Erika's bloodied wounds. *She's unconscious. I need to get her out of here.* Tyler murmured the healing spell over her stomach. Her ruptured innards and wounds sealed before his eyes, stopping the blood loss. He hoped it would be enough.

"Knucker! Knucker above!" a demon shouted to the others.

The Knucker swooped into a pile of demons crushing them underneath its weight. Pummeling those close to it with its tail, the dragon's eyes dilated before incinerating a crowd of demons with its molten breath. The flames were so intense leaves dried on trees several feet away.

Seeing the havoc the Knucker unleashed, some of the Sons were unsure which to kill first. Foxtrot set his men straight. "Demons now! Knucker later!"

Mossy cleared another row of demons beneath him. "Mr. Grayson! So good to see you again. But I must insist that you leave immediately!"

Tyler couldn't help but chuckle. "Seems you're always trying to shoo me away, Mossy."

Mossy smiled down at him. "Only because you keep stirring up trouble like the good little Scribe you are. Now go, or I'll send Annikki after you. Knucker!"

Barreling through the sky, the Knucker turned, descended from the air and rode up next to Tyler. Its eyes urged Tyler to get on its back. Grabbing Erika, Tyler secured her onto the Knucker's back before straddling behind her to keep her from falling off mid-flight.

"Until we meet again, Mr. Grayson."

"Someday soon, Mossy. Thank you!"

Clearing a runway for itself and searing any demon foolish enough to stand in its way, the Knucker stretched its wings out and, with a gallop, took flight, leaving the battlefield behind him.

CHAPTER 32
ERIKA'S PAST

The morning sun peered through the window drapes as its warm caress pried at Erika's eyes. Laying warm and comfortable in a pillowy, soft bed, Erika gingerly opened her eyes. It took her a moment to realize she was safe, especially since the last thing she remembered was getting stabbed. Jolting forward, she pulled her shirt up just enough to check her wound. The only remaining evidence was the slightest discoloration of a scar.

"Hey, you okay there?" Tyler leaned in and rubbed her shoulder from his chair.

"I think so, are we dead?" Erika smiled.

Tyler shook his head. "Told ya we'd make it out."

"You okay?"

"Yeah, just been here keeping busy," he said glancing at a pile of old textbooks littering the desk beside him.

"Where are we?"

"Gramp's new hide out. Thought I'd give you a view when you woke up."

Erika joked, "You could've given me a view of a garbage dump and I'd been happy so long as I woke to see it."

The two chuckled. They were truly safe now. They could rest after all that happened in the past few days. Their smiles lingered, but the mood soon faded. The elephant in the room could no longer go undiscussed.

"I know everything, Erika," Tyler said in a somber tone.

Erika sat uncomfortably as shame and guilt washed over her face. "I . . . I don't know what to say, Tyler. I don't think an apology is good enough at this point."

"I think the truth is the best place to start."

With a quiet nod, Erika took a deep breath. "He got me years ago."

"Like a couple years back?

"Try a couple decades," Erika clarified.

"What did he get you for? What was the Oath?" Tyler asked.

She choked on a growing lump in her throat. "I'd help him get the Codex, and he'd make me immortal . . . again."

"You?" He tilted his head. "You fell in love?"

Erika nodded. "He died months after we were engaged, an infection he picked up helping patients."

"I'm sorry. What was his name?"

"Alton."

She paused for a moment, giving Tyler time to ask, "And Ezekiel approached you soon after?"

"No. I went on with my life as though nothing had happened. We didn't get married, so maybe I was still in the clear."

"But you weren't? You were aging faster?"

Erika pulled the sheet aside so she could sit face to face with Tyler. "It scared me. I was . . . dying, aging. And he

323

was gone. I had to face mortality alone. That's when I heard through a network of acquaintances of a man who could fix my heart."

Ezekiel knows how to reverse something like that? Without the Codex?

"How?"

Erika winced at the thought. "I don't remember the whole process, but it was awful! Several weeks of potions and magic. I nearly quit so many times. But, when it was done, I wasn't aging. One year, five years, ten years, it didn't matter. I was immortal again."

"And then he had you join the Guild, for the right moment?"

Erika shook her head. "I signed up long before. He just had me reinstate and keep sharp until he needed me. Other than that, I got to live my life. So many years had passed, I honestly thought he had forgotten or something."

"Then I came around, and he knew I'd need an Adjutor."

Erika reached for his hand as their eyes met. "I know saying 'But I stopped' doesn't excuse—"

Tyler interrupted her. "When I was attacked in the pub. You stopped then."

"Y-yes, how did you know?" Erika asked with a surprised expression.

"I've had a lot of time to think while watching over you," Tyler said omitting the fact he read her mind while she was out.

He knew it invaded her privacy, but he needed to know. And he saw it all. Every moment of doubt. Every self-loathing thought as she got to know him and became a large part of his world. And then the breaking point. After another marvelous night with Tyler, her friend, she could not stand by and watch him get hurt. She would not lead him into danger again. After this, Ezekiel started invading her mind both awake and asleep. Headaches, visions, restless nights of tossing and turning. But she resisted him. She held him off by creating false thoughts and wrong turns.

Tyler continued. "I pieced it together. You were supposed to pay the tab and let them kill me. But you didn't. You stepped in."

She peered into his eyes, unsure what else she could say besides, "I'm just so so sorry, Tyler."

"Do you know what I thought when I first found out?" Tyler asked clearing his throat.

Erika shook her head fighting back sniffles. "I can only imagine."

He held her hand tighter. "Well, first I was just shocked. Hurt. Confused. Then I got angry. And for a second, I . . . well, I didn't like you very much."

"Ha! Only for a second?" Erika asked holding back the tears brimming her eyes.

"Okay, maybe two. But then I remembered back to when Ezekiel was standing over me. He was gonna kill me. But you saved me. If you truly didn't care . . . if you were on his side, you could've just let him. So, question is, why'd you save me?"

Erika could not control the tears rolling down her face. "Because you deserved better! You're kind and gentle and sweet. You did things for me just out of the goodness of your heart. You wanted nothing back from me, except friendship. You're a good person and I couldn't let that die. You deserved better from me."

"Well, lucky for me, you ended up on my side after all," he said wiping a tear from her face. "We make a pretty good team, you and me."

"You're not mad?"

"Sitting here with the woman who literally threw herself over me like a shield? No, I'm not. And no one else is either . . . this is between you and me, okay?"

Erika didn't know what to say. She was not sure if she could say the same if the shoe were on the other foot.

He tucked her back into bed. "You need to rest. I did my best, but nothing beats time and rest. I'd like us to start scribing again after the holiday. I can condition better, and we can cele—"

"Wait! Y–you still want me to be your Adjutor?" Erika assumed at least this much was over.

"Couldn't imagine doing it with anyone else," Tyler said walking back to the library door. He glanced back. "I'm gonna meet up with Amanda, Casey, and Ballsy in a bit. Charlie said he'd check up on you while I'm gone."

"Say hi for me."

Closing the door behind him, Tyler walked down the cramped stairway into the kitchen. Charlie was already hard at work cooking lunch for everyone.

Laying back, Erika gave a sigh of relief. She was unsure if she deserved a second chance, but grateful Tyler gave it to her. She silently vowed to herself she would not squander his forgiveness. This time he truly would not regret his decision.

The scar she earned was not a mark of shame. It was a lasting reminder that she made the right decision and received a second chance. Closing her eyes, the sound of silence ringing through her ears, Erika noticed something. The dull tension in her head, a pain which became so background to her, it was gone. She drifted back to sleep with peace of mind. Erika knew Ezekiel's reign over her life was, at last, over.

CHAPTER 33
THE ROAD AHEAD

The time had come once again after nearly two weeks of celebrating the holidays with family and friends. Tyler originally planned to leave the day after Christmas, but Charlie pressed him to stay just one more day to celebrate Boxing Day with them.

"Too tight?" Amanda asked helping wrap the scarf she bought Tyler for Christmas around his collar.

"Just right, thanks."

"Toasty and matching," Amanda said as Erika adjusted her own scarf.

"Thanks for spending the night," Tyler said.

Amanda reached out and gave her friend a hug. "Of course! Sorry Thomas couldn't be here to see you off."

"Ugh, just because you two are dating now doesn't mean you have to call him by his name. He's been Ballsy since forever."

"He doesn't mind. Or the other name I have for him," Amanda said with a wink.

"Woo'kay!"

"Seriously though, when're you gonna tell him? Or Case? Or Zane?"

"Maybe someday," Tyler answered. "For now, it's better they don't know."

Amanda turned and embraced Erika. "Take care of him, and yourself."

"I will."

"Alright, let's go say goodbye to everyone." Tyler said to Erika, hoping to Jump before it got dark in Belgium.

Holding the door for his friends, Tyler turned and took one last look into their empty room. Their beds were neat and made for a change. He was leaving his grandfather's watchful eye again, but he knew things would be better this time.

Coming into the kitchen space, everyone else had already gathered around waiting for Tyler.

"Chicken potato soup. These'll keep you two warm," Charlie said packing two large thermoses into Tyler's backpack.

"Thanks, Charlie," Tyler said slinging the backpack over his shoulder.

"And some holiday bread." Charlie handed him a warm, tightly hand-wrapped brown bag.

"Thank you."

Standing atop the table, Penelope reached out arms extended wide to give Tyler a hug. "When will you be coming back to visit?"

"Aiming for early spring," Tyler answered.

"Earlier if you need," Jon said in a reminding tone.

"Of course." Tyler turned to Erika with a nod. "Alright, ready?"

"When you are."

Everyone took turns giving Tyler and Erika one last goodbye hug. Both Penelope and Amanda didn't miss the opportunity to give Tyler another either.

Holding his grandson in his arms, Jon gave him a firm pat on the back. "Your mother would be proud. Keep it up." Their eyes meeting, Tyler did not say a word but cracked a smile and a nod of the head. Taking Erika's hand, the two wished everyone a happy new year and vanished.

Landing in the countryside, Tyler and Erika landed on their two feet. *Ha! Nailed it! Think I'm finally getting the hang of Jumping.* The ground was covered with a fresh coat of snow. It was thick enough to cover the grass below, but not enough to feel like they were trudging through the winter wonderland. An almost unnoticeable breeze nipped at their cheeks as their clothing kept them comfortably warm. As Erika pulled a beanie over her head, the two both grinned warmly at one another.

"Ready?" Erika asked taking a step forward still holding Tyler's hand.

"When you are," he said taking a step himself to match.

Walking down the hill, the sound of ice crunched beneath their feet. Their next adventure started along this unassuming snowy path.

Erika let out a comfortable sigh. "Wish our job was always this peaceful."

"Aw, but what fun would that be?" Tyler teased nudging her softly.

"Yeah, I guess."

"Hey," Tyler said pointing to Erika's empty hands. "No music?"

330

She gave his hand a gentle but tight squeeze. "Thought I'd just enjoy the sights with you for a change."

"It's out of battery, huh?"

There was an innocent smile on her face. "It's the thought that counts."

A NOTE FROM THE AUTHOR

Hello!

I'm Richard Gibbard. Thanks for reading *The Codex of Tyler Grayson: Creatures Among Us.* I hope you enjoyed!
If you did enjoy my book, please leave a review on Amazon and tell your friends! The sequel is already on its way. Keep your ears to the ground!

In the meantime, do you want to talk, ask questions, stay connected, and get news first?

Here's are a couple ways to follow me on Social Media and e-mail:

Gmail:
richardgibbardjr@gmail.com

Twitter:
https://twitter.com/gibbard_richard

Still craving more adventure?

Check out my good friend and fellow author, James Stevens' highly acclaimed book:

Fern Majestic & The Fall of a Dragon
https://twitter.com/FernMajestic

9 781733 938319